旅遊服務英語

主　編　許酉萍、張科
副主編　石軍、張朝政

Preface 前言

本書的編寫秉承以學習者為中心的教學理念，以旅遊實踐為導向，從旅遊從業者的角度來設計和編寫教學內容，既注重理論知識，又側重知識的應用和可操作性，注重旅遊服務過程的能力培養，體現了「以就業為導向、以能力為本位」的設計理念。本書具有以下三個特色：

第一，將會展英語納入旅遊服務英語，進一步拓展了旅遊的廣度和深度；第二，注重中國社會與文化的介紹，有助於提高旅遊從業者的文化素質；第三，將景區英語以對話的形式進行，抓住景區的重點進行介紹，可以起到舉一反三的示範作用，具有很強的可操作性。

本書以板塊設計為主，共分為五個部分，共 26 個單元：第一部分為導遊英語；第二部分為酒店英語；第三部分為會展英語；第四部分為景區英語；第五部分為中國社會與文化。

每一單元由四個模塊組成：

（1）介紹（Section 1　Introduction）。介紹本單元主要內容，瞭解工作流程，並在此基礎上提出問題進行討論，明確其任務、職責和要求。

（2）對話（Section 2　Dialogues）。對話情景的選擇貼近和涵蓋旅遊服務工作的實際，具有針對性和實用性；詞彙學習（Words and Phrases）將兩個板塊中的生詞的發音、詞義以及短語加以註釋，便於學生查閱學習；實用句型（Useful Expressions）總結有助於拓展鞏固常用句型和表達方法，便於學生模仿學習。

（3）練習（Section 3　Exercises）。根據每課的教學內容，精心設計多樣練習

類型。情景對話填空進一步拓寬了學習內容，尤其是情景對話操練中 Tips 的設定是本書的一大特色，它提供了相關場景和詞彙，可組織學生進行真實場景模擬練習，更豐富、更全面地呈現各場景學習；漢譯英、英譯漢、表格填寫以及寫作訓練都有助於學生英語應用能力的提高。

（4）拓展閱讀（Section 4 Extensive Reading）。與主題有關的拓展閱讀包括文化、習俗、禮儀介紹，將極大地提高學生的個人素質。

編寫分工如下：許西萍編寫 Part Two Hotel English 和 Part Four Scenic Spot English 中的 Unit 3~Unit 5；張科編寫 Part Five Chinese Society and Culture 中的 Unit 1~Unit 4；張朝政編寫 Part One Tour Guide English；劉志群編寫 Part Three MICE English 和 Part Four 中的 Unit 1~Unit 2；解巍編寫 Part Five 中的 Unit 5~Unit 6；石軍編寫 Appendix。

　　本書由多年從事旅遊英語教學的一線教師參與編寫。教材選材新穎、點面結合、內容豐富、圖文並茂、語言規範、實用性強，練習兼具實用性和針對性。它以應用為目的、夠用為尺度，擺脫了一般教科書場景設置單一的缺點，更接近生活實際，具有真實性、生動性和趣味性。教材注重培養學生的獨立思考能力和創造力，體現「在學中用，在用中學，學以致用」的學習理念。本書可作為高等職業學院、高等專科學校、成人高等院校、本科院校旅遊英語專業及旅遊管理專業學生的學習用書，也可作為旅遊企業服務與管理從業人員的培訓教材。

　　本書的編寫還得到了許多同事和朋友的熱情關心、幫助和指導，在此，編者一併表示感謝。在這裡，特別要感謝外籍專家 Eric Regener（加拿大）對本教材進行了認真的審閱，並提出了修改意見。

　　由於旅遊英語所涉及的內容廣泛且不斷發展，加之編者水平有限，書中不足與疏漏之處在所難免，敬請廣大讀者和同仁不吝批評指正。

編者

Contents 目錄

Part One　Tour Guide English

Unit 1　Meeting the Guests at the Airport ·············· 3

Section 1　Introduction ··· 3
Section 2　Dialogues ·· 4
　Dialogue 1　Meeting a Guest at the Lobby of the Airport ················ 4
　Dialogue 2　Meeting the Guests at the Exit of the Airport ················ 4
Section 3　Exercises ·· 6
Section 4　Extensive Reading ··· 8

Unit 2　Helping with Accommodation ·············· 9

Section 1　Introduction ··· 9
Section 2　Dialogues ·· 10
　Dialogue 1　Helping the Tour Group to Check in at the Hotel ············ 10
　Dialogue 2　Accompanying the Guest to Check in at the Hotel ············ 10
Section 3　Exercises ·· 12
Section 4　Extensive Reading ··· 14

Unit 3　Talking About the Itinerary ·············· 15

Section 1　Introduction ··· 15
Section 2　Dialogues ·· 16
　Dialogue 1　Discussing the Itinerary ································· 16

1

Dialogue 2　Discussing a Change in the Itinerary ·················· 16
Section 3　Exercises ··· 17
Section 4　Extensive Reading ·· 19

Unit 4　On the Way to the Scenery ························· 21

Section 1　Introduction ·· 21
Section 2　Dialogues ··· 22
　　　Dialogue 1　On the Way to Hailuogou Glacier ·················· 22
　　　Dialogue 2　On the Way to Mt. Emei ···························· 23
Section 3　Exercises ··· 25
Section 4　Extensive Reading ·· 27

Unit 5　Dealing with Complaints ···························· 28

Section 1　Introduction ·· 28
Section 2　Dialogues ··· 29
　　　Dialogue 1　Complaining About the Service of the Hotel ········ 29
　　　Dialogue 2　Complaining About the Service of a Restaurant ··· 30
Section 3　Exercises ··· 31
Section 4　Extensive Reading ·· 32

Unit 6　Dealing with Emergencies ·························· 34

Section 1　Introduction ·· 34
Section 2　Dialogues ··· 35
　　　Dialogue 1　A Guest's Passport Is Lost ························· 35
　　　Dialogue 2　A Guest Is Lost ····································· 36
Section 3　Exercises ··· 38
Section 4　Extensive Reading ·· 39

Part Two Hotel English

Unit 1 The Front Office 43

Section 1　Introduction 43
Section 2　Dialogues 44
　　Dialogue 1　Reservation 44
　　Dialogue 2　Check in Services 45
Section 3　Exercises 48
Section 4　Extensive Reading 50

Unit 2 The Housekeeping Department 52

Section 1　Introduction 52
Section 2　Dialogues 53
　　Dialogue 1　Cleaning the Room 53
　　Dialogue 2　Room Service 54
Section 3　Exercises 56
Section 4　Extensive Reading 59

Unit 3 The Food and Beverage Department 60

Section 1　Introduction 60
Section 2　Dialogues 61
　　Dialogue 1　Receiving the Dinner 61
　　Dialogue 2　Special Chinese Food 62
Section 3　Exercises 65
Section 4　Extensive Reading 66

Unit 4 Business Center 68

Section 1　Introduction 68
Section 2　Dialogues 69

    Dialogue 1　Ticket Services ··· 69

    Dialogue 2　Sending a Fax ··· 70

Section 3　Exercises ·· 73

Section 4　Extensive Reading ··· 74

Unit 5　The Health and Recreation Club ·································· 76

Section 1　Introduction ·· 76

Section 2　Dialogues ··· 77

    Dialogue 1　At the Health Center ··· 77

    Dialogue 2　At Beauty Salon ··· 78

Section 3　Exercises ·· 81

Section 4　Extensive Reading ··· 83

Part Three　MICE English

Unit 1　Conference Services ··· 89

Section 1　Introduction ·· 89

Section 2　Dialogues ··· 90

    Dialogue 1　Reserving a Conference Room ································· 90

    Dialogue 2　Registering at a Conference ··································· 91

Section 3　Exercises ·· 93

Section 4　Extensive Reading ··· 95

Unit 2　Expo Services ·· 96

Section 1　Introduction ·· 96

Section 2　Dialogues ··· 97

    Dialogue 1　Discussing the Preparation Work for the Exhibition ·········· 97

    Dialogue 2　Application & Booth Reservation ····························· 97

Section 3　Exercises ··· 100

Section 4　Extensive Reading ·· 101

Unit 3 Trade Fairs 103

Section 1 Introduction 103
Section 2 Dialogues 104
  Dialogue 1 Visiting a Showroom 104
  Dialogue 2 Introducing Oolong Tea 105
Section 3 Exercises 108
Section 4 Extensive Reading 109

Unit 4 Incentive Travel 111

Section 1 Introduction 111
Section 2 Dialogues 112
  Dialogue 1 Announcing a Schedule 112
  Dialogue 2 Arranging for an Incentive Travel 112
Section 3 Exercises 116
Section 4 Extensive Reading 117

Part Four Scenic Spot English

Unit 1 Dujiangyan Irrigation Project 121

Section 1 Introduction 121
Section 2 Dialogues 122
  Dialogue 1 Visiting Dujiangyan Irrigation Project 122
  Dialogue 2 Visiting Li Dui Park 123
Section 3 Exercises 127
Section 4 Extensive Reading 128

Unit 2 Mt. Qingcheng 129

Section 1 Introduction 129

5

Section 2　Dialogues ··· 130
　　Dialogue 1　Talking About Taoism ··· 130
　　Dialogue 2　Visiting Shangqing Temple ··· 131
Section 3　Exercises ··· 134
Section 4　Extensive Reading ··· 135

Unit 3　Leshan Giant Buddha ··· 136

Section 1　Introduction ··· 136
Section 2　Dialogues ··· 137
　　Dialogue 1　A Panoramic View of Leshan Giant Buddha ··· 137
　　Dialogue 2　Leshan Giant Buddha ··· 139
Section 3　Exercises ··· 142
Section 4　Extensive Reading ··· 143

Unit 4　Mt. Emei ··· 144

Section 1　Introduction ··· 144
Section 2　Dialogues ··· 145
　　Dialogue 1　Wannian Temple ··· 145
　　Dialogue 2　The Golden Summit ··· 146
Section 3　Exercises ··· 149
Section 4　Extensive Reading ··· 149

Unit 5　Jiuzhaigou Valley ··· 151

Section 1　Introduction ··· 151
Section 2　Dialogues ··· 153
　　Dialogue 1　The Shuzheng Lakes ··· 153
　　Dialogue 2　Nuorilang Falls ··· 154
Section 3　Exercises ··· 157
Section 4　Extensive Reading ··· 158

Part Five Chinese Society and Culture

Unit 1 An Overview of China 161

Section 1 Introduction 161
Section 2 Dialogues 163
    Dialogue 1 How Many Wonders Does China Boast? 163
    Dialogue 2 Chengdu — A Charming and Liveable City 164
Section 3 Exercises 166
Section 4 Extensive Reading 167

Unit 2 Main Religions in China 168

Section 1 Introduction 168
Section 2 Dialogues 170
    Dialogue 1 Talking About China's Buddhism 170
    Dialogue 2 The Taoist Temple and the Five-Peck Rice Sect 171
Section 3 Exercises 173
Section 4 Extensive Reading 174

Unit 3 Traditional Chinese Festivals 175

Section 1 Introduction 175
Section 2 Dialogues 180
    Dialogue 1 The Legend of Mid-autumn Festival — The Archer and the Suns 180
    Dialogue 2 Guessing Riddles — The Traditional Activity of the Lantern Festival 181
Section 3 Exercises 183
Section 4 Extensive Reading 184

Unit 4　Chinese Cuisine ········ 186

Section 1　Introduction ········ 186
Section 2　Dialogues ········ 188
　　Dialogue 1　Ordering Sichuan Food at a Restaurant ········ 188
　　Dialogue 2　Tasting Beijing Roast Duck ········ 189
Section 3　Exercises ········ 191
Section 4　Extensive Reading ········ 192

Unit 5　Chinese Art ········ 193

Section 1　Introduction ········ 193
Section 2　Dialogues ········ 197
　　Dialogue 1　Talking about Kung Fu Movies ········ 197
　　Dialogue 2　At a Souvenir Shop ········ 198
Section 3　Exercises ········ 200
Section 4　Extensive Reading ········ 201

Unit 6　Traditional Chinese Medicine ········ 203

Section 1　Introduction ········ 203
Section 2　Dialogues ········ 205
　　Dialogue 1　How to Keep Colds away ········ 205
　　Dialogue 2　Talking About Chinese Medicine ········ 206
Section 3　Exercises ········ 208
Section 4　Extensive Reading ········ 209

Appendix　Useful Vocabulary for Hotel English ········ 211

Reference ········ 224

Part One
Tour Guide English

Unit 1　Meeting the Guests at the Airport

● Section 1　Introduction

　　A tour guide should first do the following preparations before going to the airport: a. Get necessary information of the guests' flight; b. Just before setting off to the airport, telephone the inquiry office of the airport to confirm if the flight will arrive on time; c. Get a car and inform the people involved; d. Be sure to prepare a signboard and put the name of the leader of the tour group you are going to meet and the name of his company so as to avoid meeting the wrong person who has the same name; e. If the tour group is a VIP group, a VIP room and a VIP pass at the airport should be reserved for the guests in advance.

　　At the airport, a tour guide should do the following: a. Smile and welcome the guests warmly; b. Help the guests with their luggage; c. Ask the guests if they need to take a short rest at the airport before going to the hotel.

Discussion

　　1. What kind of preparation is necessary for a tour guide before he goes to the airport to meet an overseas tour group?

2. What should a tour guide do if the flight of the tour group is delayed?

 Section 2   Dialogues

Dialogue 1   Meeting a Guest at the Lobby of the Airport

Scene: The tour guide meets Mr. White at the lobby of the airport.
(T=Tour Guide   G=Mr. White, the guest)

T: Excuse me, but are you Mr. White from the United States?

G: Yes, that's right. I am White. You are...

T: My name is Li Ming. I'm from China International Travel Agency. Our company has assigned me to be your host here in Chengdu.

G: How do you do, Miss Li?

T: How do you do, Mr. White?

G: I'm really glad to meet you here. Thank you for coming to the airport to meet me.

T: It is my pleasure to meet you here.

T: How was your trip, Mr. White?

G: On the whole, it was pretty good, but we feel a little bit tired after the long flight.

T: Should we take a rest at the airport?

G: No, this is my first time to come to Chengdu. I am very excited to see the city.

T: You have enough time to see this city. We have set aside one day for you to visit the city in your travel plan.

G: Oh, very good.

T: It is my pleasure.

G: Now, where are we heading?

T: We are going to the parking lot first; our coach is there. Then we will go to the hotel. We have reserved rooms for the tour group in the hotel.

G: How long will it take to get to our hotel?

T: About 40 minutes.

G: Okay, let's go.

Dialogue 2   Meeting the Guests at the Exit of the Airport

Scene: The tour guide meets Mr. Tom and his wife Susan at the exit of the airport.

(T=Tour Guide   G=Mr. Tom, the guest   S= Susan)

T: Excuse me, sir, are you Mr. Tom from New York?

G: Yes, I am. And you must be our tour guide?

T: Yes, I am. My name is Wang Li. I'm from China Youth Travel Agency. I'm here to meet you.

G: Nice to meet you, Miss Wang.

T: Nice to meet you, Mr. Tom.

G: This is my wife, Susan.

T: Nice to meet you.

S: Nice to meet you, too.

T: Did you have a pleasant trip?

G: Yes, I enjoyed it very much.

T: It's a long way to China, isn't it? I think you must be very tired. We have ordered a VIP room where you can rest for a while.

G: Thank you. You are so thoughtful. But I think I am OK, if everything is ready, we can start for the hotel.

T: No problem. We have already reserved a room in the City Hotel.

G: Do you know where the baggage claim area is?

T: Yes, I do. It is at the corner of the airport lobby.

T: How many pieces of luggage do you have?

G: Three pieces.

T: Let me help you with your luggage.

G: Thank you very much.

T: It is my pleasure.

G: What shall we do then?

T: We will go to the hotel.

G: Where is our hotel?

T: The hotel is in the center of the city.

G: Oh, very good. It is very convenient to visit the city.

T: Let's go to the parking lot first. Our car is waiting for us there.

G: OK, Let's go.

Words and Phrases

the parking lot   停車場

the exit 出口

luggage ['lʌgidʒ]　　*n.* 行李

lobby ['lɒbi]　　*n.* 大廳

duty　　*n.* 關稅

dutiable articles　　應納稅物品

duty-free article　　免稅物品

contraband ['kɒntrəbænd]　　*n.* 違禁品

Useful Expressions

1. How do you do?
2. You must be Mr. Tom from… .
3. It is nice to meet you here.
4. It is my pleasure to meet you here.

Section 3　Exercises

I. Complete the following dialogue according to the Chinese in brackets.

(O = Customs Officer　G = Guest)

G: Good morning, sir.

O: Good morning, ___1___ (有任何需要申報的物品嗎)?

G: Well, _____2_____ (我帶了一部數字照相機和手提電腦供自己用).

O: ___3___ (還有其他東西嗎)?

G: Nothing else.

O: Well, _____4_____ (請你填一下表好嗎)?

O: ___5___ (有違禁品嗎)?

G: No, just things for personal use.

O: _____6_____ (介意打開你的手提箱嗎)?

G: Of course not, sir.

O: What is that?

G: Some apples I bought at the New York airport.

O: Sorry, _____7_____ (我必須把這些蘋果沒收).

G: Why?

O: _____8_____ (食品是不許帶入境的).

O: What is more, I am afraid you have to pay some duty for the three gold necklaces because they are _____9_____ (應納關稅的物品). The others in your suitcase are duty-free.

G: How much should I pay for the necklaces?

O: 200 Yuan RMB.

G: Here is the money.

O: Thanks, _____10_____ (這是你的收據).

G: Is that all?

O: Yes, thank you for your cooperation.

II. Translate the following sentences into English.

1. 打擾一下, 你是來自英國的懷特先生嗎?
2. 你簽證的有效期是三個月。
3. 請問你來中國的目的是什麼? 是觀光還是經商?
4. 能否請你打開手提箱檢查?
5. 這些物品都是要納稅的。

III. Make dialogues according to the given situations. Your dialogue should include the following points.

Situation A: Suppose you are a tour guide. You are going to meet a guest named Tom at the airport. Tips:

1. Meet Mr. Tom at the exit of the airport.
2. Introduce yourself to Mr. Tom.
3. Ask Mr. Tom how he feels about his trip.
4. Help Mr. Tom with his luggage.
5. Tell Mr. Tom that the car is parking at the parking lot of the airport.

Situation B: Suppose you are a tour guide. You are going to meet a tour group at the airport. Mr. Tom is the leader of the tour group. Tips:

1. Meet Mr. Tom and the tour group at the lobby of the airport.
2. Mr. Tom introduces himself to you first.
3. You are somewhat surprised to know that Mr. Tom can recognize you first.
4. You ask Mr. Tom how he can recognize you.
5. You ask Mr. Tom about his trip.

6. You ask Mr. Tom whether the tour group would like to take a rest at the airport because there are some old people in the group.

Section 4　Extensive Reading

A Welcome Speech on the Coach to the Hotel

Good morning, ladies and gentlemen.

Welcome to Chengdu. Welcome to Sichuan.

Please sit down and relax. Your luggage will be sent to our hotel by another coach, so you don't have to worry about it.

Now please let me introduce myself to you. My name is Wang Li. You can call me Xiao Wang in the traditional Chinese way or use my English name: Jane. I am a tour guide from China International Travel Agency, Chengdu Branch. I am assigned by my travel agency to be responsible for you during your stay in Sichuan. This is my card. If you need any help, just let me know. I will be staying with you during your time in Sichuan.

Now, let me introduce my colleague Mr. Zhang to you. He is also from China International Travel Agency. He has 20 years' driving experience. He will drive the coach for you throughout your trip in Sichuan. Please remember the number of this coach: 998866.

During your stay in Sichuan, we will try to make your trip a pleasant one. If you have anything special in your mind that you want to see, please tell me or your tour leader. I hope you will enjoy your stay here.

It will take about 40 minutes to drive to the hotel. If you are tired, you can take a nap on the coach. If you have any questions, you can ask me.

Unit 2
Helping with Accommodation

Section 1   Introduction

To help the guests with the accommodation, the tour guide should do the following: a. Be familiar with the various kinds of hotels in the city including their prices, locations, services and facilities, etc.; b. Understand how to help the foreign guests to check in at the hotel; c. Reserve a room for the guests; d. Have a clear picture of the general situation of the hotel in the city; e. Have a good command of language expressions in helping foreign guests to check in; f. Introduce the services and facilities of the hotel; g. Ask the guests if they are satisfied with the hotel; h. Help the guests to solve possible problems in the hotel.

Discussion

1. Is it useful to know the services of the hotel you are going to recommend to a foreign guest?

2. What can you do to help a guest with his accommodations?

Section 2 Dialogues

Dialogue 1 Helping the Tour Group to Check in at the Hotel

Scene: The tour guide and the guests are at the reception desk of the hotel.
(R=Receptionist   T=Tour Guide   L=the Leader of the Tour Group)

R: Can I help you, sir?

T: Yes, I have reserved some rooms for some American guests under the name of Wang Li.

L: This gentleman is the leader of the tour group. Miss Wang has reserved some rooms for us, and we'd like to check in now, if we may.

R: Yes, Miss Wang has reserved five single rooms and eight standard rooms for you. Is that right?

L: Yes, the number of rooms is correct.

R: Would you please ask all the guests to give the passports to you, sir? Then we can fill in the registration form.

L: Yes, I will collect the passports at once.

L: Here are the passports.

R: Now, would you please fill in this registration form, sir?

L: (Filling in the form) Here you are. Thank you.

R: OK. Thank you. Here are the key cards to the rooms of all the guests.

L: Thank you.

T: What do you think of this hotel?

L: It is a very nice hotel.

T: It is one of the best hotels in Chengdu.

L: Oh, thank you for your help.

Dialogue 2 Accompanying the Guest to Check in at the Hotel

Scene: The tour guide and Mr. Tom are at the reception desk of the hotel.
(R=Receptionist   T=Tour Guide   G=Guest)

R: Good morning, sir. Welcome to our hotel. Can I help you?

G: Good morning. I'd like to have a room in your hotel.

R: Certainly, sir. Do you have a reservation with us?

G: No. Is there a vacant room?

R: Yes, we have some rooms available this evening. What kind of room do you want? We have some vacant single rooms and standard rooms.

G: I want a quiet room.

R: These single rooms are all quiet. They do not face the street.

G: Okay, please give me a single room.

R: How long will you be staying?

G: One night.

R: May I have your passport, please?

G: Here you are.

R: Thank you. Would you please fill in the registration form?

G: No problem. Here you are. How much do you charge for this room?

R: 400 Yuan RMB per night. Would you pay 200 Yuan RMB as deposit?

G: Here you are.

R: Thank you. Here's the key card to Room 2118.

G: Thank you.

T: Mr. Tom, what do you think of this hotel?

G: It is very nice. Thank you for your recommendation of the hotel.

T: It is my pleasure. Just let me know if you need any help.

Words and Phrases

reception desk　服務臺，接待處，前臺

check in　辦理入住手續

reserve [ri'zɜː(r)v]　vt. 預訂

room service　客房服務

banquet ['bæŋkwit]　n. 宴會

dinner party　晚餐會

a standard room　標準間

a single room　單人間

a double room　雙人間

suite [swiːt]　n. 套間

deposit [di'pɒzit]　n. 押金，定金

accommodation [əkɒməˈdeiʃ(ə)n]　　n. 住宿
charge [tʃɑː(r)dʒ]　　vt. / n. 收費
recommend [ˌrekəˈmend]　　vt. 推薦
accompany [əˈkʌmp(ə)ni]　　vt. 陪伴
registration form　住宿登記表
IDD　國際長途電話
DDD　國內長途電話

Useful Expressions

1. Do you have a reservation in our hotel?
2. Would you please fill in the registration form?
3. How much do you charge for a standard room?
4. What do you think of this hotel?
5. Thank you for your recommendation of this hotel.

Section 3　Exercises

I. Complete the following dialogue according to the Chinese in brackets.

(R = Receptionist, T = Tour Guide, G = Guest)

R: Good evening, May I help you?

T: Good evening, ＿＿＿＿＿1＿＿＿＿＿ (有空餘的房間嗎)?

R: Yes, there are some double rooms and single rooms available.

T: (To the Guest) ＿＿＿＿＿2＿＿＿＿＿ (你需要什麼樣的房間，先生)?

G: ＿＿＿＿＿3＿＿＿＿＿ (我要一個可以看海景的房間).

T: (To the receptionist) Is there any room facing the sea that is available?

R: (To the guest) You are very lucky, there is only one room facing the sea that is vacant now.

G: Okay, I will take it.

R: (To the guest) How long will you stay here?

G: Two days.

R: ＿＿＿＿＿4＿＿＿＿＿ (請你填一下這個表好嗎)?

G: OK. (Filling in the form) _____5_____ (這是什麼意思)?

T: _____6_____ (它指你呆在中國的理由). You just write down the reason here. That will be OK.

G: (To the receptionist) Is that OK?

R: Yes, this is your key card to room 3118. _____7_____ (希望你在我們酒店過得愉快).

G: Thanks. _____8_____ (能不能叫門童把我的行李送到我房間)?

R: No problem, just go to your room. Your luggage will be sent to your room.

G: Thank you.

R: It is my pleasure.

II. Translate the following sentences into English.

1. 請你填一下房間登記表好嗎?
2. 你在我們這預訂了房間嗎?
3. 還有空餘的雙人間嗎?
4. 一個單人間的價格是多少?
5. 我需要一個不臨街的安靜單間。

III. Make dialogues according to the given situations. Your dialogue should include the following points.

Situation A: Suppose you are a tour guide. You go to the reserved hotel with Mr. Tom to check in. Tips:

1. Tell Mr. Tom that you have reserved a hotel for him.
2. Tell the receptionist at the hotel that the reservation is under your name.
3. The receptionist at the hotel asks Mr. Tom to show his passport.
4. Help Mr. Tom to fill in the registration form.
5. Ask Mr. Tom what he thinks of the hotel you reserved.

Situation B: Suppose you are a tour guide, you help Mr. White to check in at a hotel. Mr. White has not reserved a room in the hotel. Tips:

1. Mr. White asks you to recommend a hotel.
2. You recommend a hotel and introduce the services to Mr. White.
3. You and Mr. White arrive at the hotel and check in.
4. There are vacant rooms in the hotel.
5. Mr. White wants to have a room that faces the sea.

6. You ask Mr. White if he is satisfied with the hotel.

Section 4   Extensive Reading

Serviced Accommodation

Serviced accommodations include hotels, motels, inns and guest houses which tend to cater to specific markets; for example, city center hotels for businessmen and conferences, hotels for coach groups, and hotels for different social and income sectors. Airport hotels have become important in catering for air travellers, but often because of their strategic location they attract business meetings and conferences.

Youth hostels have played a very important role in supporting the youth travel. The members of the European Federation of Youth Hostel Associations operate some 1,500 youth hostels offering the youth travel and adventure holiday markets offering 150,000 beds every night and account for 15 million bed nights each year.

In recent years, universities and other educational institutions have entered the market. They cater to young people during term time, but design their student accommodations to be suitable for the adult conference and course markets during vacation periods. They utilize their built-in recreation facilities to offer sports holidays and many other special-interest products.

In Europe, as agriculture has continued to play a less important role in the economy of the countryside, farm tourism has become popular as a means to diversify and supplement farm incomes.

Unit 3 Talking About the Itinerary

Section 1 Introduction

   A tour guide should consider the following elements when planning the itinerary for the guests: a. The choice of the right airlines with good services; b. The time available to the guests; c. How much money the guests will spend for their travel; d. The proper order in which to visit different scenic spots or places of interest; e. The proper choice of entertainment programs for guests; f. The use of different means of transportation; g. All the arrangements should consider carefully such things as the age, physical condition, professions, interests, food preferences, and religions of the guests.
   In addition to the above-mentioned points, the tour guide should discuss the itinerary with the guest and ask the guest if any change is needed.

Discussion

   1. What are the basic elements that a tour guide should consider when he is writing a draft of an itinerary?
   2. What is important when a tour guide talks about the itinerary with a guest?

Section 2 Dialogues

Dialogue 1 *Discussing the Itinerary*

Scene: The tour guide discusses the itinerary with Mr. Tom.
(T = Tour Guide   G = Mr. Tom, the guest)

G: Everything is okay. Shall we start discussing the itinerary?

T: Certainly, Mr. Tom. Have you got any special place in your mind that you would like to visit?

G: I think you know Sichuan much better than I do. We only have seven days in Sichuan. In such a short time, is it possible for us to visit a province with such a long history and so many famous places of interest? The time seems far from sufficient.

T: Don't worry about it. I'll make full use of the time and try my best to let you see the most important places of interest in Sichuan.

G: Thank you. It's really very thoughtful of you.

T: It is the second time you visit Sichuan. This time I have drafted an itinerary for Sichuan tour before your arrival. Let us examine it together. You will visit Hailuogou Glacier, Bifeng Gorge, and Mount Siguniang. They are all very beautiful natural scenic spots.

G: That sounds fascinating.

T: Is this draft all right?

G: It is excellent.

T: Anything else you want to change about your itinerary?

G: No, your plan is very wonderful, you needn't make any change.

Dialogue 2 *Discussing a Change in the Itinerary*

Scene: The tour guide discusses the change of the itinerary with Mr. Tom.
(T = Tour Guide   G = Mr. Tom, the guest)

T: Good morning, Mr. Tom.

G: Good morning, Miss Wang.

T: Mr. Tom, are you free now?

G: Yes, I am.

T: Mr. Tom, this is your itinerary. Is there anything you would like to change?

G: Thank you. Let me see. It is very nice on the whole. May I ask you to change the plan for tomorrow evening? Some members of the tour group want to go to some pubs in the city tomorrow evening. The pubs are said to be very famous in the city.

T: Oh, we have organized a party for you and other guests in the tour group at that time. If you want to go there to enjoy yourselves, can we change the party to this evening?

G: Ok. No problem.

T: Mr. Tom, do you have any other question about the itinerary?

G: No, the only change I want is for tomorrow evening. Your travel plan is very good. I really appreciate it. Thank you very much.

T: It is my pleasure to do that.

Words and Phrases

itinerary [ai'tinərəri]　　n. 行程安排

schedule ['ʃedju:l]　　n. 計劃

change the itinerary / make some changes in the itinerary　　改變行程安排

rearrange the itinerary　　重新安排行程

the draft of the itinerary　　草擬的行程

Useful Expressions

1. What do you think of the itinerary?

2. Is there any special place in your mind that you want to visit?

3. If you have any questions about the itinerary, we can make some changes.

Section 3　Exercises

I. Complete the following dialogue according to the Chinese in brackets.

(T=Tour Guide　　G=Guest)

G: Good morning, Miss Wang.

T: Good morning, Mr. Tom.

G: Excuse me, _____1_____ (我妻子和我今天下午不想隨旅行團看川劇), is that OK?

T: But _____2_____ （川劇十分美妙）, and it is the only chance for you to watch it in Sichuan. I think it is a pity for you not to watch the performance of the artists.

G: It does not matter. We are not interested in operas. _____3_____ （我們想去市中心商業區為朋友買一些特產）.

T: Ok, if you are really not interested in the performance, there is no reason not to go downtown. By the way, will you have supper with us this evening?

G: No, _____4_____ （我們自己在市中心吃飯）. By the way, _____5_____ （我們怎樣去市中心商業區）?

T: It is not far from here. You can take a taxi there.

G: Thank you.

T: It is my pleasure.

II. Translate the following sentences into English.

1. 懷特先生，你現在空嗎？我們可不可以商討一下旅遊的行程安排？
2. 你是否有很想去遊覽的地方？
3. 如果你對旅遊行程安排不滿意，我們可以立即修改。
4. 我可不可以修改一下明天晚上的行程安排？我想見幾個老朋友。
5. 在你到成都之前，我們制定了一個你的旅遊行程的草稿。

III. Make dialogues according to the given situations. Your dialogue should include the following points.

Situation A: Suppose you are a tour guide. You discuss with Mr. Jack the concrete arrangements in his itinerary. Tips:

1. Mr. Jack is a businessman visiting Sichuan. He wants to visit some factories in Sichuan.
2. Mr. Jack wants to spend one day to see his friends in Chengdu.
3. He wants to see some scenic spots in Sichuan.
4. Recommend some scenic spots to him.
5. Recommend some famous Sichuan food to him.
6. Tell him you will make a draft of his itinerary.

Situation B: Suppose you are a tour guide. You discuss with Mr. Tom, the leader of a tour group, some changes of their itinerary. Tips:

1. The flight of the tour group is delayed because of the bad weather, so the

itinerary needs to be changed a little bit.

2. Ask Mr. Tom his opinions on how to change the itinerary.

3. Mr. Tom tells you that some guests want to see their friends in China, so they want to have a half day free to see their friends.

4. Mr. Tom tells you that some members of the tour group are very interested in Sichuan food. So he hopes you can meet their needs when you arrange meals for them.

5. Tell Mr. Tom that you will rearrange the itinerary as quickly as possible.

● Section 4   Extensive Reading

The Itinerary of a Three-day Tour Around Chengdu

Day One Chengdu

Arrive in Chengdu, capital of Sichuan. Meet the local guide at airport and transfer to hotel. Stay overnight at the Holiday Inn.

Day Two Chengdu-Leshan-Mt. Emei

Leave for Leshan in the morning. Upon arrival in Leshan visit the Giant Buddha in Lingyun Temple. The Giant Buddha, completed in Tang Dynasty after 90 years' construction, enjoys a fame as the biggest sitting stone sculpture in the world with a height of 71 meters. Carved on the cliff face, the sculpture is well designed with perfect balance and an effective water drainage system. After visiting the Lingyun Temple and the Giant Buddha, boat on the Mingjiang River to see the front side of the Giant Buddha and 「the Hidden Buddha」. Afterwards head for Mt. Emei, the main ritual place of Samantabhadra Bodhisattva (Puxian Pusa) and one of the four most celebrated Buddhist Mountains in China. Visit Baoguo Temple at the foot of Mt. Emei. Overnight at Emeishan Grand Hotel.

Day Three Mt. Emei-Chengdu

Early in the morning take the sightseeing bus to the Leidongping Bus Station along the 52-kilometer zigzag mountain road. Upon arrival, take the cable car to the Golden Summit. With an elevation of 3099 meters, if it is fine, you find your visions broadened; the verdant forest waves surge along the mountain; Mingjiang River, Qingyi River, and Dadu River are like three pieces of silk; Mt. Daxue and Mt. Gongga seem to stretch to the horizon; the sun emerges with shimmering rays through the surging clouds. Luckily enough, the Buddhist halo is available to see. After visiting Huazang Temple and the golden statue of Samantabhadra Bodhisattva (Puxian Pusa), take the cable car and the sightseeing bus down to the foot of Mt. Emei, drive back to Chengdu. Overnight at the Holiday Inn.

Unit 4
On the Way to the Scenery

Section 1 Introduction

A tour guide's preparations before going to places of interest should include the following: a. Take the tour flag with oneself and carry the tickets for places of interest or for some tourist programs; b. Remind the driver of the car or coach to do full preparations for his driving in advance; c. Make sure that dinners for the guests are well-arranged and prepared; d. Before starting off to the places of interest, the tour guide should arrive at the meeting place at least ten minutes in advance so that the tour guide can have some time to deal with emergencies or to politely greet the guests and talk with them a little to better understand them and their needs; e. Tell the guests about things they should be careful of, for example, the tour guide should remind the guests of the geographical conditions of the scenic spots and remind especially old guests of some possible dangers while visiting certain areas; f. The tour guide should be in time to ask the guests to get on the coach; The guide should stand at the side of the coach politely and count the guests; g. If the tour guide finds some guests have not arrived at the meeting place on time, he should try to deal with the situation and make proper arrangements.

In the coach, on the way to the scenic areas, the local tour guide should do the following: a. Repeat today's sightseeing arrangements, including the time and places for lunch and supper; b. Tell the guests how much time is needed to arrive at the scenic spots; c. Introduce the guests to local customs and geographical conditions of the scenic spots; d. Give a brief introduction to the scenic spots to arouse the guests' interest and answer the guests' questions about them; e. If it takes a long time to arrive at the place of interest, the tour guide can do something to keep the guests from getting bored. For instance, the tour guide can tell some interesting Chinese stories or sing some songs to the guests.

Discussion

1. What should a tour guide do when the guests are on the bus to visit a scenic spot?
2. What kind of preparations should a tour guide make before going to the scenery?

● Section 2 Dialogues

Dialogue 1 On the Way to Hailuogou Glacier

Scene: On the way to Hailuogou Glacier, the tour guide is introducing some information about Ya'an city.

(G = Tour Guide   T = Tourist)

G: Today, our tour destination is Hailuogou Glacier. We are now driving on the Chengdu—Ya'an expressway. The total distance is about 300 kilometers, 8 hours bus ride. After 2 hours drive, we will arrive at Ya'an, a city located at the western rim of the Sichuan Basin. It used to be the starting point of the southern Silk Road in China, which is also called the ancient Tea-Horse Path. As a commercial passage for barter, it begins from Ya'an, passes Liangshan in Sichuan, Lijiang and Diqing in Yunnan, Lhasa in Tibet and finally gets into Bhutan, Nepal and India.

T: Wow. It's amazing that Ya'an has such an important role. Could you say something about the city?

G: Yes. It is famous for three characteristics: Ya rain, Ya girl, Ya fish. Ya'an is called 「the Rain City」because it rains more than 250 days a year. Many people are very curious about this weather phenomenon and want to know the reason. There is a local legend that a mythological figure called Nüwa, just like Eva in western mythology, could not find the five-colored stones to mend the collapsed sky, and left a hole above Ya'an. So it often rains in Ya'an. In fact, Ya'an lies in a geographical location — so-called 「Huaxi Rain Belt Zone」, at the conjunction of two big mountain ranges-the Qionglai Mountain Range and the Longmeng Mountain Range.

T: It's an interesting story. What does Ya girl mean? Does it mean the girls here are beautiful?

G: Yes. the humid climate and rich rainfall give the local girls a beautiful complexion.

T: How about Ya fish? Is this fish different from others?

G: Yes. Ya fish is very delicious. After eating it, you will never forget the delicacy. Besides these, the humid climate and abundant rainfull and vegetation make Ya'an one of the birthplaces of the tea culture in the world. It is also a birthplace of the Giant Panda. If you are interested in Chinese tea and tea culture, you can select and brew tea here. Well, we have arrived at Ya'an city. It's time to show you around the city! After two hours in Ya'an, we will continue our trip to Hailuogou Glacier.

Dialogue 2　On the Way to Mt. Emei

Scene: On the way to Mt. Emei, the tour guide introduces Mt. Emei.

(T=Tour Guide　G1=Guest1　G2=Guest 2　G3=Guest3　G4=Guest 4)

T: Ladies and gentlemen, we are on the way to Mt. Emei. It will take us about 20 minutes to go to this famous mountain resort. During this time I'll give you a brief introduction.

Mt. Emei rises 3,099 meters above sea level in Emei County, 160 kilometers southwest of Chengdu. It is known as 「Beauty under Heaven」, 「Botanical Kingdom」, 「Paradise of Animals」 and 「Geological Museum」 and 「Fairy Mountain and Buddhist Kingdom」. In 1996, it was made a UNESCO world natural and cultural heritage.

There are four scenic areas on Mt. Emei: Baoguo Temple, Qingyin Pavilion and Jiulao Cave, Wannian Temple and the Golden Summit. Standing on the top of the Golden Summit, you can not only enjoy the snowy mountains in the west and the vast plain in the east but also appreciate four spectacles: the Clouds Sea, the Sunrise, the Buddhist halo and the Magic Lanterns.

The weather on Mt. Emei is changeable. There is 14℃ temperature difference between the foot of the mountain and its peak. The average temperature during July and August is around 11.8℃. Mt. Emei is a natural「Oxygen Bar」, where the average Negative Oxygen Ions in one cubic meter are up to 1 million, which is 500-1,000 times more than that in its city cousins. So it is an appealing summer resort.

G1: How long will we stay on the mountain?

T: We will stay there for two days. For the first day, we will visit Baoguo Temple, Wannian Temple, Qingyin Pavilion. We will stay at the hotel on the top of the mountain: The Golden Summit.

G2: Excuse me, will we have the chance to watch the wonderful sunrise at the top of the mountain?

T: Certainly. We have arranged that. But the weather at the top is changeable. It often snows or rains at this season. If we are lucky, the weather will be fine tomorrow morning, and then we can watch the wonderful sunrise. I hope so.

T: It is hard to climb to the top of the mountain. So we'd better leave everything we don't need on the coach. What is more, if you do not want to climb to the Golden Summit at the top of the mountain, you can get there by cable car.

G3: You said it often snows at the top of the mountain in summer. Should we take more clothes in our bag?

T: Yes, it is a little cold there. You'd better carry a jacket or sweater. We have to put on more layers of clothes on the top of the mountain.

G4: What else should we be careful about during the mountain tour?

T: Very good question. There are many monkeys on Mt. Emei. The monkeys are very cute, but please keep your distance from them. Also, be careful not to make the monkeys angry. If you want to feed the monkeys, please remember to follow the advice of the working staff standing nearby.

G4: Sure, thank you.

T: It is my pleasure.

Words and Phrases

on the way to the scenic spot　在去景點的路上
a natural oxygen bar　天然氧吧
the temperature difference　溫差
meet at the parking lot　在停車場匯合
take the cable car　乘纜車

a layer of clothes 一層衣服

article ['ɑː(r)tik(ə)l] n. 物品

Useful Expressions

1. It will take us about 20 minutes to go to the scenic spot.
2. The scenic spot is very crowded at this season, please follow me.
3. Some places in the mountain are very dangerous, please be careful.

Section 3　Exercises

I. Complete the following dialogue according to the Chinese in brackets.

(T = Tour Guide　G1=guest 1　G2 = guest 2)

T: Ladies and gentlemen, we are on the way to _____1_____ (樂山大佛). It will take us about 30 minutes to go to this famous resort. _____2_____ (在此期間,我想對景區簡單介紹一下).

T: Are you clear about the scenic spot now?

G1: I have one question. How long do we have to wait to see the Buddha?

T: _____3_____ (在這個旅遊旺季,恐怕至少要排隊等候半個小時才能看到大佛).

G2: That's too long to wait on such a hot day. _____4_____ (有些體質弱一點的人可能忍受不了長時間的等待).

T: _____5_____ (如果不想排隊看大佛,可以乘船觀看).

T: Do any guests want to take the boat to see the Buddha?

(Some guests want to take the boat. The guide counts the number of the guests to take the boat)

T: Then our tour group can be divided into two parts.

T: _____6_____ (本地導遊帶領排隊參觀大佛的團員).

I will go with those who take the boat. We will meet at the parking lot at 12 o'clock. Next we'll go for our lunch.

T: Any other questions about the arrangement?

G2: You say there are so many tourists in this busy season. _____ 7 _____（如果我沒跟上本地導遊，該怎麼辦）？

T: If you can't see the guide, then follow other members of the tour group. If you can't see them, meet us at the parking lot at 12 o'clock or call me for help.

II. Translate the following sentences into English.

1. 從酒店到峨眉山腳大約需要 20 分鐘。
2. 步行到山頂需要大約 3 小時，如果你體力不夠，可以乘纜車到山頂。
3. 山頂和山腳溫差很大，山頂夏天經常下雪，請多帶幾件衣服。
4. 即將去的景點遊客很多，請盡量跟在導遊後面。
5. 景區有些地方有點危險，遊覽時請小心。

III. Make dialogues according to the given situations. Your dialogue should include the following points.

Situation A: Suppose you are a tour guide. You have a conversation with some tourists on the coach to the scenery. Tips:

1. Give a brief introduction of the scenic spot.
2. Tell the guests to be careful when visiting the scenic spot because some places in the scenic spot are somewhat dangerous.
3. Tell the guests to bring enough clothes because the top of the mountain is cold.
4. Answer some guests' questions about the scenic spot.
5. Tell the guests to follow the tour guide. If someone is lost, he can phone the tour guide for help.

Situation B: Suppose you are a tour guide. You have a conversation with some tourists before getting on the bus to the scenery. Tips:

1. Some guests ask you questions about the scenic spot first.
2. You give a very brief introduction about the scenic spot and will give a more detailed introduction on the bus.
3. You tell the departure and arrival time.
4. You tell the old guests to bring more layers of clothes because the mountain top is cold.
5. You introduce the scenery to the tourists.

Section 4 Extensive Reading

Tourism Resources in Sichuan

Sichuan is abundant in tourism resources. It has many tourist attractions. It boasts of beautiful landscapes and brilliant culture. Some scenic spots have been made UNESCO World Heritage sites, such as Jiuzhai Valley and Huanglong and Dujiangyan Irrigation System and Qincheng Mountain, Mt. Emei and Leshan Giant Buddha, as well as the stone forest in Xingwen County, the world geological park.

Sichuan has a great many scenic spots at state level, 20 tourist attractions, 15 scenic spots, and nature protection areas, 5 national forest parks, 8 national geological parks, 62 important cultural relic protection units, 5 places for「Forty Best Tourist Attractions in China」, 12 Outstanding National Tourist Cities, 7 Chinese History & Culture cities. Wuhou Temple, Dufu Thatched Cottage Museum and the Sanxindui Cultural Relics are well known in China and abroad. Hailuogou Glacier, the Four Girls Mountain, and the South Sichuan Bamboo Sea are of breath-taking beauty. The minority flavors in A'ba, Ganzi and Lianshan prefectures are colorful with diversified culture reflecting each other. Tourism has become an important industry in Sichuan.

Unit 5
Dealing with Complaints

Section 1 Introduction

When a guest makes complaints, the tour guide should first find out the reasons. Knowing the reasons may help the tour guide understand the problem quickly and help the tour guide to deal with the complaints in time. The following are some possible causes of complaints: a. Unsatifactory service or delayed service at the hotel or restaurant; b. Services or places of interest are not so good as promised; c. Problems are not dealt with in time; d. Scenic spots are too crowded and noisy; e. Some working staff at hotels or restaurants or at some scenic spots may be impolite or even rude; f. Some Chinese tourists may not be polite to the guest; g. The guest may be unsatisfied with the tour guide's service sometimes.

When a guest makes complaints, the tour guide must go up to the guest in time to deal with the situation. To better deal with complaints, the tour guide should: a. Be very patient; b. Smile to the guest and listen carefully; c. Try to understand the reasons why the guest makes complaints; d. While listening to the guests' complaints, try to comfort the guest with soft words and a smiling face.

After listening to the guest's complaints, discuss with the guest and the parties concerned (the hotel manger or restaurant manager, etc.) about how to deal with them.

Discussion

1. Is it important for a tour guide to listen to the complaints of a guest?
2. What should a tour guide do to comfort a guest when he/she is complaining?

Section 2　Dialogues

Dialogue 1　Complaining About the Service of the Hotel

Scene: The tour guide deals with the guest's complaint at the hotel.

(T= Tour Guide　G = Guest)

T: Good morning, Mr. Tom.

G: Good morning, Miss Wang.

T: Is everything ok here, Mr. Tom?

G: Well, actually something is wrong in my room. I didn't sleep well last night. The pillowcases in my room are not comfortable. The water was too hot when I took a shower. I tried to change the temperature of the shower, but it didn't work. I had to wash myself in a rush yesterday evening. It is really annoying.

T: I am really very sorry to hear that. I will tell the hotel manager about all this. He will have someone to send you more comfortable pillowcases and have the shower fixed.

G: That's not all. The most troublesome is the noise. This room faces the street, and I didn't know that there would be so much noise at night. I especially cannot stand the noise of the heavy trucks. I woke up sevaral times last night. I am still a little sleepy this morning. Is it all right to change to a quieter room?

T: No problem, Mr. Tom. I will talk to the manager of the hotel about it.

T: (After talking with the manager) Well, Mr. Tom, you can move to Room 2718, which doesn't face the street. Everything in the room is ready. I will ask a porter to help you to take your luggage there.

G: Thank you, Miss Wang.

T: It is my pleasure. If you need any help, just let me know.

Dialogue 2 Complaining About the Service of a Restaurant

Scene: The tour guide deals with the guest's complaint at a restaurant.

(T=The tour guide   G = Guest   M=Manager)

T: Good evening, Mr. Tom. Are you satisfied with services and dishes of this restaurant?

G: No, the beef the waiter recommended is not very fresh.

T: Oh, I'm sorry to hear that. I will ask the manager to deal with this.

(The manager of the restaurant comes to Mr. Tom.)

M: I am really very sorry about it. This is most unusual. We have fresh beef every day.

G: It smells terrible and I feel unhappy with it.

M: I am very sorry. Would you like me to change it for another one for you? It would be on the restaurant, sir.

G: No, I don't want to try your beef again. It is really disgusting.

M: Maybe you can try our twice-cooked pork. It's a famous Sichuan dish. We will cross the beef off your bill.

G: That's all right.

T: Mr. Tom, I am sorry for the bad service of this restaurant.

G: Do not worry about it. The manager of the restaurant will solve the problem. Thank you very much.

T: It is my pleasure. Just tell me if you have any more trouble.

Words and Phrases

complain [kəmˈpleint]   vt. 投訴
make a complaint   投訴
disgusting [disˈgʌstiŋ]   adj. 令人討厭的
twice-cooked pork   回鍋肉
be on the restaurant   餐館買單（意為：顧客免費）

Useful Expressions

1. Sorry to trouble you, but something seems wrong with the air conditioner in the room.

2. Excuse me, but I don't think the pork is fresh.

3. Sorry, but the heating system does not seem to work in my room.

4. I have got a small problem here. This cake was cooked too long. It tastes dry.

5. I am afraid I have a complaint to make about the service in your restaurant.

6. I am very sorry to hear that. I will ask the hotel manager to solve your problem.

Section 3　Exercises

I. Complete the following dialogue according to the Chinese in the brackets.

(T = Tour Guide　G = Guest　M = Manager)

T: _____1_____ (這兒的一切讓你滿意嗎)?

G: No, _____2_____ (服務員推薦的豬肉不新鮮). What is more, the service is slow. I have had to wait a long time.

T: _____3_____ (很抱歉聽說這種情況). I will ask the manager to deal with this.

M: I am sorry to hear your complaint. _____4_____ (你可不可以嘗試其他菜)? It is on the restaurant.

G: I do not want to try the pork again. It is annoying to think of it.

M: Can you try some steak? _____5_____ (它是我們的特色菜).

G: That is OK.

M: As for the slow service, I will look into the matter. I do apologize to you for the unsatisfactory services.

T: I apdogize for the service here.

G: That is all right. _____6_____ (你已經叫餐廳經理處理這件事了).

II. Translate the following sentences into English.

1. 打擾一下，我覺得這道菜不新鮮。

2. 這個房間太熱了，房間的空調有問題。

3. 這個房間太吵，我經常聽到貨車的噪音，一夜都沒有睡好。

4. 恐怕今天早晨你送的牛奶是酸的。

5. 對不起，我會安排人修理空調。

III. Make dialogues according to the given situations. Your dialogue should include the following points.

Situation A: Suppose you are a tour guide; a guest comes to you to complain about the unsatisfactory facilities in the hotel. Tips:

1. First listen carefully to the guest with a smiling face.
2. Comfort the guest with soft words.
3. Tell the guest that you will ask the manager to deal with the problem.
4. The manager first says sorry to the guest and then gives his suggestion to deal with the problem.
5. The guest accepts the manager's suggestion to deal with the problem.

Situation B: Suppose you are a tour guide; a guest comes to you to complain about poor service in the restaurant. Tips:

1. Ask the guest if he is satisfied with his meal.
2. The guest complains about the poor service in the restaurant.
3. Comfort the guest.
4. Ask the manager of the restaurant to deal with the matter.
5. The manager apologizes and gives his suggestion to deal with the problem.
6. The guest accepts the manager's solution.

Section 4　Extensive Reading

Dealing with Complaints

Tour guides are bound to receive complaints and criticisms. Some of the complaints and criticisms are well justified and very constructive. They are perfect reminders of the areas of the tourism industry that still leave something to be desired. Other complaints are just results of fastidious and difficult personalities. People who make complaints and criticisms can be friendly and reasonable; they can also be rude and abusive. No matter how the person behaves the tour guides should always try to be nice to them. An argument with the guest is the most undesirable thing that can happen to a staff member or a travel agency.

In handling complaints, the guide should always be polite and helpful. He/she should always be ready to lend an attentive ear to what the guest is saying and always hear the guest through. He/she must not interrupt the guest unless necessary. It is advisable for him/her to jot down what the guest has said. He/she should then make a short apology and express his/her understanding of the guest's situation or sympathy with the guest. Only when he/she puts himself/herself in the guest's shoes can he/she look at the problem from other person's perspective. And only when the staff member can look at the guest's problem in the guest's way can he/she is ready to sympathize with the guest. After that the staff members should take actions quickly to remove the complaint, either by making polite, patient and detailed explanations, or making swift, effective corrections and remedies, or reporting the complaint to a superior.

But what he/she intends to do, he/she must keep the guest informed of the measures or actions he/she plans to take and when he/she will carry them out.

Unit 6
Dealing with Emergencies

Section 1   Introduction

    The principles to deal with emergencies are as follows: a. Try to prevent emergencies from happening; b. If an emergency does happen, the tour guide should deal with the situation calmly; c. Try to minimize the damages of guests and the travel agency, if an emergency occurs.

    If a guest's passport is lost, a tour guide should do the following: a. First, try to comfort the guest because the passport is the most important official paper for a person in a foreign country; b. Help the guest to try to find the passport in his luggage or the places at which he has stayed; c. If the passport can not be found, go to the local police station with the guest for help; d. If the passport is not found by the police and all concerned, the tour guide should report the incident to the travel agency; e. The foreign guest should report his loss to the local Public Security Bureau with a written testimonial offered by the travel agency with the guest's photo; f. Then, with this testimonial, the guest should apply for a new passport at his own country's Embassy in China; g. Next, with the new passport, the guest can apply for a new visa in the office of entry and exit visas for foreigners at the Public Security Bureau.

Discussion

1. Do you think it important for a tour guide to know the basic principles of handling emergencies?

2. What can a tour guide do to help a guest if his passport is lost?

Section 2   Dialogues

Dialogue 1   *A Guest's Passport Is Lost*

Scene: Miss Zhang, the tour guide, deals with the loss of a guest's passport.

(Z= Miss Zhang, the tour guide   B = Mr. Black)

B: Excuse me, I have a bad problem to tell you about.

Z: Take it easy. What has happened?

B: Ennnh... I... I can't find my passport. It is very important for me, you know. What can I do? Could you help me?

Z: Don't worry too much. I will try my best to help you to find it. By the way, when did you see it last?

B: I saw it the day before yesterday. But this morning after breakfast when I packed my luggage, I couldn't find it any more.

Z: Then Let's return to your hotel room and search for it carefully. I hope we will be lucky enough to find it.

B: I hope so.

(After looking for it carefully in the hotel room, the passport is not found.)

Z: Do not be nervous, Mr. Black. It seems that we cannot find the passport now.

B: What can we do now, Miss Zhang?

Z: It is a big headache now. First, I have to report this to my travel agency and ask my colleagues for help. As for you, you have to write a report about this incident. Then our travel agency will offer you a testimonial about your loss of the passport.

B: I will do as you told me to. By the way, should I take some pictures of my own?

Z: Of course. You should have some pictures of your own.

B: Then, what can we do next?

Z: We will take the testimonial from our travel agency and report the incident to the

Public Security Bureau. The police will give us a testimonial about the loss of the passport. With the testimonial issued from the police, you can go to the Embassy of your country in China to apply for a new passport. With the new passport, you can apply for a new visa in the office of the entry and exit visas for foreigners at the Public Security Bureau.

B: Thank you very much, you are so nice and helpful.

Z: It is my pleasure to do that.

Dialogue 2　A Guest Is Lost

Scene: The tour guide deals with the emergency that a guest, Mr. Tom, has gotten lost.

(T = Tour Guide　G = Mr. Tom, the guest　G1 = Guest1　G2 = Guest2　G3 = Guest3　L = the leader of the tour group　R = the receptionist)

T: Have you seen Mr. Tom? It seems that he hasn't returned to the restaurant for supper.

G1: I last saw him this afternoon in the lobby of the hotel sitting on the couch. Then I went back to my own room to call my wife and kids to go downtown. When we came to the lobby, he was not there any more. Since then, I haven't seen him at all.

G2: I saw him walk out of the hotel alone this afternoon.

G3: He likes walking on his own. Perhaps it is just hard for us to find him. He is a bit undisciplined. Don't worry too much about him.

T: I am the tour guide. It is my duty to find him.

T: (To the leader of the tour group) Will you please take care of the guests in our tour group for the time being? I will look for Mr. Tom.

L: That's OK.

T: Thank you.

L: Not at all.

(The tour guide searches the restaurant inside and out for a few minutes, but she does not find Mr. Tom. She comes back to the leader of the tour group.)

T: Is Mr. Tom back?

L: He hasn't come back.

T: Perhaps he has returned to the hotel already and then gone to the restaurant. Let's phone the hotel to see whether he has come back.

L: I remember his room number at the hotel. His room is next to mine. His room number is 3118.

T: (Calling the receptionist of the hotel) Is that the City Hotel?

R: Yes, what can I do for you?

T: This is Wang Li, the tour guide for the tour group from America. I want to see if Mr. Tom of this tour group is in his hotel room. His room number is 3118.

R: Ok. I will ask the floor attendant to check. Just wait for a few minutes.

R: Miss Wang, Mr. Tom is not in his room.

T: Thank you.

R: It is my pleasure.

T: (To the leader of the tour group) Mr. Tom is not in his hotel room. Will you take all the members of the tour group to the hotel first? The coach is at the back of the restaurant, the driver is on the coach. I will phone the driver of the coach about this. Please make sure all the other guests in the group get on the coach. I will stay here to wait for Mr. Tom.

L: No problem.

T: Thank you very much.

L: Do not mention it.

(Just as the foreign guests are going out of the restaurant, Mr. Tom comes to the restaurant.)

T: It is nice to see you again, Mr. Tom. We have been looking for you everywhere.

G: I am really sorry for that. The city center is really so beautiful. I was busy taking photos. I forgot the time. I am sorry for the trouble.

T: It doesn't matter. Next time, you'd better follow us and come back to the meeting spot on time.

G: It is very kind of you.

Words and Phrases

emergency [iˈmɜː(r)dʒ(ə)nsi]　　n. 緊急情況

passport [ˈpɑːspɔː(r)t]　　n. 護照

visa [ˈviːzə]　　n. 簽證

the Public Security Bureau　　公安局

embassy [ˈembəsi]　　n. 大使館

apply for a new visa 申請新簽證

testimonial [testiˈməʊniəl] *n.* 證明

The Entry and Exit Visa Department for Foreigners at the Public Security Bureau 公安局出入境管理處

Useful Expressions

1. When did you see your passport last?
2. Do not worry too much. I will try my best to help you to find your luggage.

Section 3　Exercises

I. Complete the following dialogue according to the Chinese in brackets.

(T = Tour Guide　G = Guest　D = Doctor)

T: Good morning, Mr. Tom.

G: Good morning, Miss Wang.

T: _____1_____（你面色蒼白）. What happened?

G: I have a cold.

T: _____2_____（需要看醫生嗎）?

G: Yes, I think so.

T: Let me go to the nearby hospital with you.

G: Thank you very much, you are really very helpful.

T: _____3_____（這是我的職責）.

(at the hospital)

D: _____4_____（你有什麼問題嗎）?

G: I think I have a cold, doctor.

D: _____5_____（你有些什麼症狀）?

G: _____6_____（我流鼻涕，頭痛）.

D: _____7_____（咳嗽嗎）?

G: No, I don't.

D: _____8_____（嗓子痛嗎）?

G: Yes, my throat feels swollen.

D: _____9_____（我檢查一下你的喉嚨）. Open your mouth.

Please say「Ah」.

D：It is a common cold. Do not worry.

G：Thank you, Doctor.

II. Translate the following sentences into English.

1. 你最後看到你的簽證在什麼時候？

2. 護照掉了先要由中國的公安機關開一個遺失證明。

3. 外國遊客可以憑中國公安機關開具的護照遺失證明到本國的中國大使館申請護照。

4. 我們徹底地找一下你的房間，看能否找到你的錢包。

5. 別擔心，我們會盡力幫你找回行李。

III. Make dialogues according to the given situations. Your dialogue should include the following points.

Situation A：Suppose you are a tour guide; one of the guests' luggage is lost. Tips：

1. Comfort the guest.

2. Try to help the guest to find the luggage.

3. If the luggage is not found, you should help the guest to deal with the trouble.

Situation B：Suppose you are a tour guide leading a group of foreign guests, and one of the guests is sick. Tips：

1. Ask the guest if something is wrong.

2. The guest tells you that he is ill.

3. Comfort the guest.

4. Go to the hospital with the guest.

Section 4　Extensive Reading

Tips for Dealing with Cases of Emergencies in Travel

1. Delayed Flight or Ship

a. Contact the airlines to confirm when the flight will take off.

b. Work together with airlines to arrange a hotel for the guests for the time being.

c. Work with the parties concerned to minimize the damage.

d. Try to comfort the guests.

e. Talk with the leader of the tour group to make adjustments to the sightseeing plan.

f. If there is any change in the travel plan, tell the local guide for the next stop of the tour to make changes accordingly.

2. A Guest's Luggage is Lost

a. Try to help the guest to find it.

b. If it is not found, report it to the travel agency.

c. Help the guest to ask for compensation from the insurance company.

d. Help the guest to deal with the trouble brought about by the loss of the luggage.

3. A Guest Has Lost His Way in Sightseeing

a. Try to find the guest with his family members or his friends.

b. The local tour guide goes on with the sightseeing with other members of the tour group.

c. Contact the travel company or the working staff of the scenic spot to seek help to find the lost guest.

d. If the guest is found, encourage him to apologize to other members of the tour group for the trouble brought about by his actions.

4. A Guest is Sick

a. First, try to comfort the guest because it is somewhat miserable for a person to be ill in a foreign country.

b. Go to the hospital with the guest.

c. Help the guest to communicate with the doctor.

d. Pay attention to the guest and say warm words to him to show your love and care.

國內外一些主要的旅行社及網址：

中國國際旅行社(China International Travel Service) http://www.cits.cn/

中國旅行社(China Travel Service) http://www.ctsho.com/

上海春秋旅行社(Shanghai Spring and Autumn Travel Service) http://www.spring-tour.com/

西安天馬旅行社(Xi'an Tianma International Travel Service) http://www.tm-silkroad.com/

中國青年旅行社(China Youth Travel Service) http://www.cytsonline.com/

美國運通(American Express) http://www.americanexpress.com.cn

中旅途易有限公司(TUI China Travel Co.Ltd) http://www.tui.cn/mice/

Part Two
Hotel English

Unit 1　The Front Office

Section 1　Introduction

　　The Front Office of a hotel is generally considered as the 「shop window」 of a hotel because the guest's first and last impressions take place here. It is a liaison between the guest and the hotel and the focus of guests' requests for information and service as well as the profit center of room sales. It primarily deals with reservations, reception, concierge, room allocation, check in and check out, payments and so on. As the nerve center of a hotel, it also provides assistance to guests during their stay, completes their accommodation, offers food and beverage, provides information, exchanges foreign currencies, handles guests' complaints/difficult situations to create 「a home away from home」 for guests. The Front Office staff's efficiency and personality are of great importance to the realization of the hotel's aim. To fulfill these tasks, the staff must have a neat and smart appearance, good manners, adaptability, good knowledge of languages and a head for figures. But the most important of all the qualities is a real liking for people and a warm desire to help them.

Discussion

1. What are the functions of the Front Office? According to you, what are the duties of a hotel receptionist?

2. What qualities should the Front Office staff have?

Section 2   Dialogues

Dialogue 1   Reservation

Scene: Mrs. Houston is calling to the Shanghai International Hotel to make a room reservation.

(R = receptionist   G = Guest)

R: Shanghai International Hotel. Good morning, Madam. May I help you?

G: Yes. I'm Whitney Houston. I'm phoning from the U.S.A.. I'd like to book a room in your hotel.

R: What's the arrival date and how long will you be staying, please?

G: I'm going to arrive on September 30th and will stay for 4 days inclusive.

R: Very good. What kind of room would you like? We have single rooms, double rooms, standard rooms, suites and deluxe suites.

G: A double room with bath. Do you have a room available?

R: Wait a moment, please. Oh, yes, there are still some.

G: That's right. How much do you charge?

R: 880 Yuan RMB per night.

G: That's quite expensive. Do you give any discount?

R: I'm very sorry. We usually have high occupancies in the peak seasons. I will give you a room which commands a good view of Huangpu River.

G: That'll be fine. I will take it. Please keep the room blocked for me. Do you need a deposit?

R: No. We'll keep your reservation until 6:00 p.m. on that evening. May I have your phone number?

G: Ok, my phone number is 001-886-356-2495.

R: Very well, Mrs. Houston. I would like to confirm your reservation. A double room with bath from September 30th to October 3rd. Is that right?

G: Exactly. Thank you very much.

R: You're welcome. We're looking forward to seeing you next Tuesday.

Dialogue 2   Check in Services

Scene: Mr. Smith has just arrived in the lobby of the hotel. He is busying checking in at the reception desk.

(R = receptionist   G = Guest)

R: Good afternoon, sir. Welcome to our hotel. May I help you?

G: Yes. I booked a room one week ago.

R: May I have your name please, sir?

G: John Smith.

R: Just a moment, sir. Let me look through the list. Yes, we do have a reservation for you, Mr. Smith. A twin room with shower for 4 days. The room rate is 500 Yuan RMB per night including breakfast. You've paid 500 Yuan RMB as a deposit. Is that correct?

G: That's it.

R: Would you please fill in this registration form, sir?

G: Sure. Here you are. Is that all right?

R: Let me see... name, address, nationality, forwarding address, passport number, signature and the date of departure. Oh, here, sir. You have forgotten to fill in the date of departure. May I confirm your departure date?

G: October 24th.

R: May I see your passport, please? Thank you, sir. Now everything is in order. This is the receipt and key card. Your room is 1820, overlooking a large lake. Please make sure that you have the key card with you all the time. You need to show your card when you sign for your meals and drinks at the restaurants and the bars.

G: Yes, thank you. By the way, do you have a western style restaurant here? We are not quite used to Chinese food yet, you know.

R: Don't worry, Mr. Smith. We have three authentic foreign restaurants on the second floor, one French restaurant, one Muslim restaurant and one Japanese restaurant. Besides, we also have two Chinese restaurants on the third floor. So you'll have a variety of choices. And the breakfast is from 7:30 a.m. to 9:00 a.m..

G: Wonderful! We can vary our meals every day. Thank you very much.

R: You are welcome. The elevator is behind you. You can go to your room directly, and the bellman will deliver your baggage to your room later. I hope you enjoy your stay with us.

G: Thank you.

Words and Phrases

concierge [ˌkɔːnsiˈɛəʒ]   *n.* 看門人
receptionist [riˈsepʃənist]   *n.* 接待員
reservation [ˌrezəˈveiʃn]   *n.* 預定
inclusive [inˈkluːsiv]   *adj.* 包括的
twin room   雙人間
triple room   三人間
junior suite   普通套房
suite [swiːt]   *n.* 套房；隨員
duplex suite   復式套房

deluxe suite　豪華套房

Presidential suite　總統套房

available ［əˈveiləbl］　*adj.* 可提供的

discount ［ˈdiskaʊnt］　*vt. /n.* 打折, 折扣

occupancy ［ˈɒkjəpənsi］　*n.* 佔有

peak season　*n.* 旺季

slack season　*n.* 淡季

command ［kəˈmɑːnd］　*n.* 命令；指揮　*vt.* 命令；指揮；俯瞰

confirm ［kənˈfɜːm］　*vt.* 確認

lobby ［ˈlɒbi］　*n.* 大廳

look through　瀏覽

forwarding address　投遞地址

departure ［diˈpɑːtʃə(r)］　*n.* 離開；起程

receipt ［riˈsiːt］　*n.* 收據, 發票

overlook ［ˌəʊvəˈlʊk］　*n.* 遠眺；瞭望

authentic ［ɔːˈθentik］　*adj.* 真正的

elevator ［ˈeliveitə(r)］　*n.* 電梯

bellman ［ˈbelmən］　*n.* 行李員；門童

deliver ［diˈlivə(r)］　*vt.* 遞送；交付

Useful Expressions

1. What kind of room would you like (prefer)?

2. A double room with a front view is 140 US dollars per night.

3. A double room with a rear view is 115 US dollars per night.

4. Could you tell me under whose name the reservation was made?

5. May I have your name and phone number, please?

6. How long will you be staying?

7. Would you please fill in this registration form, sir?

8. Do you have any vacancies (vacant rooms)?

9. I'm very sorry, we have no room available. But I can recommend you another hotel here.

10. We won't be able to guarantee you a room for... (date)

11. A single room is 800 Yuan RMB per night, with a 15% service charge.

12. We offer 10% discount for group reservations.

13. What credit card are you holding, sir?

14. Can I pay with traveller's cheques?

15. You have to change the US dollars into RMB at the exchange counter over there.

16. The credit limit by the visa card office is $10,000 every day, we need their permission to extend credit over the amount. Would you like to pay difference in cash?

Section 3　Exercises

I. Complete the following dialogue according to the Chinese in brackets.

(C = Clerk　　G = Guest)

C: Good morning, sir. ＿＿＿＿1＿＿＿＿ (有什麼能為您效勞的嗎)?

G: Yes, ＿＿＿2＿＿＿ (我想支付我在酒店的帳單).

C: Your name and your room number, please?

G: John Smith, room 1102.

C: Yes, Mr. Smith, have you used any hotel services since your staying here?

G: I used the mini-bar and I drank two cans of beer. ＿＿＿＿3＿＿＿＿ (我叫了早餐但我付了現金).

C: All right. ＿＿＿＿4＿＿＿＿ (您的帳單總計1,500美元, 給您, 請檢查一下).

G: Correct.

C: ＿＿＿＿5＿＿＿＿ (您用什麼支付方式, 先生)?

G: ＿＿＿＿6＿＿＿＿ (您這裡可用什麼樣的卡)?

C: American Express, Master, International Diner's Club, Visa card, Euro card, International Great Wall and so on. ＿＿＿＿7＿＿＿＿ (請問您有什麼卡)?

G: Visa card. Here it is.

C: Fine. ＿＿＿＿8＿＿＿＿. (讓我為您刷卡吧). Wait a moment, please.... Sorry to have kept you waiting, ＿＿＿9＿＿＿ (請您在這裡簽名, 好嗎)?

G: OK. Here you are.

C: Thank you, sir. ＿＿＿＿10＿＿＿＿ (這是您的卡,

零錢和收據/發票). Hope you had a nice stay in our hotel.

II. Translate the following sentences into English.

1. 登記住宿時，客人應該填寫登記表格並出示護照才可拿到房卡。
2. 對不起，我們酒店不打折，因為現在是旅遊旺季。
3. 請問您想定單人間還是雙人間？
4. 你確定 10 月 1 日我們有一個單人間嗎？
5. 我可以給您安排一個房間，可以俯視黃浦江的景色。

III. Fill in the registration form of temporary residence for foreigners (外國人臨時住宿登記表).

The Registration Form

Names in Full(全名)　　Sex(性別)	Date of Birth(出生年月)　　　Nationality(國籍)
Permanent Address(永久地址)	Occupation and Place of Work(職業及工作處所)
Purpose of Stay (停留事由)	Visa or Travel Document Numbers and Date of Validity (護照或旅遊證號碼及期限)
Where from and to (何處來何出去)	Date of Arrival(抵達日期)
Room No.(房間號碼)	Duration of Stay (擬住日期)
Received by (接待單位)	Date & Signature (日期及簽名)

IV. Make dialogues according to the given situations. Your dialogue should include the following points.

Situation A：Suppose you are Jack Wilson. You will make a reservation in a hotel by phone. Tips：

1. You need a single room with shower.
2. The room rate is 300~500 Yuan RMB.
3. You need pay a deposit.
4. You need pick-up service at the airport.
5. Your arrival time and departure time.

Situation B: After checking in, Mr. Smith wants to keep his luggage at the Cloakroom / at the Bell Captain's Desk. The clerk serves him. Tips:

1. He has two pieces of luggage to keep at the Cloakroom.
2. There are valuable or breakable items in his bag.
3. His name tag / claim tag is 28.
4. This cloakroom is open until…
5. The hotel offers 24-hour service here.

Section 4 Extensive Reading

The Genre of Hotel

The hotel industry is a mature industry marked by intense competition. It rebounded during and immediately after World War II, as the volume of travel increased. Different types of hotels meet the varied needs of today's traveling public. In America, common American hotel classifications are as follows:

Commercial Hotels cater mainly to business clients and usually offer room service, coffee-shop, dining room, cocktail lounge, laundry and valet service as well as access to computers and fax services.

Airport Hotels are located near airports and are a conveniently located to provide any level of service from a simple room to room service. They may provide bus or limousine service to the air lines.

Economy Hotels provide a limited service and are known for clean rooms at low prices, meeting just the basic needs of travelers.

Suite or All-Suite Hotels are hotels which offer spacious layout and design. Business people like the setting which provides space to work and entertain separate from the bedroom.

Residential Hotels used to be very popular. The typical residential hotel offers long-term accommodations.

Casino Hotels are often quite luxurious. Their main purpose is in support of the gambling operation. Casino hotels often offer top name entertainment and excellent restaurants.

Resort Hotels are the planned destination of guests, usually vacationers. This is because resorts are located at the ocean or in the mountains away from inner cities. Resort hotels may offer any form of entertainment to keep their guests happy and busy.

「Green」Hotels are environmentally-friendly properties whose managers are eager to institute programs that save water, save energy and reduce solid waste—while saving money—to help PROTECT OUR ONE AND ONLY EARTH!

Motels or motor hotels are usually located outside the center of town near major roads and are less expensive than hotels.

Unit 2
The Housekeeping Department

Section 1 Introduction

The Housekeeping Department is the backbone of a hotel. It must ensure that the hotel's reputation and impression with guests remains at a high level. Housekeeping staff, such as floor clerks, house-maids and room boys, all have direct contact with guests and contribute to the guests' overall experience with the hotel. As the main source of economic income of a hotel, the guest room income accounts for 50% of its total income. The main duty of the staff is to see to the cleanliness and tidiness and comfortableness of all rooms and places in the hotel. Besides, the staff should provide good and reasonable services which coordinate closely with the Front Office, such as chamber services, laundry services, special services, personal services, miscellaneous services, maintenance services, to make guests really enjoy their stay in the hotel and determine whether they will return.

This department demands a well-organized and well-trained staff who can do a great deal to assure a high business repeat and occupancy rate, not only through the efficiency in their jobs but also through their heart-felt warmth in serving the guests. So the qualities of housekeeping department staff – enthusiasm, patience, politeness and professional spirits–can ensure that the staff fulfill their tasks.

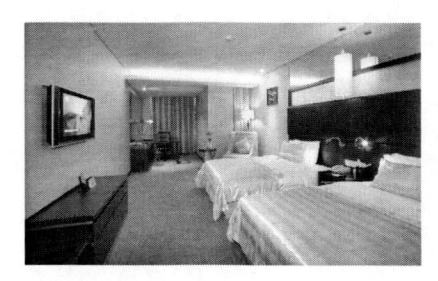

Discussion

1. Do you think the Housekeeping Department is the backbone of a hotel? Why?
2. What are the duties of the housekeeping staff? How can you do your duty as a room attendant?

Section 2　Dialogues

Dialogue 1　Cleaning the Room

Scene: Mr. White is sitting in the room when a chamber maid knocks at the door.
(CM = Chamber Maid　　W = Mr. White)

CM: Housekeeping. May I come in?

W: Yes, please.

CM: Good morning, Mr. White. Would you like me to clean your room now, sir?

W: You can do it half an hour if you like. I am preparing some data now. By the way, would you please do me a favor?

CM: Yes, sir. I'm always at your service.

W: My son is coming to see me. Could I have an extra bed, a kind of roll-away?

CM: Please contact the Front Office first. I'll get you the extra bed with their permission.

W: How much does an extra bed cost?

CM: It's 100 Yuan RMB for one night.

W: Ok, I'll call the Front office. By the way, would you please bring two extra pillows and two blankets, I feel a little bit of cold at night. And I would like to have a few more hangers. I will stay here for a whole week and I have a lot of clothes.

CM: Certainly, sir. I will prepare them well. I do wish we had known earlier.

W: It's kind of you to say so.

CM: It's my pleasure. I hope you are enjoying your stay with us.

Dialogue 2　Room Service

Scene: Mr. Black is calling to order breakfast for tomorrow morning, the operator receives his call.

(O = Operator　　B = Mr. Black)

O: Good evening, Room service. May I help you?

B: Yes, this is Room 1506. I'm Jackson Black. I'd like to order breakfast for tomorrow morning.

O: Certainly, sir. We offer three types of breakfast: American, Continental and Chinese breakfast. Which one would you prefer?

B: What is in the American breakfast?

O: Fried eggs, juice, coffee, sausage, bacon or ham, bread or toast.

B: That would be fine. I will have the American breakfast. I'd like two fried eggs, sunny-side up, a piece of bread, ham and grapefruit juice, please.

O: Would you like any cereal?

B: Yes, a dish of Cream of Wheat. That's all. Thanks.

O: What time would you like your breakfast served, sir?

B: 8:30.

O: Yes, sir. Let me confirm your order. Mr. Black, Room 1506, American breakfast, fried eggs, sunny-side up, a piece of bread, ham and grapefruit juice and a dish of Cream of Wheat, is that right?

B: Exactly.

O: Your order will be ready tomorrow morning. Thank you for calling. Have a good evening.

Words and Phrases

Housekeeping Department　客房部
ensure　[inˈʃʊə(r)]　　vt. 確保
see to　注意、負責
backbone　[ˈbækbəʊn]　　n. 脊梁, 脊柱, 骨幹

cleanliness ［ˈklenlinəs］　　n. 清潔
coordinate ［kəʊˈɔːdineit］　　vt. 協調
chamber ［ˈtʃeimbə(r)］　　n. 房間
laundry ［ˈlɔːndri］　　n. 洗衣
miscellaneous ［ˌmisəˈleiniəs］　　adj. 多種多樣的，多方面的，混雜的
maintenance ［ˈmeintənəns］　　n. 維修
go sightseeing　　觀光
do sb. a favor　　幫忙
pillow ［ˈpiləʊ］　　n. 枕頭
extra ［ˈekstrə］　　adj. 額外的
blankets ［ˈblæŋkits］　　n. 毯子
hanger ［ˈhæŋə(r)］　　n. 衣架

1. Room service 送餐服務
2. American breakfast 美式早餐（generally including juice, coffee, milk, sausage, bacon and ham, egg, bread or toast）
3. Continental breakfast 歐式早餐（generally including bun, butter, honey, jam, coffee and tea）
4. Chinese breakfast 中式早餐（generally including millet congee, fried eggs, dumpling, steamed dumpling/ bread, spring roll, soybean milk）
5. fried eggs 煎蛋（sunny-side up 只煎一面，over easy 兩面稍微煎一下），poached egg 水煮蛋，scrambled egg 炒雞蛋
6. medium rare 中等偏生（牛排生熟度分為：rare 三分熟，medium rare 中等偏生，medium 半熟，medium well 八成熟，well done 熟透）
7. tomato juice 番茄汁，grapefruit juice 葡萄柚汁，orange juice 橙汁，pineapple juice 菠蘿汁，lemonade juice 檸檬汁

Useful Expressions

1. Housekeeping / Room service. May I come in?
2. Would you like me to do your room / do the turn-down service now, sir?
3. What time would be convenient / better for you, sir?
4. What kind of fruit would you like: apple, orange, watermelon, banana or grape?
5. What kinds of breakfast do you prefer?

6. The baby-sitting service charges 20 Yuan per hour, with a minimum of 4 hours.

7. Do you think it is necessary for me to send for a doctor?

8. Do you need some aspirin / painkillers / plasters / bandages / sleeping pills?

9. We also provide express service, but it will cost 50% more.

10. Special laundry bags with lists are placed in your wardrobe. Washing handed in by 9:00 a.m. will be returned to you after 5:30 p.m. on the same day.

Section 3   Exercises

I. Complete the following dialogue according to the Chinese in brackets.

(R = Room Attendant   B = Mr. Bellow   C = Mrs. Bellow)

C: Room attendant, can you come to Room 1280, please?

R: Yes, madam. _____1_____ (有什麼需要幫忙的嗎)?

C: _____2_____ (我丈夫在衛生間滑到了). One of his legs and head are bleeding and he cannot stand up.

R: How unfortunate! Don't worry, Mrs. Bellow. Leave it to me.

(Few minutes later, the room attendant arrives.)

Mr. Bellow, _____3_____ (請靠在我身上, 我把你扶到床上去).

B: (almost in tears) Go slowly.

R: _____4_____ (貝婁先生, 請讓我給你按住腿以阻止流血).

B: Oh, my goodness!

R: Mrs. Bellow, bring a towel and wash Mr. Bellow's leg and head, please. Mr. Bellow, please press here, otherwise it will bleed again. Do you feel better now?

B: Yes, _____5_____ (但我的右膝蓋仍然很痛).

R: Everything will be all right, sir. _____6_____ (我去請醫生。請放松一點).

(The doctor confirms it is a minor injury with no fracture or concussion.)

B: It's lucky I haven't injured heavily. _____7_____ (否則我就不能去桂林看那兒的美麗景色了).

R: Sure, Mr. Bellow, but all you have to do now is to take a good rest in the room. _____8_____ (我希望你不久就會康復的).

C：You are most helpful. Thank you ever so much.

R：My pleasure.

II. Translate the following sentences into English.

1. 除非客人有要求，否則我們先整理已退的房間。
2. 我們為客人提供洗衣服務、托嬰服務、24 小時客房服務和叫早/ 喚醒服務。
3. 我房間的電視機壞了，圖像是搖擺的，可以請人過來修一下嗎？
4. 先生，你希望我什麼時間來做夜床服務？
5. 早上好，我來取您要洗的衣服。您要快洗服務還是要當日取？

III. Writing.

客人損壞物品賠償表
REPORT OF DAMAGES

＊＊＊國際大酒店
GOLDEN DOME INTERNATIONAL HOTEL

編號：　　　　　　　　　　　　　　　　　　　　日期：
NO.　　　　　　　　　　　　　　　　　　　　　　DATE

房號 ROOM NO.		國籍 NATIONALITY		姓名 NAME	
品名 ITEM		數量 QTY		單位 UNIT	
原因 REASON					
修理費用 REPAIRING COSTS		賠償費用 PAID FOR THE DAMAGE			

製表　　　　　　　　　　　　　　　　　批准
PREPARED BY _____　　　　　　　　　APPROVED BY _____

備註：
　第一聯：存根　第二聯：財務　第三聯：客人　第四聯：樓層

IV. Translate the following into Chinese.

Floor Supervisor　（　　）　　　PA Supervisor（　　）

FC ＝Floor Captain（　　）　　　PA Captain　（　　）

FA ＝Floor Attendant（　　）　　RA＝ Room Attendant（　　）

BS ＝Butler Service（　　）　　　CO＝ Check-out Room（　　）

High Occupancy（　　）　　　　　VC＝ Vacant & Clean（　　）

Low Occupancy (　　　)　　　　HR = Hour Room (　　　)
O = Occupied　(　　　)　　　　Long Stay (　　　)
DL = Double Lock (　　　)　　　Stayover　(　　　)
DND= Do not Disturb (　　　)　 Skipper　(　　　)
PMU = Please Make Up (　　　) 　Chambermaid (　　　)
Bellman (　　　)　　　　　　　 Bell Captain (　　　)
Master Key (　　　)　　　　　　Golden Butler (　　　)
Baby Sitting (　　　)　　　　　 Pet Concierge (　　　)

V. Make dialogues according to the given situations. Your dialogue should include the following points.

　　Situation A: Mrs. Wilson will attend a party tonight. She wants to have a silk dress and a shirt cleaned. She phones the laundry clerk to send a valet to her room to pick up them. When the valet arrives at her room, she asks some information about the laundry. Tips:

　　1. Get some information about the laundry service items. (same-day service, next-day service, express service, express pressing service)

　　2. Know whether the color will run in the wash.

　　3. Dry-clean the silk dress and starch and valet the shirt.

　　4. Have an extra charge 50% more for express service; have the laundry back before 5:00 p.m.

　　5. Fill in and sign on the laundry list.

　　Situation B: Mr. Michale has just arrived in Shanghai. He is suffering from jet-lag and is confused with the time difference. He wants to have a good sleep to get up early for a scene spot tomorrow morning. So he goes to the floor attendant to require a turn-down service and an wake up call tomorrow morning. Tips:

　　1. Mr. Michale requests a mornimg call before 7:30.

　　2. He requires a turn-down service to have a good sleep.

　　3. He wants the chamber maid to do the turn-down service one hour later because he is going to meet his friend in the room.

　　4. He wishes the chamber maid to buy some fruits and take some fresh tea for him.

Section 4 Extensive Reading

The Characteristics of A Les Clefs d'Or Concierge

Les Clefs d'Or concierges handle all duties with efficiency and zeal. Recommendations, reservations, travel, meeting and party planning, personal shopping and assistance are all in a day's work for Les Clefs d'Or concierges. They are also ultimate social advisors, business expediters, and personal confidantes.

On those rare occasions when guests' requests cannot be met single-handedly, Les Clefs d'Or concierges have a never-ending network of acquaintances, friends and colleagues from around the world to assist in fulfilling guests' wishes.

Les Clefs d'Or members have dedicated many years of hard work and training to the concierge profession. They are pleasant and welcoming and remain calm in hectic environments. Discretion and integrity are hallmarks of a Clefs d'Or concierge.

As Les Clefs d'Or concierges, they have their fingers on the pulses of the cities in which they work. They advise guests on restaurants, night life, sporting and theater events, sightseeing tours, shopping and all the venues and services our cities offer. They can direct guests to any location or product, at any time of day or night.

Motivated by a genuine desire to serve, Les Clefs d'Or concierges are known for being creative, resourceful, prudent, kind, dedicated, gracious, disciplined and tenacious. They're a traveler's best ally.

The global environment of today's business world demands that concierges be able to converse with all travelers, from Albania to Zaire. Many Clefs d'Or members are multilingual and most are well versed in many cultures.

Les Clefs d'Or concierges have worked hard to obtain their keys. Whether requesting something simple or complex, you can be sure they are trusted resources to business travelers and vacationers alike, always keeping guests' safety, enjoyment and satisfaction in mind.

Unit 3
The Food and Beverage Department

Section 1 Introduction

The food and beverage department is a very important part of a hotel. It is often one of the foremost income earners for the hotel. In many large hotels, it brings in more income than room rentals and can account for two fifths to one half of a hotel's profit. There are a number of different areas offering a variety of meals and services all within a hotel—the restaurant, grill room, different bars, cafeteria and coffee shop as well as room service, lounge service and banqueting.

This department requires well-trained employees and highly skilled and versatile managers in the kitchen, bar and service areas. The department employees, especially waiters, waitress and bartenders, can play an extremely important role in creating a pleasant atmosphere and satisfying the requirements of customers and the restaurant at once. High quality service is dependent on the waiter, and other food and beverage department staff as well, having a love for his job and a knowledge of its working right down to the last detail. So, good knowledge and skill, a cordial smile, plenty of courtesy with sincere effort and efficiency will bring into full play the motto —「Reputation first, customer foremost」.

Discussion

1. Why is the food and beverage service a major factor in the hotel operation?

2. How can a waiter or a waitress try to satisfy the requirements of both the customer and the restaurant at once? How do you understand 「high quality service」?

● Section 2　Dialogues

Dialogue 1　Receiving the Dinner

Scene: A couple, Mr. Bruce and Mrs. Bruce, comes to the restaurant to have their dinner, but there is no vacant seat at the moment. The receptionist receives them.

(H= Head waiter　　B= Mr. Bruce　　B1 = Mrs. Bruce)

H: Good evening, sir and madam. Welcome to our restaurant. Do you have a reservation, sir?

B: No, I am afraid we don't.

H: I'm sorry that the restaurant is full now. We don't have a vacant table at the moment. You will have to wait for about half an hour. Would you please care to have a drink at the lounge until a table is available?

B: No, thanks. We'll come back later. May I reserve a table for two?

H: Yes, of course. May I have your name, sir?

B: Yes, John Bruce.

H: Thank you, Mr. Bruce.

B1: By the way, can we have a table by the window in a non-smoking section? I want to be away from the kitchen, if possible.

H: Our restaurant is all non-smoking. I'll note your preference and try to arrange it, but I can't guarantee, Madam.

B1: That's fine. Thank you.

(Half an hour later, the couple comes back.)

R: Sorry to have kept you waiting, Mr. Bruce and Mrs. Bruce. Your table is ready, Would you step this way, please?

B: Thank you.

H: Please take your seats. Here's the menu. The waiter will take your order.

Dialogue 2　Special Chinese Food

Scene: Mr. Smith and his friends want to try some Chinese food, the waiter recommends some Chinese food to them.

(W = Waiter　　G = Guest)

W: Good evening, sirs. Welcome to our restaurant. Do you have a reservation?

G: Yeah, we have a reservation under Mr. Smith for four people.

W: Ok, is it in Jinjiang room, a private room with river view?

G: That's right.

W: It's on the second floor. This way, please.

(Two minutes later, Mr. Smith and his friends are sitting around the table.)

W: Good evening, sirs. May we take your order now?

G: Yes, We'd like to try some real Chinese cuisine. But we have no idea about it. What would you recommend?

W: Well. You see, there are eight famous Chinese cuisines, such as Sichuan food, Cantonese food, Hunan food, Zhejiang food, and so on.

G: Is there any difference between Cantonese food and Sichuan food?

W: Yes, Cantonese food is light and fresh while Sichuan food is spicy and hot. Sichuan food tastes different. It is now very popular in China.

G: Oh, really, I'd like to have a taste of Sichuan food. Are there any special Sichuan dishes that you can recommend?

W: I think Mapo bean curd, twice-cooked pork, spicy deep-fried chicken, spicy pork lung slice, sauted kidney and water-cooked fish.

G: It sounds great. We'd like to take these dishes.

W: What about some vegetables and soup?

G: Can you recommend some?

W: Yes, sir. We have a very nice vegetable「broccoli with crabmeat sauce」. It's delicious and worth a try. Besides, we have a choice of fresh asparagus, green beans, spinach and grilled tomatoes. The soup includes hot and sour soup and tomato and egg soup, etc..

G: We will take broccoli with crabmeat and tomato and egg soup. Besides, we will have 10 bottles of Snow-flake beer.

W: Yes, sir. Your dishes will be served in ten minutes. Here's the tea for you.

Words and Phrases

vacant ['veikənt]   *adj.* 空的

lounge [laʊndʒ]   *n.* 休息室

guarantee [ˌgærən'ti:]   *vt.* 保證

recommend [ˌrekə'mend]   *n.* 推薦

cuisine [kwi'zi:n]   *n.* 烹飪，烹調法

spicy ['spaisi]   *adj.* 香的，多香料的，辛辣的

hot [hɒt]   *adj.* 熱的，辣的

mapo bean curd   麻婆豆腐

twice-cooked pork   回鍋肉

spicy deep-fried chicken   辣子雞

spicy pork lung slice   夫妻肺片

sauted kidney   炒腰花

water-cooked fish   水煮魚

crispy fried duck   香酥鴨

broccoli with crabmeat sauce   蟹汁花椰菜

asparagus [ə'spærəgəs]   *n.* 蘆笋

green beans *n.* 豆角

spinach ['spinitʃ]   *n.* 菠菜

grilled potato   烤熟的土豆

tomato and egg soup   西紅柿雞蛋湯

a private room   包間

a room with river view   河景房

waiting room　候餐室

Table D' hote　套餐（也稱為客飯，由餐廳配置好菜式組合，分為A、B餐等，價格比較大眾化。）

A La Carte　零點餐（由客人照菜單點菜，選擇比較靈活，價格比較高。）

French Service　法式服務（服務員在餐桌旁將每種菜直接從大盤中送到每位客人的小盤中）

General order of Chinese food and Western food.

Chinese food order: cold dishes, wine, drinks, hot dishes, soup, dessert, rice or noodles etc., fruit.

Western food order: starter, soup, main course, dessert, coffee and tea.

中國的八大菜系：Sichuan cuisine, Cantonese cuisine, Shangdong cuisine, Hunan cuisine, Anhui cuisine, Jiangsu cuisine, Fujian cuisine, Zhejiang cuisine.

Useful Expressions

1. Would you like a table in the dining room or in a private room?
2. How many people are there in your party?
3. Do you have any special requirements for the celebration?
4. Could you please tell me in whose name the reservation was made?
5. I'm afraid that table is reserved for 8:00 p.m..
6. We don't have a vacant table at the moment.
7. I'm sorry. The table by the window has been reserved.
8. Would you like to have table d' hote, or a la carte?
9. Why not try our buffet dinner?
10. Which flavor would you prefer, sweet or chilly?
11. Would you like to try our house specialty?
12. Today's special is…, with a 20% discount.
13. What would you like to drink? We have a great variety of wines. Which kind do you prefer?
14. Would you like your beer draught or bottled?
15. Would you like your coffee with milk and sugar?
16. With ice or without ice, sir?
17. I do apologize for giving you the wrong dish. I'll exchange it for you at once.
18. I'm terribly sorry. I will go to check it out and bring it to you as soon as possible.

19. Could I offer you a complimentary drink?

20. Please accept our apologies. I assure you this won't happen again.

Section 3　Exercises

I. Complete the following dialogue according to the Chinese in brackets.

（B = Barman　　G1= Guest 1　　G2= Guest 2　　G3= Guest 3）

B：Good evening, Lady and gentlemen. Welcome to Moonlight Bar. _____ 1_____（先生，您喜歡來杯什麼）?

G1：Whiskey, please.

B：_____ 2 _____（先生，請問要加冰還是不加冰）?

G1：With lots of ice. How about you, Sally?

G2：I don't drink at all. _____ 3 _____（你們這有飲料嗎）?

B：Of course, madam. How about a non-alcohlic cocktail?

G2：It sounds good. I'll take it.

B：What would you like to drink, sir?

G3：I would like a beer, please.

B：_____ 4 _____（您喜歡哪種牌子的啤酒）?

G3：San Miguel.

B：_____ 5 _____（先生，您要瓶裝的還是散裝的）?

G3：Draught, please.

B：Here you are, sirs! Enjoy your drinks.

G1：_____ 6 _____（我可以把帳記在我的房卡上嗎）?

B：Certainly, sir.

G1：Here's my key card.

B：Thank you, sir.

II. Translate the following sentences into English.

1. 很抱歉，餐廳已經滿座了。您大概要等15分鐘才會有空桌。
2. 這道菜是我們當地一道著名的美食，一直是我們顧客最喜歡的菜。
3. 我想來點清淡些的，你能推薦什麼嗎？
4. 按中國的方式是先上菜再上湯；如果你喜歡，我們可以先上湯再上菜。
5. 我想要一份中式早餐，一碗小米粥，一個雞蛋，兩個蒸餃，兩個春卷和一

杯豆漿。

III. Please surf the Internet to know some information about the Chinese food and the Western food.

IV. Make dialogues according to the given situations. Your dialogue should include the following points.

Situation A: Mr. Smith, the office manager of a company, is making a reservation for 100-people banquet by phone. Before the banquet, they will hold a meeting. So Mr. Smith asks the restaurant receptionist to arrange a room for the meeting and recommend delicious food for them. Tips:

1. The time of the banquet and the purpose of the banquet.
2. The restaurant can provide a medium-sized meeting room.
3. Hall 2 is large enough to accommodate 600 quests.
4. The restaurant can cater for gourmet dishes, liquor or wine.

Situation B: Mr. White orders a well-down steak. But the waiter gives him a rare down steak. He asks the waiter whether they make a mis-serving. The head waiter comes to Mr. White and apologies for giving him the wrong dish. The head waiter promises to change it immediately. Tips:

1. It will take 10 minutes to prepare a new well-done steak.
2. Mr. White will have an appointment at 7:00 p.m., but it is now 6:45 p.m..
3. The head waiter apologizes to Mr. White and decides to ask the Room Service to serve Mr. White the well-done steak as a snack at 9:30 p.m. without payment.
4. Mr. White expresses his thanks.

Section 4 Extensive Reading

Table Manners

Do not play with the table utensils or crumble the bread.
Do not put your elbows on the table, or sit too far back, or lounge.
Do not talk loudly or boisterously.
Be cheerful in conduct or conversation.
Never, if possible, cough or sneeze at the table.
Never tilt back your chair while at the table, or at any other time.

Do not talk while your mouth is full.

Never make noise while eating.

Do not open the mouth while chewing, but keep the lips closed. It is not necessary to show people how you masticate your food.

Never indicate that you notice anything unpleasant in the food.

Do not break your bread into the soup, nor mix it with gravy. It is bad taste to mix food on the plate.

Never leave the table before the rest of the family or guests, without asking the host or hostess to excuse you.

Eat soup with the side of the spoon, without noise.

The fork is used to convey the food to the mouth, except when a spoon is necessary for liquids.

Tea or coffee should never be poured into the saucer to cool, but sipped from the cup.

If a dish is presented to you, serve yourself first and then pass it on.

Unit 4   Business Center

● Section 1   Introduction

The Business Center at hotels and resorts provides a variety of comprehensive secretarial and translation services and business support by experienced and friendly staff for guests. Generally speaking, high-end hotels may have a moderately equipped business center on one level and a nicely equipped one on the club or concierge level. The Business center services are offered 24 hours a day, including Internet, audio and video conference, binding, facsimile, equipment rental, computers, printers and scanners, photocopying and faxing services, translation and interpretation services. 24-hour Business Center services can meet all the needs of busy business guests.

Nowadays, with IT technology developing, the traditional Business Center has changed a great deal. The hotel operators focus more on the guests' personal requirements. The guest rooms in most hotels are equipped with computers, so guests can surf the Internet in their bedrooms. Besides, the hotels also offer Wi-Fi and a plug panel to let the guests connect their laptops to the flat-screen TVs. At the same time, the interior and the exterior of the hotel, including bedrooms, the pool, the lobby and terraces and gardens, offer Wi-Fi as a convenience for the guests.

Discussion

1. What equipment does the Business Center have? According to you, what quality should a business clerk have?

2. What's the difference between a traditional Business Center and a modern one?

Section 2　Dialogues

Dialogue 1　Ticket Services

Scene: Mr. Smith is going to the Business Center to ask the clerk to help him reserve a ticket from Beijing to London.

(B = Business Clerk　S = Mr. Smith)

B: Good afternoon. What can I do for you?

S: Yes. I'd like to book one plane ticket from Beijing to London on June 24th.

B: Please wait a moment. Ok, Air China has a flight from Beijing to London that day, with one stopover in Frankfurt.

S: Oh no. I prefer a non-stop flight. Could you please check to see if there's any direct flight that day?

B: Just a second please. Let me see. Oh, there is only a direct flight to London on the 25th. There are still seats available on that flight.

S: What time will the plane take off?

B: The plane takes off at 14:10 p.m. and lands in London at 17:45 p.m. local time.

S: The time is fine. How much is it?

B: Which class do you prefer, First, Business or Economy?

S: Economy, please.

B: How about seat? A window seat or an aisle seat?

S: A window seat, please.

B: One- way or round -trip tickets?

S: One -way.

B: Fine. The total price is 7,860 Yuan RMB, including tax and 40 Yuan service charge. May I have your passport, please?

S: Here you are.

B: Fine. One ticket for the Flight CA937,300 to London, for Mr. Smith, on June 25th. Is that right, sir?

S: Yes. When can I get my ticket?

B: Tomorrow morning at around 9:30 a.m.. May I have your room number?

S: Room 1080.

B: Fine. We'll send it up to your room as soon as we get it.

S: Thank you.

B: You are always welcome, sir.

Dialogue 2 Sending a Fax

Scene: Mr. White is coming to the Business Center. He requests the business clerk to help him type some manuscripts and send a fax for him.

(B= Business Clerk   W= Mr. White)

B: Good morning, sir. Can I help you?

W: Yes. I'd like to send an important fax to America. But at first I want to have some manuscripts typed.

B: Ok, sir. How many pages?

W: About 6 pages.

B: When do you need it?

W: I hope it will be ready before 11:00 a.m.. It's urgent. Here you are.

B: Is this whole document in English? I'm sorry your handwriting is a little illegible to me. I'm hard to make it out. But I will try my best.

W: Thank you. How much do you charge for one page?

B: For typing, it's 10 Yuan RMB for each A4 page, and for copying it is only 1 Yuan RMB for each.

S：A4, please. By the way, I'd like to make a copy of this and then send it to America. What's the rate for a fax to America?

B：It's 20 Yuan RMB per minute, plus service charge 10%.

S：That's fine. Here is the fax number. 0018-3759-2976. Can you do it as soon as possible?

B：Certainly, sir. Could you please sign your name on the bill here? It will be on your account.

S：Can I pay it in cash? How much should I pay altogether?

B：Certainly. That'll be 96 Yuan RMB.

S：Here you are.

B：Thank you, sir. Here is the receipt and changes. Please keep them.

Words and Phrases

comprehensive [ˌkɒmprɪˈhensɪv]　　*adj.* 廣泛的；綜合的

high-end　*n.* 高端

equip [ɪˈkwɪp]　*vt.* 裝備，配備

printer [ˈprɪntə(r)]　*n.* 打印機

scanner [ˈskænə(r)]　*n.* 掃描器

photocopy [ˈfəʊtəʊkɒpi]　*n.* 影印本；複印件

fax [fæks]　*n.* 傳真

stopover [ˈstɒpəʊvə(r)]　*n.* 停靠（尤指飛行旅程中的）中途停留

direct flight / non-stop flight　直航航班

First Class　頭等艙

Economy Class　經濟艙

Business Class　商務艙

aisle seat　靠近通道的座位

one-way tickets　單程票

round-trip tickets　雙程票

manuscript [ˈmænjuskrɪpt]　*n.* 手寫稿

document [ˈdɒkjʊmənt]　*n.* 文件

illegible [ɪˈledʒəbl]　*adj.* 難辨認的；模糊不清

service charge　服務費

Useful Expressions

Typing

1. What font and size would you like?
2. What size would you like?
3. Could you tell me the rate of typing and copying?
4. Please indent the first line of each paragraph.
5. Would you like me to staple these for you?
6. Shall I staple them on the left side or at the top?

Photocopying

1. How many copies would you like?
2. How small / large / big would you like it?
3. Would you like me to make it a little darker / lighter / to reduce it smaller?
4. Your original is not very clear. I can't guarantee the copy will be good.
5. Shall I enlarge / reduce this to fit A4 paper?
6. Shall I copy these on both side of the paper?

Fax

1. We can meet the need of guests. We can send a fax / type a document / send an e-mail / photocopy the document for you.
2. May I have the fax number / your name / your room number / the country code / the area code / the address of the company?

Mail service

1. I want to mail the letter by express. How much is it for express service?
2. Here is your fax / EMS we received this morning.

Others

1. Hard berth tickets /soft berth tickets are not available now.
2. A lower berth ticket, please.
3. Where can I change some money?
4. The money exchange is in the hotel lobby.
5. Today's rate of exchange is 8.09 to the dollar.
6. How many participants will be attending your conference?
7. What size of conference do you have?

Section 3　Exercises

I. Complete the following dialogue according to the Chinese in brackets.

（B＝ Business Clerk　　G＝ Guest）

B：Good afternoon, sir. Can I help you?

G：Yes, ＿＿＿＿＿＿1＿＿＿＿＿＿（你能幫我打印並複印這些資料嗎）?

B：Certainly. How many pages?

G：About 10 pages and two copies for each.

B：＿＿＿＿＿＿2＿＿＿＿＿＿（您要什麼字體, 多大字號的）?

G：Times New Roman. 5 size, A 4. ＿＿＿＿＿3＿＿＿＿＿（請問打印和複印的費用是多少）?

B：We charge each page 8 Yuan for typing and 2 Yuan for copying, sir. ＿＿＿＿4＿＿＿＿（請問你想裝訂在左邊還是上邊）?

G：On the left side.

B：Sure. What time do you expect it?

G：＿＿＿＿＿＿5＿＿＿＿＿＿（這是是急件。我需要5點以前拿到）.

B：No problem, sir. I'll send your original and the copies to your room as soon as I finish typing.

G：Thank you. How much should I pay?

B：That'll be 100 Yuan. (bring the bill) ＿＿＿＿＿6＿＿＿＿＿（請您在這兒簽上你的姓名和房號, 好嗎）? It will be on your account.

G：Sure. Thank you.

B：You're always welcome.

II. Translate the following sentences into English.

1. 我把原件放在這兒, 等複印好了就打電話通知我吧。
2. 史密斯先生, 您有一份發自上海的傳真, 請到商務中心來取。
3. 您想買哪種臥鋪票, 硬臥還是軟臥?
4. 我是不是把它放大／縮小到適合 A4 紙大小呢?
5. 我們酒店有設備完備的會議中心可滿足客人的各種需要。這是我們的設備清單及價格。

III. Make dialogues according to the given situations. Your dialogue should include the following points.

Situation A: Mr. Black goes to the Business Center to mail two urgent letters to his business partners. One is to be mailed to Shanghai, and the other to Singapore. The Business clerk suggests that he could have express service here. After sending letters, Mr. Black wants to use the computer to type some documents and e-mail them. Tips:

1. A letter by air to Singapore costs 20 Yuan RMB under the weight of 20 g.
2. A letter by mail to Shanghai costs 1.2 Yuan RMB and it needs 3 days or 4 days.
3. Pay 10 Yuan for using the computer per hour.
4. Save the data on our disks, in case of any viruses.

Situation B: Mr. Scoot's company is going to have a seminar in the hotel next week. He comes to the Business Center to ask for some information about the facilities. Tips:

1. Two fully-equipped convention center for conference and exhibition hall.
2. Three Multi-function halls / media-sized meeting room / breakout room.
3. Excellent audiovisual equipment—TV set, multi-media projector, video, laptop, microphone.

Section 4 Extensive Reading

Telephone Etiquette

The Front Office staff will use professional telephone etiquette at all times to promote and enhance the first professional, luxurious image of the hotel to all callers.

Procedures:

1. Answer all calls promptly within 3 rings, using the appropriate greeting.
2. When answering a call, pause briefly before speaking.
3. Speak into the telephone mouthpiece or receiver.
4. Speak clearly and slowly, and maintain a friendly tone and pitch.
5. Listen carefully to the caller's request—DO NOT interrupt. Repeat back to the caller to confirm understanding.
6. Use the guest's name where known, or sir/madam at all times. (If internal call room number or extension will be displayed on the screen of telephone. Use the inquiry

screen in Fidelio or printed guest list to confirm the guest's name where necessary).

7. Use correct, professional language at all times, including 「Yes」 or 「Certainly」 「OK」 or 「Yeah」 is not acceptable language in responding to a caller. Avoid jargon or slang words.

8. Whenever the call is interrupted for any reason, including paging or locating a guest, the call must be put on hold. Always ask guest's permission before putting a caller on hold. If the caller is not prepared to wait, enquire if they would prefer to be contacted back, and take appropriate details.

9. Never chew or drink when on the telephone.

10. Close the call, thanking the caller.

11. Allow the caller to hang up the telephone first.

12. You do not end the call with 「Goodbye or Bye Bye」. Use phrases such as 「Thank You or Have a Nice Day!」

Unit 5
The Health and Recreation Club

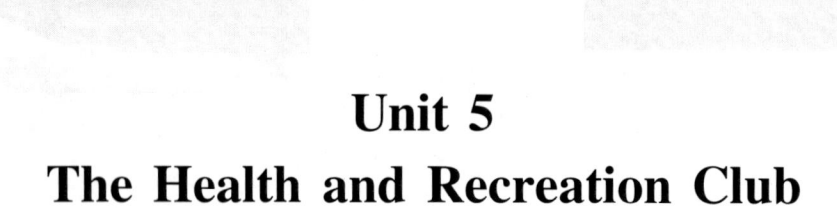

Section 1 Introduction

The Health and Recreation Club strives to offer a range of well-maintained facilities and quality programs to meet the needs of the guests in the hotel. It can help the participants enjoy a pleasant atmosphere and hopefully increase their level of fitness and general wellbeing, such as reducing stress, looking better, feeling more mentally alert, sleeping better and generally feeling happier. The Health and Recreation Club enlarges the hotel's management scale. It is both the imperative way of attracting the customers and the critical income of the hotel. It is also an important symbol to validate the status of the hotel in comparative rankings.

There are various kinds of recreation facilities in different hotels, mainly including Hair & Beauty Salon, Gymnasium, Sauna Bath and Spa, Yoga, Aerobic, Taekwondo, Swimming pool, Bowling room, Tennis, Billiards room, Snooker, Chess room, Golf, KTV, Nightclub and so on.

Discussion

1. Why is the Health and Recreation Club playing an important role in running hotels?

2. As the staff in the Health and Recreation Club, how can you provide satisfactory services for the guests?

● Section 2　Dialogues

Dialogue 1　At the Health Center

Scene: Mr. Robert wants to take some exercises, so he comes to the Health Center. The gym clerk serves him and introduces the facilities to him.

(C = Gym Clerk　R = Mr. Robert　)

C: Good afternoon, sir. Welcome to our Health Center. Can I help you?

R: I'd like to take some exercises. Could you tell me what facilities you have here?

C: Certainly, sir. Our gym consists of two sections, an equipment section and an aerobics section. We have a well-equipped gym with all the latest recreational sports apparatus, including stationary bike, electric treadmill, weights, nautilus machines, dumb bells, bar bells, spring grips, chest-expanders and muscle builder sets. We also have swimming pools and tennis courts. There is no fee for the registered guest.

R: That sounds terrific! I'm wondering if there is a coach around here supervising the exercises.

C: Yes. The men standing over there are our resident coaches. They are certified exercise instructors. They will supervise all the activities and give guidance to the guests. After taking exercises, you can enjoy our excellent sauna with a free supply of towels, bathrobes and soap. We have a dry sauna, a wet sauna, a steam sauna, a herbal sauna and so on.

R: That's great. I will try a dry sauna. By the way, do you have aerobic class here?

C: Yes, It's an open class. All the guests who are living in our hotel can join in at any time.

R: That sounds good. So I can continue my aerobics class here during my stay in your hotel.

C: Sure. If you are interested in the aerobics class, I will also prepare a timetable for you.

R: It's really kind of you. If I take the aerobics class, should I go through any procedure?

C: No need. Just bring your room card with you. It will be all set.

R: Ok. Thank you very much.

C: You are welcome.

Dialogue 2 At Beauty Salon

Scene: A woman wants a facial and massage, but she doesn't know much about them. A beautician gives some introductions to her.

(B=Beautician   G=Guest)

B: Good afternoon, madam, May I help you?

G: Yes. I feel very exhausted after a long flight journey. I would like to take a facial and a body massage. Could you give me some suggestions?

B: Yes, let me check your skin. Yours is very dry and tarnish. It needs to supplement some moisture and nutrition. I suggest you can use our own line of organic anti-aging facial products. We have many kinds of famous facial treatment brands, which have the highest quality and professional status that are internationally recognized.

G: What should you do?

B: First, we will massage your back for ten minutes to relax your body. Then we start with a through facial cleaning with cleansing milk, followed by exfoliation treatment — a peeling or scrubing mask that removes the dead cells that make the skin look dull. After that we'll massage your face and neck with oil or cream to improve the facial blood circulation and relieve tension, followed by a mask to moisturize and soften the skin to leave the skin feeling intensively hydrated, fresh and smooth. In the end, we will have a make-up for you to make you more beautiful.

G: That's exactly what I want. How long does it take and what's the rate?

B: One and half hours for 80 Yuan. If you really feel tired, I suggest you try a spa to have a complete relaxation.

G: Really? Could you please tell me the details?

B: The spa is a heavenly retreat devoted to wellness. Guests can indulge in the heated indoor hydro-pool and outdoor lap pool, sauna, steam room and the crystalline waters of the swimming pool at their own leisure. In a word, the spa can revitalize your mind, body and soul in an excellent and elegant setting with full spa facilities and amenities, leaving you with a deep feeling of relaxation and a restored natural balance.

G: It sounds good. I will take both the facial treatment and the spa.

Words and Phrases

stationary bike　固定腳踏車
electric treadmill　電子跑步機
weights　舉重
nautilus machines　全身型健身器
dumb bell　啞鈴
bar bell　杠鈴
spring grips　握力器
chest-expanders　擴胸器
muscle builder sets　肌肉鍛煉器
supervise ['suːpəvaiz]　vt. 監督；管理
resident coach　住店教練

relieve ［riˈliːv］　　vt. 解除；緩解
herbal ［ˈhɜːbəl］　　adj. 藥草的；草本的
sauna ［ˈsɔːnə］　　n. 桑拿
bathrobe ［ˈbɑːθˌrəʊb］　　n. 浴袍
massage ［ˈmæsɑːʒ］　　n. 按摩
cleanse ［klenz］　　vt. 弄乾淨；清洗
tarnish ［ˈtɑːnɪʃ］　　vt. / vi. （使）失去光澤
moisture ［ˈmɔɪstʃə(r)］　　vt. 給……增加水分；使濕潤
nutrition ［njuˈtrɪʃn］　　n. 營養，滋養
cleansing milk　　n. 潔面乳
exfoliation treatment　　n. 去角質護理
circulation ［ˌsɜːkjəˈleɪʃn］　　n. 流通，傳播
peel ［piːl］　　n. 皮　vt. 削皮
mask ［mɑːsk］　　n. 面膜
scrub ［skrʌb］　　vt. 用力擦洗
soften ［ˈsɒfn］　　vt. 變軟
eye cream　　眼霜
hydrated ［ˈhaɪdreɪtɪd］　　adj. 含水的
make-up　　n. 化妝，化妝品
hand care　　n. 手護
manicure ［ˈmænɪkjʊə(r)］　　n. 修指甲
pedicure ［ˈpedɪkjʊə(r)］　　n. 修趾甲

Useful Expressions

1. Could you tell me what facilities you have here?

2. We have many kinds of apparatus in this room.

3. We have spring expanders, dumb bells, parallel bars, band rings and many others.

4. Aerobic exercise is a popular system of exercises keeping your heart and lungs in top health as well as for overcoming weight problems.

5. We offer yoga, Pilates, martial arts, and Taiji classes.

6. You'd better do some stretches before you work out.

7. We have snookers and pools, what would you like?

8. Swimming is the most recommended exercise to achieve both a good figure and a healthy body.

9. We have safe-deposit boxes to keep guests' valuables.

10. Would you like me to put your clothes at the cloak room?

11. The men standing over there are our resident coaches.

12. What color would you like to dye your hair?

13. Would you like me to shave your mustache, sir?

14. I'd like to have my hair cut. Just a trim, and cut the sides fairly short, but not so much at the back.

15. By the way, could you give me a manicure? Use a light nail polish, please.

16. You can enjoy our excellent sauna with a free supply of towels, bathrobes and soap.

17. We have a dry sauna, a wet sauna, a steam sauna, a herbal sauna and so on. Which one do you prefer?

18. There are also lots of treatments you can have to help relax.

Section 3　Exercises

I. Complete the following into English according to the Chinese in brackets.

(C= Clerk　　G= Guest)

C: Good evening, sir. Can I help you?

G: Yes, I'd like to have a swim. _____1_____ (你們的游泳池怎麼樣)?

C: Our swimming pool is a newly-decorated and newly-equipped one and _____2_____ (對住店客人游泳是免費的, 只收小吃的費用).

G: Great! I'm in Room 1820. I'm not good at swimming. How deep is the pool?

C: _____3_____ (有深水區和淺水區). Its depth is from 1.5 meters to 3 meters. Don't worry. _____4_____ (我們這兒每天都有全職的教練可給游泳者提供指導並確保其安全). Besides, we have live belt.

G: That's very kind of you. I can't wait. I will take it.

C: This way please. _____5_____ (更衣室在那邊, 你的櫃門鑰匙是 26 號). We have safe-deposit boxes to keep guests' valuables. You have to wear a swimming cap in the pool.

G: I'm sorry. I just brought my swimming trunks and I forgot to bring a swimming cap along. By the way, I still need a pair of goggles. Where can I get them?

C: _____6_____ （你可在商務中心旁的商店裡買）.

G: I see. Thank you. I will come back soon.

C: My pleasure.

II. Match the English expressions in column A with those Chinese expressions in column B.

A	B
1. bobbed style	A. 寄物櫃
2. conventional saunas	B. 電子跑步機
3. Karaoke	C. 衣帽間服務員
4. seaweed mask	D. 修眉
5. eyebrow-trim	E. 普拉提
6. electric treadmill	F. 傳統桑拿
7. swimming trunks	G. 海藻面膜
8. locker room	H. 剪短髮
9. Pilates	I. 泳褲
10. cloakroom attendant	J. 卡拉 ok

III. Translate the following sentences into English.

1. 我想洗個桑拿，做個身體按摩，消除一下近期的疲勞和緊張。

2. 我們這裡的健身房設施完善，擁有最新的娛樂運動設施。

3. 我們的娛樂中心營業時間從上午 9 點到凌晨 4 點。每位最低消費 50 元，包括飲料。

4. 星期六和星期日我們通常客滿。請坐下來稍等會兒吧。

5. 對住店客人，唱歌是免費的。我們只收飲料和小吃的費用。

IV. Make dialogues according to the given situations. Your dialogue should include the following points.

Situation A: Mr. Wang and his four friends go to the KTV Bar to relax themselves by singing and dancing. They ask the charge and have a private room. The clerk serves them. Tips:

1. First-class audio apparatus and light to let you enjoy both classical music and pop music, video cassettes, laser discs, D. J..

2. Song lists, select songs by computer and you can dance to the music.

3. 180 Yuan per hour for a medium room, 200 Yuan per hour for a large room, 280 Yuan per hour for a private room.

4. Drink lists, charge for the drinks, beers, wines and snacks.

Situation B: Mrs. White will attend an important party. So she goes to the Beauty Salon to have her hair waved. She asks some information about the most fashionable styles and the prices. Tips:

1. Have one's hair done, have a trimming, layer.

2. Cold wave or permanent wave, leave the fringe.

3. The latest hair styles— bobbed style, swept-back style, chaplet style, shoulder-length style, hair done in a bun.

4. Hair cream, tonic water, the prices.

Section 4　Extensive Reading

Etiquette and Policies

In order to ensure that all guests benefit from the quiet, tranquil atmosphere that befits Arabella Spa, you are requested to keep noise to a minimum.

In the interest of our guests' privacy, the use of cameras and cell phones is prohibited.

We recommend that all valuables be left in the guests' hotel rooms.

No glass objects are permitted in the spa. Plastic glasses are provided for your convenience.

Hotel guests are requested to use their robes & slippers from their rooms when using spa facilities.

When using the Fitness Centre:

please:

- Wear appropriate clothing and non-marking footwear.
- Keep a sweat towel with you at all times.
- Wipe all machines after use with the wipes provided.
- Do not drop weights on the floor or remove them from the Fitness Centre.
- Do not move any machines.
- Always shower after a workout and before entering any of the other facilities in

the spa.

When using the sauna and steam room：

please：

- Shower before entering.
- Wash down the seat with the hand shower before and after use.
- Sit or lie on a dry towel if you are not wearing a Roman skirt.
- Have a cool shower before re-entering if you feel any distress.
- Be aware that a time limit of 10 to 15 minutes is recommended.

Pool Area

- Spa guests must shower before and after using the lap pool or hydro-pool.
- Costumes must be worn in this area at all times.

國內外著名的酒店管理集團及網址：

希爾頓酒店集團(Hilton Hotels Corp.)http://www.hilton.com/

馬里奧特集團(Marriott International)http://marriott.com/

喜達屋國際酒店集團（Starwood Hotels & Resorts Worldwide）http://www.starwood.com/

雅高國際酒店集團(Accor International Hotels Group) http://www.accor.com/

精品國際酒店集團(Choice Hotels International)：http://www.choicehotels.com/

洲際國際酒店集團(Intercontinental Hotels Group)http://www.ichotelsgroup.com/

四季國際酒店集團(Four Seasons Hotels & Resorts) http://www.fourseasons.com/

凱賓斯基國際酒店集團(Kempinski Hotel)http://www.kempinski.com/

凱悅國際酒店集團(Hyatt International Hotels Group) http://www.hyatt.com/

香格里拉酒店集團(Shangri-La Hotels & Resorts)http://www.shangri-la.com/

最佳西方國際酒店集團（Best Western International）http://www.bestwestern.com/

聖達特國際酒店集團(Cendant Corporation)http://www.cendant.com/

錦江國際酒店集團(Jinjiang Internationa Hotel Group)http://www.jinjianghotels.com/

如家酒店集團(Homeinns Hotel Group)http:// www.homeinns.com/

首旅集團(Beijiang Tourism Group)http:// www.btg.com.cn/

天倫國際酒店管理集團(Tianlun International Hotel)http://www.tianlunhotels.com/

金陵飯店集團（Jinling Hotel）http：//www.jinlinghotel.com/
上海東湖集團　http：//www.donghugroup.com/
北京酒店網　http：//www.bjhotel.cn
中國酒店網　http：//www.china-hotel.com.cn/
中國飯店網　http：//www.zm8888.com/

Part Three
MICE English

Unit 1　Conference Services

Section 1　Introduction

　　Meetings and conferences are get-togethers of many people to hold a discussion on certain topics or to have some activities. People come to attend conferences from different fields of life: business, society, religion, and so on. The number of attendees may be so large that it needs to be organized in a hotel or a specially designed conference room or training center where the environment is right for discussions. Conferences are formal affairs. So a particular agenda has to be discussed and focused upon and invitations are often sent in advance. Nowadays, conferences, especially international conferences, as an important part of the exhibition industry, play an important role in city and business images, promote urban development, and create social and economic benefits.

Discussion

1. How many types of meetings do you know about? Can you name some of them?
2. What do organizers and receptionists often do at a conference?

● Section 2 Dialogues

Dialogue 1 Reserving a Conference Room

Scene: Nancy, a receptionist, is answering Eric Smith's telephone call to reserve a convention hall.

(R= Receptionist   S= Mr. Smith)

R: Good morning, Conference Service Center of Beijing Hotel, Nancy speaking. How can I help you?

S: This is Eric Smith from General Motors Corporation. I'd like to reserve a conference room in your hotel.

R: Certainly. What size do you expect it to be?

S: For about one hundred and fifty people. We're holding a press conference from 5:00 p.m. to 7:00 p.m., and a cocktail party from 7:00 p.m. to 9:30 p.m..

R: For the press conference, what seating style would you prefer?

S: Theater style, please.

R: Sure. May I know the time and date, please?

S: Our plan is for a Sunday in November. What's your suggestion?

R: Just a minute, Mr. Smith. I'll check the reservation schedule. Thank you for waiting, What about late November? That is, Nov. 16th or 23rd.

S: Nov. 23rd, please. What facilities do you offer with the room?

R: The convention room is equipped with three cable microphones, one LCD projector with screen, laptop connection and wireless network access.

S: Great! That will do. What is the charge for the convention room?

R: We have two convention rooms for you to choose from. One is 150m^2 at US $ 1,980 per night and the other is 200m^2 at US $ 2,480 per night. The second one is more luxurious and spacious. Which one would you prefer?

S: The second, please.

R: Would you like to make a guaranteed reservation with your credit card?

S: All right. Do you accept American Express?

R: Yes. May I know the number?

S: It's 9934256.

R: 9934256. May I have your passport number?

S: A20395.

R: A20395. Thank you. Let me repeat your reservation: a conference room for Mr. Eric Smith, at US $2,480 per night, on Sunday, Nov. 23rd, from 5:00 p.m. to 9:30 p.m.. Is that right?

S: Yes.

R: My name is Nancy Stone. Please just call me if there is anything I can help you with. Thank you for calling, and we look forward to serving you.

Dialogue 2   Registering at a Conference

Scene: Mr. Smith comes to register at a conference. A receptionist and a clerk receive him.

(S= Mr. Smith   R= Receptionist   C= Clerk)

R: Good morning, sir. May I help you?

S: Yes. I've got an invitation to attend this conference. I'm here to register.

R: May I have your invitation letter please?

S: Here it is.

R: Mr. Smith, since there are so many people registering here, you can go to the self-registration point to save on waiting time. We have staff to help you there.

S: All right. Thank you.

C: Good morning, sir. Are you coming to register?

S: Yes.

C: You can use our iPad to complete the registration. Please feel free to ask us if you run into any problems.

S: Okay. No problem.

C: Here is our iPad. You just need to fill in the form following the instructions.

S: All right. Thank you. Ok, it's done. Here it is.

C: Thank you, sir. You've registered successfully. Here is a badge. Please wear it when attending the conference.

S: Okay. Thank you.

C: You are welcome. Have a nice day! Goodbye.

S: Goodbye.

Words and Phrases

conference [ˈkɒnfərəns]　　n. 會議；大會

attend [əˈtend]　　vt. 出席

attendee [ˌætenˈdiː]　　n. 出席者

affair [əˈfeə(r)]　　n. 事情；事務

agenda [əˈdʒendə]　　n. 議程；日常工作事項

in advance　　提前地

a convention hall　　會議室

a press conference　　新聞發布會

a cocktail party　　雞尾酒會

equip [iˈkwip]　　vt. 裝備；配備

projector [prəˈdʒektə(r)]　　n. 投影儀；放映機

laptop [ˈlæptɒp]　　n. 筆記本電腦

access [ˈækses]　　n. 通路；進入

　　　　　　　　vt. 使用；接近

luxurious [lʌgˈʒʊəriəs]　　adj. 奢侈的

spacious [ˈspeiʃəs]　　adj. 寬敞的；廣闊的

invitation letter　　邀請函

self-registration point　　自助註冊點

instruction [ɪnˈstrʌkʃn]　　n. 指示

provide [prəˈvaid]　　vt. 提供

badge [bædʒ]　　n. 徽章

Additional Words and Phrases

convention　　會議

symposium　　討論會

seminar　　講習會，學習討論會

banquet　　酒宴

plenary meeting　　全會

forum　論壇
session　會期
representative　代表
secretary general　秘書長
executive secretary　執行秘書
procedure　程序
schedule　日程表
item on the agenda　議程項目
memorandum　備忘錄

Useful Expressions

1. Hello, can you show me the documents? I'd check your information, thank you.

2. Here is a copy of the itinerary we have worked out for you. Would you please have a look at it?

3. How many people can you accommodate?

4. This big auditorium can accommodate over three hundred people.

5. What kind of meeting facilities are there?

6. We have the most modern conference equipment: air-conditioned auditoriums, microphones, overhead projectors, slide projectors, film projectors, tape recorders, etc.

7. How much do you charge for the use of your auditorium for the whole day?

8. I will discuss the details with you later.

Section 3　Exercises

I. Complete the following dialogue according to the Chinese in brackets.

(R = Receptionist　S = Mr. Smith)

S: Good morning, sir. I'm Mr. Smith. ＿＿＿＿1＿＿＿＿ (我來參加今天的會議).

R: Good morning, sir. ＿＿＿＿2＿＿＿＿ (請出示您的身分證和邀請函好嗎)?

S: Here you are.

R: Thank you. Please wait a moment. Please look at the webcam behind me. We'll take a picture for you.

　　S：All right.

　　R：Sir, this is your attendance card. ＿＿＿＿3＿＿＿＿ （請佩戴好出席證）so that you can walk about freely in the company.

　　S：Thank you. ＿＿＿＿4＿＿＿＿ （請問會議在哪裡舉行）？

　　R：You take the escalator to the second floor, ＿＿＿5＿＿＿ （左轉，第二間房間就是會議室）. You can see signs. ＿＿＿＿6＿＿＿＿ （如果找不到，您也可以問問我們的工作人員）.

　　S：Thank you very much!

　　R：You are welcome.

II. Translate the following sentences into English.

1. 我想和您協商一下會議服務的一些細節。
2. 這個會議室可以容納 300 餘人。
3. 我們有最現代的會議設備。
4. 使用一天會議室收費多少？
5. 請把貴賓的名單交給我，以便為他們安排恰當的房間。

III. Writing practice.

Surf the Internet to learn about a famous hotel or an international conference center, then write a brief introduction to the hotel or center in 200 words in English, including its location, capacity, facilities, good reputation and so on.

IV. Make dialogues according to the given situations.

Situation A：Li Ping is phoning Wu Dong about the meeting to be held in Room 306 at two o'clock next Friday afternoon. It's about how to improve the service. The manager of the company will chair on the meeting. Wu Dong is expected to attend the meeting.

Situation B：Li Ping is serving Mr. Smith, who comes to reserve a conference room for a business meeting. He asks for a room that can accommodate fifteen people comfortably and equipped with a television set and a video recorder. He inquires about the rate and books the room.

Section 4　Extensive Reading

Business Etiquette—Conference Room Layout

Conference room layout refers to the design of the conference room. A proper conference room layout is very important for a successful and meaningful conference. It covers all the necessary requisites that are within and around the conference room. A well planned conference room layout must make the room ideally suitable for the conferences and meetings.

Conference rooms can be arranged in various ways, where there should be flexible seating arrangements, syndicate rooms, adaptable staging and simultaneous conference link-ups for administrative assistance. Therefore telephones and internet facilities are required.

Unit 2 Expo Services

Section 1 Introduction

    An exposition (Expo) provides a focal point for visitors around the world to learn about the latest developments in new technologies, new products and innovations. Through expositions, visitors can also learn the cultural aspect of a country or a company. Therefore, a global expo and trade show company offers many quality services, which include exhibit advertisment and invitations, booth design and construction, graphics and installation, dismantling and trussing, storage and more. The professional and successful expo and trade show companies are dedicated to serving their customers' needs. They strive to bring the best in quality service and pursue the goal of perfect customer satisfaction. Hence, the environment they provide ensures that suppliers, customers, as well as many other sides benefit and feel content with. And, a wide range of objectives can be achieved in an exhibition.

Discussion

1. How do we select qualified staff for working at an exhibit booth? What qualities are preferred?

2. What's your impression of the services provided for the visitors during Expo 2010 Shanghai China? Make some remarks.

Section 2　Dialogues

Dialogue 1　Discussing the Preparation Work for the Exhibition

Scene: Mr. Brown is asking Miss Wang, the secretary, about the preparation work for the exhibition.

(B = Mr. Brown　W = Miss Wang)

B: Miss Wang, how is the preparation for the fair going?

W: I am worried about the hall decorations.

B: Yes?

W: They should be completed by next Monday and we have only one more week.

B: I think we will have to try our best. What about the transport of the exhibits?

W: So far so good! I think they'll be here on time.

B: Good. I want everything in good order before the fair. By the way, Miss Wang, the opening ceremony will be held next Tuesday. Have all the visitors been notified?

W: Yes, I sent them formal invitations a week ago.

B: Have you prepared the guidebook, including the introduction and schedules of the fair?

W: Yes, I have. I have also prepared a fair memo.

B: Good. By the way, will you help me to type these letters and mail them immediately?

W: Yes, sir.

Dialogue 2　Application & Booth Reservation

Scene: Thomas Brown is applying by phone for an exhibition booth. A receptionist is talking to him.

(B= Mr. Brown   R= Receptionist)

R: Good morning. Sichuan Exhibition Center. Can I help you?

B: Yes, please. I'm from Jill Motorcycle Co.. I'd like to register for the International Motorcycle Exhibition.

R: May I have your name, sir?

B: I'm Thomas Brown.

R: Let me check, Mr. Brown…Thank you for waiting. Fortunately, there are still some booths available. If you send us your registration form and registration fees within two weeks, it is still possible for you to get a booth.

B: May I register for it now on the phone?

R: Certainly. May I know your phone number, email and your company's name?

B: My phone number is 867-932-294; my email is thomasbrown@ jillmotors. com; my company's full name is Jill Motorcycle Assembling Corporation.

R: Mr. Thomas Brown at 867-932-294 from Jill Motorcycle Assembling Corporation; and your email is thomasbrown@ jillmotors.com. Is that right?

B: Yes!

R: Are you looking for a standard package booth or non-standard package booth?

B: What is the charge for each?

R: The nine-square-meter booth costs at least 23,000 Yuan RMB per unit while the six-square-meter booth is at least 17,000 per unit. Which one would you prefer?

B: One nine-square-meter booth, please.

R: Where do you wish your booth to be located?

B: Can I reserve a space in the center?

R: Sorry. All center booths have been booked up. We have only corner booths left. There is a corner stand to the right of the entrance. Will that be all right?

B: Okay, that's fine. I'll take it. May I pay by Visa Card?

R: Certinly, sir. You have reserved one nine-square-meter corner booth to the right of the entrance. The booth number is A-092. May I have your credit card number?

B: The number is 8453-1940-0327.

R: Thanks. I'll send you a letter to confirm your reservation. Anything else we can do for you?

B: No, thank you very much. Goodbye!

R: Thanks for calling. Goodbye!

Words and Phrases

expo (abbr., exposition)　博覽會
exhibition ［ˌeksɪˈbɪʃn］　　n. 展覽；展覽會
provide ［prəˈvaɪd］　　vt. 提供
graphics ［ˈɡræfɪks］　　n. 製圖
installation ［ˌɪnstəˈleɪʃn］　　n. 安裝
dismantle ［dɪsˈmæntl］　　vt. 拆開；拆卸
truss ［trʌs］　　vt. 捆綁
storage ［ˈstɔːrɪdʒ］　　n. 貯存；貯藏
dedicate ［ˈdedɪkeɪt］　　vt. 奉獻；獻身
be dedicated to　致力於
strive ［straɪv］　　vi. 奮鬥；力爭
strive for　為……而奮鬥
pursue ［pəˈsjuː］　　vt. 繼續；追求
ensure ［ɪnˈʃʊə(r)］　　vt. 確保
profitable ［ˈprɒfɪtəbl］　　adj. 獲利的；賺錢的
qualified ［ˈkwɒlɪfaɪd］　　adj. 合格的；有資格的
booth ［buːθ］　　n. 展臺；貨攤
exhibit ［ɪɡˈzɪbɪt］　　n. 展覽品
　　　　　　　　　　vt. 展覽；顯示
exhibit booth　展臺
exhibitor ［ɪɡˈzɪbɪtə(r)］　　n. 參展商
fair ［feə(r)］　　n. 展覽會
decoration ［ˌdekəˈreɪʃn］　　n. 裝飾，裝潢
ceremony ［ˈserəməni］　　n. 典禮，儀式
notify ［ˈnəʊtɪfaɪ］　　vt. 通告；通知
memo ［ˈmeməʊ］　　n. 備忘錄
fortunately ［ˈfɔːtʃənətli］　　adv. 幸運地
available ［əˈveɪləbl］　　adj. 有效的；可得的
package booth　包價展位（含所有費用的攤位）
corner booth　角落展位
corner stand　角落處

entrance ['entrəns]　　*n.* 入口；進入

Additional Words and Phrases

exposition　博覽會
pamphlet　小冊子
brochure　宣傳冊，說明書
showcase　陳列，陳列櫃
exhibitor manual　參展商手冊
information pack　會展資料袋
exhibitor profile　展商簡介
row booth　標準展臺
indoor exhibition space　室內展區
floor plan　展館平面圖
minimum area　起租面積
raw space　展覽空地

Useful Expressions

1. Your booth number is…
2. Which one would you like?
3. We'll send you a layout of the exhibition hall, and mark the available booths on it.
4. I'm afraid we're fully booked.
5. We still have some corner booths available.

Section 3　Exercises

I. Complete the following dialogue according to the Chinese in brackets.

（C = Miss Chen　　D = Douglas）

C: Good morning, sir. ＿＿＿＿＿1＿＿＿＿＿（歡迎光臨北京國際汽車展覽會）.

D: Good morning, sir. ＿＿＿＿＿2＿＿＿＿＿（我想瞭解一下整個展覽的情況）.

C: ＿＿＿＿＿3＿＿＿＿＿（這是我們展覽會的導遊手冊）, you can have a

look.

D: Oh, thank you. By the way, _____4_____ (請問寶馬公司的展位在哪裡)?

C: _____5_____ (在A座6號展位,沿這條路直走再轉右就可以看到了)。

D: Thank you very much.

C: You're welcome.

II. Translate the following sentences into English.

1. 你們有展區中心的空地(raw space)嗎?
2. 對不起,已經預訂滿了。
3. 我們把可預訂的攤位標出來了。
4. 我建議您現在就用信用卡預訂,否則我們無法保證您的攤位。
5. 取消展位必須於截至日期前以書面形式提出。

III. Writing practice.

Suppose you are Mr. Su Jian, General Manager of a manufacturer specialized in sanitary ware. Please write a letter of invitation to some company managers or representatives to invite them to visit your booth at The Continental Exhibition Center. The letter must cover the dates, position of the exhibition and the products displayed at the booth.

IV. Make dialogues according to the given situations.

Situation A: Mr. Li is inviting Mr. Peter to take part in their car exhibition. Mr. Peter is interested in it and leaves Mr. Li his phone number to contact.

Situation B: Mr. Li is showing Mary, Mr. Peter's assistant, around the exhibition hall. Mary asks about the price for the booth near the door. They do some bargaining and finally reach agreement.

Section 4 Extensive Reading

The Development of Macao's Convention and Exhibition Industry

Macao has long been a meeting point for Eastern and Western business and cultural exchanges with the city functioning as a co-operation platform. Having a rich cultural background and tourism resources, the city possesses unique advantages for the development of the convention and exhibition sector. More than 30 million people visit Macao annually. Macao possesses world-class international convention and exhibition venues which are equipped with diverse features to meet the needs of different events. There are an increasing number of events being held in Macao. Meanwhile, a number of large convention and exhibition venues are being constructed in the city. In 2011, a total of 1,045 conventions and exhibitions were held in Macao, with the number of participants and attendants totaling around 1.28 million. As the branding effect of local conventions and exhibitions is becoming more obvious, various overseas fairs and events are also being attracted to Macao. During 2012, the 2nd International Infrastructure Investment and Construction Forum and the 3rd China Catering Expo were two major overseas events organized in Macao.

Unit 3   Trade Fairs

Section 1   Introduction

A trade fair is an exhibition organized so that companies in a specific industry can showcase and demonstrate their new products or services. The convention and exhibition industry has been one of the fastest-growing industries in recent years. The organization of conferences and exhibitions brings business opportunities to a variety of sectors and promotes the development of the entire industry chain. Suppliers can launch new products, build their brand image, make sales and create profitable leads, learn more about customers' needs, and thus improve their products and services. Visitors can evaluate and compare products and suppliers. They can see, touch, taste, smell, hear, learn and judge for themselves. The IMEX Group (IMEX Frankfurt, IMEX America, etc.) runs the world's largest and most diverse exhibitions for meetings, incentive travels and events. It gathers global exhibitors in a comprehensive range, including tourist boards, international hotel companies, airlines, destination management companies, technology providers and many more. It's also renowned for attracting buyers, so along with trade visitors, senior decision-makers to do business with.

Discussion

1. Can you name some famous trade fairs or expositions in China and abroad?
2. Would you like to make some comment on Expo 2010 Shanghai? What were its main achievements?

Section 2 Dialogues

Dialogue 1 Visiting a Showroom

Scene: Miss Zhang is showing a Korean businessman around her showroom. She expects some orders from him.

(Z = Miss Zhang Tong   Y = Young Kin, the Korean businessman)

Z: Mr. Young, I'd like to show you around our showroom. This way, please.

Y: Thank you. What an array of products!

Z: Yes, we market about 2,000 different items; 2,300, if we include the trial products.

Y: That's impressive.

Z: This is our digital camera. This is our software area. We have CAD, accounting software, etc. And here are our various electronic toys.

Y: This one looks like an instrument used in space technology.

Z: That's right. It is used for satellite orientation and navigation. The surface is treated with a special coating.

Y: You have lots of attractive products.

Z: Yes. I hope you'll place some orders after you see our displays.

Y: Well, let me see. We still have some very important matters to discuss.

Z: You mean prices. I don't think you have to worry about prices. Our goods are sold at the lowest price. Here is our catalogue with the latest quotations.

Y: Thank you. I am interested in the electronic toys.

Dialogue 2　Introducing Oolong Tea

Scene: Liu Jun, a business representative of a tea company, is introducing Oolong tea to Mr. Green and especially emphasizes the quality of the tea.

(L=Liu Jun　G=Mr. Green)

L: Good morning, welcome to our display. I'm the business representative of Guangdong Mingxiang Tea Corporation. Can I help you?

G: Good morning, I'm the purchasing manager of Palatable Taste Company. I'm glad to see so many of your products at this fair. I am interested in them. May I ask what your main products are?

L: Green tea and Oolong tea. They remain fresh and natural with our new techniques.

G: Do you mean they contain no preservative additives?

L: That's right. Our products are free from any chemicals that are harmful to health. Look at the certificates issued by ISO and the national inspection authorities. Some of our products have gained many awards in both national and international exhibitions. And they sell very well.

G: That's good. I believe your products are high quality. I'm interested in your Oolong tea. Can I have a look at it?

L: These series of Oolong tea are from fine and tender tea leaves grown in the mountains. They have a very pleasant aroma. Why not take a seat and taste some?

G: That's wonderful! It smells refreshing and tastes mellow and clean. Would you please give me your quotation?

L: Sure. This is our catalogue with the latest quotations. Could you please leave me your phone number?

G: OK. This is my business card.

L: Thank you. This is my card. You are welcome to contact us at any time, Mr. Green.

G: Fine.

L: Thank you for your visit. Have a pleasant day.

Words and Phrases

specific [spəˈsifik]　　*adj.* 具體的；特定的
showcase [ˈʃəʊkeis]　　*vt.* 陳列；使展現
demonstrate [ˈdemənstreit]　　*vt.* 展示；展現
supplier [səˈplaiə(r)]　　*n.* 供應廠商；供應者
a variety of　各種的，多樣的
launch [lɔːntʃ]　　*vt.* 發射（導彈、火箭等）；發起，
brand [brænd]　　*n.* 商標，牌子
the IMEX Group　會展集團
IMEX Frankfurt　法蘭克福會展
IMEX America　美國會展
Korean [kəˈriən]　　*n.* 韓國人
　　　　　　　　　adj. 韓國人的
showroom [ˈʃəʊruːm]　　*n.* 陳列室；樣品間
array [əˈrei]　　*n.* 排列；列陣
impressive [imˈpresiv]　　*adj.* 給人以深刻印象的
digital [ˈdidʒitl]　　*adj.* 數字的
CAD (abbr. for computer-aided design)　計算機輔助設計
software [ˈsɔftwɛə]　　*n.* 軟件
electronic [iˌlekˈtrɒnik]　　*adj.* 電子的
navigation [ˌnæviˈgeiʃn]　　*n.* 導航；航海
catalogue [ˈkætəlɒg]　　*n.* 目錄；產品目錄
quotation [kwəʊˈteiʃn]　　*n.* 報價單；報價
representative [ˌrepriˈzentətiv]　　*n.* 代表
oolong tea　烏龍茶
technique [tekˈniːk]　　*n.* 技巧；手法
contain [kənˈtein]　　*vt.* 包含；含有
preservative [priˈzɜːvətiv]　　*adj.* 防腐的
　　　　　　　　　　　　n. 防腐劑
additive [ˈædətiv]　　*n.* 添加物；添加劑
chemical [ˈkemikl]　　*n.* 化學製品；化學藥品
　　　　　　　　　　adj. 化學的

certificate [səˈtifikət]　　n. 證書；執照

ISO（abbr. for the International Organization for Standardization）國際標準化組織

inspection [inˈspekʃn]　　n. 視察；檢查

authority [ɔːˈθɒrəti]　　n. 權威；權力；當局

award [əˈwɔːd]　　vt. 授予
　　　　　　　　　n. 獎品

tender [ˈtendə(r)]　　adj. 溫柔的；柔軟的

aroma [əˈrəʊmə]　　n. 芳香；香味

refreshing [riˈfreʃiŋ]　　adj. 提神的；使清爽的

mellow [ˈmeləʊ]　　adj. 柔和的；成熟的；芳醇的

contact [ˈkɒntækt]　　vt. 接觸；聯繫

Additional Words and Phrases

specification　規格

pattern　款式

design　設計

manufacture　生產

reputation　信譽

quality　質量

quantity　數量

franchise　特許經銷權

agreement　協議

order　訂購，訂單

contract　合同

payment　支付

payment term　支付條件，付款方式

best price　最優價格

Useful Expressions

1. How do you like the quality of our products?

2. What about having a look at a sample first?

3. We are offering you our best prices.

4. I'm sure the prices we have submitted are competitive.
5. We are always improving our design and patterns to conform to the world market.
6. Therefore, we always put quality as the first consideration.
7. Could you tell me which kind of payment terms you would prefer?
8. What do you think of the payment terms?

Section 3　Exercises

I. Complete the following dialogue according to the Chinese in brackets.

(M＝Manufacturer　　I＝Importer)

I：_____1_____（你們製作的陶瓷作品真美）.

M：Thanks. I have 50 employees. _____2_____（我希望能成為臺灣地區最大的陶瓷出口商）.

I：Well, _____3_____（對陶瓷的需求量愈來愈大）in my country.

M：Yes, a large proportion of our sales are to the U.S..

I：_____4_____（您能給我介紹一下你們的設計嗎）?

M：This is an eight-foot decorative vase. It's hand-made and the inlaid designs are etched in. It takes 45 days to make. Its retail price will be US＄3,000.

I：The result is certainly worth the effort. _____5_____（這個式樣呢）?

M：It's quite expensive to make and because of its small size, buyers balk at its high price. We feel we could sell more if we could reduce the price.

I：Well, thank you for showing me your beautiful ceramic ware. _____6_____（你們的設計和產品質量讓我印象深刻）.

II. Translate the following sentences into English.

1. 我敢肯定我們的價格是非常有競爭力的。
2. 就質量而言，沒有任何廠家能和我們相比。
3. 我們的價格取決於你們的訂單有多大。
4. 我很高興這次洽談圓滿成功。
5. 雖然我們感謝貴方的合作，但是很抱歉，我們不能再減價了。

III. Fill in the poster for Macao Franchise Expo (MFE) 2014 with proper information.

　　Date：_____

　　Location：Convention and Exhibition Center at The Venetian Resort, Macao

　　Detail：Building on foundations laid down last time, MFE will assemble franchisors, _____, _____ from mainland China, Japan, _____, _____, etc. The Franchise brands will include food and beverages, sales, and _____. It will be a great place to promote exhibitions, expositions, forums and presentations.

　　Tel： 　　(853) 2872, 8212

　　Website： 　　http://www.mfe.mo/

IV. Make dialogues according to the given situations.

　　Situation A：Wang Ying is visiting a booth, and Peter Brown is introducing to her a new type of mobile phone being displayed.

　　Situation B：Ellen is interested in ordering some diamonds at the manufacturer's booth in the exhibition. She asks for some discount of the price. A salesman is serving her.

● Section 4　Extensive Reading

The Canton Fair

　　The Canton Fair is a trade fair held in the spring and autumn each year since 1957 in Canton (Guangzhou), China. Its full name since 2007 has been China Import and Export Fair (中國進出口商品交易會), renamed from Chinese Export Commodities Fair (中國出口商品交易會), also known as Canton Fair (廣州交易會), whose Chinese abbreviation is「廣交會」。

　　The Fair is co-hosted by the Ministry of Commerce of China and the People's Government of Guangdong Province, and organized by China Foreign Trade Centre. It is the larges trade fair in China. Among China's large trade fairs, it has the largest assortment of products, the largest attendance, and the largest number of business deals made at the fair. Like many trade fairs, it has its traditions and functions as an event of international importance. The gross exhibition space is nearly 1,125,000 m^2. It has over 55,800 standard stands and more than 150,000 varieties of products. In the 105th Session, business turnover reached 262.3 million US dollars, attracting 203 trading countries and regions as well as 165,436 visitors. The fair has three phases per session and two sessions per year, usually with the spring session in April to May and the autumn session in October. The 115th China Import and Export Fair (2014) is the largest biannual Chinese trade fair held in Guangzhou.

Unit 4　Incentive Travel

Section 1　Introduction

　　Incentive travel is a global management tool that uses an exceptional travel experience to motivate participants for increased levels of performance in support of organizational goals. It is usually undertaken as a type of employee reward by a company or institution for targets met or exceeded, or for jobs well done. This kind of travel is generally designed to help motivate employees or partners and thus to enhance productivity or achieve business objectives. Nowadays, a good deal of business travel is related to incentive travel. Unlike a meeting, a conference, or other events, incentive travel is usually conducted purely for entertainment, rather than professional or education purposes. Depending on cultural and social factors, incentive travel differs in its application and understanding in different countries. In the USA, for instance, there are many types of individual incentives using catalogue offers as incentive programmes. In some developing markets, incentive travel implies a simple arrangement or only a plane ticket and paid accommodation.

Discussion

　　1. How are incentive tours different from other tours?
　　2. What do you think are the key elements in arranging a successful incentive tour?

Section 2 Dialogues

Dialogue 1 *Announcing a Schedule*

Scene: Miss Wang is introducing the schedule of the business trip to the group tourists from Shanghai.

(W= Miss Wang   T= Tourist)

W: Good afternoon, I would like to take this opportunity to talk briefly about our schedule in the coming days.

On the first day, we will visit Shenzhen Economic & Technical Development Zone, and a free discussion will be held after the visit. A visit to the Silicon Valley of China—Shenzhen Technological Park and a business discussion will be arranged in the afternoon. On the second day, leaders from the Shenzhen municipal government will give us a briefing on the investment environment and merchant financing. You can do a business survey in the morning. In the afternoon, we will pay a visit to two renowned enterprises located in Shenzhen — Huawei Technological Co. and Konka Co.. On the third day, sightseeing at the 「Window of the World」and 「the Splendid China」will be on our schedule. On the fourth day, we will arrange a professional discussion with local entrepreneurs and a Cantonese style dinner party after that.

I am honored to accompany you throughout your travel here. I will be glad if I can answer some of your questions now and address others as we tour.

T: Thank you. Miss Wang, when and where will we gather tomorrow morning?

W: I'm sorry. We will meet at the lobby of the hotel at 8 o'clock. Please be on time.

T: Thank you. See you tomorrow.

W: See you tomorrow. I hope you have a good rest tonight.

Dialogue 2 *Arranging for an Incentive Travel*

Scene: Mr. Brown has visited Mr. Zhang's factory and placed an order for products. Mr. Zhang and his secretary Hanmei are entertaining him in a restaurant, and they also plan an incentive trip as a reward for their business relationship.

(B= Mr. Brown   Z= Mr. Zhang   H= Hanmei, the secretary)

Z: Mr. Brown, I really appreciate our cooperation. Let's cheer for it, Gan Bei!

B: Gan Bei!

H: Gan Bei!

Z: As it's your first time here in Chengdu, we've made travel arrangements for you. We hope you will like this excursion.

B: Thank you for your arrangements.

Z: We will first tour Dujiangyan Irrigation Project after breakfast tomorrow morning.

B: Oh, great. I've heard about it. When was it built, Miss Han?

H: In 256 B. C.. Li Bing diverted the fast-flowing Min River via weirs into irrigation canals.

Z: It is a major landmark in the development of water management and technology, and is still discharging its functions perfectly.

B: Great!

Z: Mr. Brown, we hear you like climbing mountains.

B: Yeah, it's a kind of aerobic exercise.

Z: So the next place is Mt. Qingcheng.

H: It is a holy Taoist mountain. The trails are lined with plum and palm trees. The air is fresh. Picturesque vistas and dozens of picturesque temples dot the route. A very attractive and intriguing scenic spot. I bet you will like it.

B: What's the weather like?

H: The weather is always fine, with a comfortable temperature of 16℃ at this time of the year. There is saying that Mt. Qingcheng is the most peaceful and secluded mountain under heaven, which means that it enjoys the most tranquil beauty among the famous mountains.

B: Oh, good. What's the height of the mountain?

H: 1,260 meters, that's about 4,000 feet.

B: Yeah.

Z: After climbing the mountain, we'll go to a hot spring resort, bathe in a spa and have a barbecue in a club.

B: I'm sure I'll have a great relaxing time. Thank you very much.

Z: Once again, for our cooperation, (H joins) Cheers!

B: Cheers!

Words and Phrases

incentive [inˈsentiv]　　*adj.* 激勵的；刺激的
global [ˈgləubəl]　　*adj.* 全球的；總體的；球形的
management [ˈmænidʒmənt]　　*n.* 管理；經營
undertake [ˌʌndəˈteik]　　*vt.* 從事；著手做
reward [riˈwɔːd]　　*n.* 報答；酬謝
　　　　　　　　　　v. 獎勵；獎賞
institution [ˌinstiˈtjuːʃn]　　*n.* 機構
target [ˈtɑːgɪt]　　*n.* 目標；靶子
motivate [ˈməutiveit]　　*vt.* 刺激；激發……的積極性
partner [ˈpɑːtnə]　　*n.* 合夥人
enhance [inˈhɑːns]　　*vt.* 提高；加強
productivity [ˌprɒdʌkˈtivəti]　　*n.* 生產力；生產率
objective [əbˈdʒektiv]　　*n.* 目的；目標
conduct [ˈkɒndʌkt]　　*vt.* 進行，實施
professional [prəˈfeʃənl]　　*adj.* 專業的；職業的
differ [ˈdifə(r)]　　*vi.* 相異；不同
imply [imˈplai]　　*vt.* 意味；隱含
arrangement [əˈreɪn(d)ʒm(ə)nt]　　*n.* 安排
accommodation [əˌkɒməˈdeiʃn]　　*n.* 住處，膳宿
schedule [ˈʃedjuːl]　　*n.* 時間表；計劃
silicon [ˈsilikən]　　*n.* 硅
Silicon Valley　　硅谷
renowned [riˈnaʊnd]　　*adj.* 著名的；有聲望的
enterprise [ˈentəpraiz]　　*n.* 企業；事業
entrepreneur [ˌɒntrəprəˈnɜː(r)]　　*n.* 企業家
entertain [ˌentəˈtein]　　*vt.* 招待；宴請
excursion [iksˈkɜːʃn]　　*n.* 遊覽；短途旅行
irrigation [ˌiriˈgeiʃn]　　*n.* 灌溉
weir [wiə(r)]　　*n.* 堰，壩
landmark [ˈlændmɑːk]　　*n.* 標誌；里程碑

discharge ［dis'tʃɑːdʒ］　　vi. 排放；流出
aerobic ［eə'rəʊbɪk］　adj. 有氧的
trail ［treil］　　n. 小徑
picturesque ［ˌpiktʃə'resk］　adj. 如畫的
vista ［'vistə］　n. 遠景
secluded ［si'kluːdid］　adj. 幽靜的；僻靜的
tranquil ［'træŋkwil］　adj. 安寧的；安靜的
resort ［ri'zɔːt］　n. 度假勝地
hot spring　溫泉
spa ［spɑː］　n. 水療
barbecue ［'bɑːbikjuː］　n. 烤肉；烤燒

Additional Words and Phrases

tour escort / director　旅行團領隊
group / package tour　團隊 / 包價旅遊
to combine sightseeing with holiday-making　觀光與度假相結合
special interest program / tour　專項 / 特色旅遊
professional tours　專業 / 職業旅遊
local / national guide　地 / 全陪

Useful Expressions

1. The quotation for each tour includes all expenses in the destination country.

2. This includes the cost of accommodation, meals, transportation, sightseeing, guides, airport departure tax, and a round-trip international airfare.

3. If you have any questions on the details, feel free to ask.

4. We'll leave some evenings free, if it is all right with you.

5. I wonder if it is possible to arrange shopping for us.

Section 3　Exercises

I. Complete the following dialogue according to the Chinese in brackets.

（J = Jean Simmons　K = Kyle Mathews）

J：Hey Kyle, guess what !＿＿＿＿＿1＿＿＿＿＿（老板下月要我去西岸參加一個市場營銷研討會）.

K：Ah hah, you must be happy. You've been looking forward to going on a business trip for months.

J：Yeah, and he said there'll be more coming up, so I should get a corporate card. Problem is, I don't know how to proceed, and I don't want the boss to know. Can you fill me in?

K：Sure, no problem. First, go see the secretary and tell her where you're going and when.＿＿＿＿2＿＿＿＿（她將為你安排交通和酒店）through our travel agent, and ＿＿＿＿3＿＿＿＿（並在幾天內給你票和旅程表）in a few days. At the same time, ask her for an application form for the card.

J：Will I use the card for everything?

K：No, ＿＿＿＿＿4＿＿＿＿＿（我們和一些主要航空公司和酒店都有公司信用協議）. For this trip, you'll probably only use it for food. Not all restaurants accept the card, so you may have to pay cash.

J：＿＿＿＿＿5＿＿＿＿＿（我要花自己的錢嗎）?

K：Afraid so. We used to have cash advances, but the company stopped that when they started issuing cards.

J：Will the company reimburse everything?

K：No, ＿＿＿＿6＿＿＿＿（每日有最高限額）. I'll give you a list. Of course, personal items aren't covered. And make sure you keep all your receipts. ＿＿＿＿7＿＿＿＿（你得把他們貼在報銷單上）when you get back.

J：Anything else?

K：No, thank you very much.

II. Translate the following sentences into English.

1. 我是中安科技外貿部的李華，歡迎來深圳。
2. 我們已經為你在花園酒店準備了房間。

3. 我們會盡量安排好你的中國之行。

4. 這是我們為你擬定的活動日程安排。

5. 我們安排了在「粵唯鮮」的晚宴，讓你感受一下廣東的飲食文化。

III. Writing practice.

Please write a tour itinerary, including when you will set out and return, the route of the visit, where you will stay, etc.

IV. Make dialogues according to the given situations.

Situation A: Li Hua is meeting his business partner Mr. Smith, who arrives in Shenzhen from London at the airport. He briefly introduces the two days' business tour to him, including some interesting incentive programs.

Situation B: Wanghai is introducing a three-day tour arranged for their business partners, which includes a typical Sichuan dinner in Jinjiang Hotel as well as the trip to Jiuzhaigou Nature Reserve.

Section 4　Extensive Reading

Wonder Works Orlando

Wonder Works Orlando is an amusement park for the mind, featuring over 100 interactive exhibits for visitors of all ages to experience. The Wonder Works exhibits utilize some of the most sophisticated graphic and audio presentation techniques available. Throughout Wonder Works, you will be able to actively participate in some of the most imaginative displays and exhibits found in any facility in the United States.

When you enter Wonder Works Orlando, you'll quickly notice something different—everything will be upside down! So you will quickly be inverted, and then your journey can begin. You will be blown away by 71-mile-per-hour hurricane force winds, get shaken by a simulated 5.3 degree earthquake, put yourself inside a bubble, and be raised up on a bed of 3,500 nails! You can make a 3-D impression of your entire body, design and ride your own roller coaster moving 360 degrees in any direction!

推薦展會場館及網址：

中國國際展覽中心（老館）——地址：北京朝陽區北三環東路 6 號

上海展覽中心，亦稱上海展覽館——地址：上海市中心靜安區延安中路 1000 號

上海新國際博覽中心——地址：上海浦東新區龍陽路 2345 號

上海光大會展中心——地址：中國上海漕寶路 66 號 B 座 5 樓

中國進出口商品交易會展館——地址：廣州市海珠區閱江中路 380 號

深圳會展中心場館——地址：深圳市中心區福華三路

成都國際會議展覽中心——地址：中國成都沙灣路 258 號

成都世紀城新國際會展中心——地址：中國四川省成都市世紀城路 198 號

法蘭克福國際會展　http://www.imex-frankfurt.com/

美國國際會展　http://www.imexamerica.com/

紐約市官方旅遊網站　http://www.nycgo.com/

澳門展貿協會　http://www.macaufta.com/

中國會展網　http://www.expo-china.com/

中國企業會議　http://www.micechina.com/

中國 2010 上海世博會　http://www.expo2010.cn/

會展旅遊集團　http://www.etgcn.com/

好展會　http://www.haozhanhui.com/

Part Four
Scenic Spot English

Unit 1　Dujiangyan Irrigation Project

Section 1　Introduction

　　Dujiangyan irrigation project is an irrigation infrastructure built by Governor Li Bing of the Qin State in 256 B. C., during China's Warring States Period (476 B. C. —221 B. C.). It is located the Min River in Sichuan province, 45 kilometers north of Chengdu. The Dujiangyan irrigation project is the only existing ancient hydro-power project and has produced comprehensive benefits in flood control, irrigation, water transport and general water consumption. It is still in use today, irrigating over 5,300 square kilometers of the region's land. There is a saying which goes「There would be no Land of Abundance without Dujiangyan」. The irrigation system is an amazing feat of engineering and construction, a wonder of the world, and is a UNESCO world heritage site. Nowadays visitors come to the site to appreciate the ingenious work of Yuzui (Fish-Mouth Levee), Feishayan (Sand-Flying Weir) and Baopingkou (Bottle-Neck Channel), as well as Two Kings Temple, Dragon-Taming Temple, Anlan Bridge, and other sights.

Discussion

1. Do you know the three great hydraulic engineering projects of the Qin Dynasty?
2. How is the Dujiangyan irrigation system different from other water conservancy projects?

Section 2　Dialogues

Dialogue 1　Visiting Dujiangyan Irrigation Project

Scene: Miss Qin, a tour guide, is showing the tourists around Dujiangyan Irrigation Project. They are arriving at Yu Zui (Fish-Mouth levee).

(Q= Miss Qin, the guide　T= Tourist)

Q: As I told you on the coach, Dujiangyan irrigation project is a major landmark in the development of water management and technology. Now, we are on the spot. We will appreciate the ingenious work in person.

T: What is the river called?

Q: Min Jiang, a tributary of the upper Yangtze River.

T: The whitewater is rolling, isn't it?

Q: Yes, it is a raging torrent as it flows quickly down from the mountains. In the past, water surging down the river from the Minshan mountain range destroyed property and killed people. Local farmers in the Chengdu plain frequently suffered from the water disasters. Therefore, Li Bing and his son designed this water control system and organized thousands of local people to construct the project.

T: Great job!

Q: Look at this part. What shape do you suppose it is?

T: A long and narrow part.

Q: Right. Is it shaped like a fish mouth?

T: Ah, exactly.

Q: So, this is called Yu Zui, Fish-Mouth Levee. Li Bing's irrigation system consists of three main constructions. This Fish-Mouth Levee is the key part. More than 2,000 years ago, when Li Bing worked as the local governor, he organized the people to build the levee in the middle of the river according to the natural geographic conditions. The

Fish-Mouth Levee's function is to divide the river into an inner and outer streams, and to control the amount of water that enters the two streams. The inner stream carries approximately 60% of the river's flow into the irrigation system during the dry season, while during the flood, this amount decreases to 40% to protect the people from flooding.

T: Marvelous work. But how did they make it? Was it originally like that?

Q: Of course not. This project was initially constructed by Li Bing around 256 B. C.. A lot of renovations and annual maintenance were carried out in the following dynasties and periods. Especially after 1949, a large-scale expansion was undertaken and it came to be as you see it now. In the past, they used Zhulong or Zhulou, long sausage-shaped baskets of woven bamboo filled with stones, and Macha, wooden tripods, to construct the levee.

T: Now it is concrete and steel.

Q: Yes. Li Bing's immortal contribution to the irrigation system lies in that he ingeniously took the advantage of the topography. As you see, the river bends here and the outer side of the bed was actually higher than the inner side. Li Bing chose the site of the project here, which works in harmony with Feishayan, there, on the right, the Sand-Flying weir, and Baopingkou or the Bottle-Neck channel, right down there, to ensure the work of diverting water, discharging sand and overflow, and, irrigation. This fully expresses the importance of utilizing natural features. It is a masterpiece of the world's hydropower culture.

T: Thank you for your wonderful introduction. You are really an orator.

Q: Am I? I am so flattered. We still have to visit the other two major constructions of the project and Two Kings Temple. There, we can see many of Li Bing's mottos about water conservancy carved on the cliff.

Dialogue 2 Visiting Li Dui Park

Scene: Miss Qin, the tour guide, is introducing Baopingkou—the bottle neck channel and Li Dui to the tourists from Australia.

(Q= Miss Qin, the guide   T= Tourist)

Q: We are arriving at Li Dui park.

T: What a beautiful park! Can we take some pictures here?

Q: Sure. Just stand in front of the stela with the characters inscribed in — THE WORLD HERITAGE DUJIANGYAN. A well certificate for your travel here, isn't it?

T: Good idea. Would you please take photos of us, Miss Qin? Just press this button, thanks.

Q: Cheese. Great. Done. Let's hurry up. Many other spots are waiting for us.

Q: Now I'd like to tell you the story of Li Dui. Is there any of you who knows the two Chinese characters? What do they mean?

T: No, sorry.

Q: Li means 「separated」 or 「isolated」. Dui means 「a mound」 or 「a heap」. Li Dui means 「a separated mound」. It was originally a part of the Yulei mountain over there. To make use of the inner stream, Li Bing had the idea of carving out of Mt. Yulei an opening to let in water to irrigate the region. Cutting the opening proved to be a great problem as the tools available to Li Bing at the time were unable to penetrate the hard rock of the mountain.

T: They could use gunpowder to explode the mountain. Chinese invented gunpowder.

Q: No. This was before the invention of gunpowder. So he used a combination of fire and water to heat and cool the rocks until they cracked and could be removed. It took eight years to cut a trunk canal through the mountain. So, we've got the isolated hill, Li Dui, and Baopinkou.

T: We see.

Q: Let's have a close look at Baopinkou. This way, on the right, please.

T: Wow, the water has a narrow entrance here. It's really like the neck of a bottle. But why?

Q: You know, this part was for irrigation purposes, so the neck works as a check gate to control and maintain the water flow. During the flood seasons, the water will not overflow into the inner canal. Instead, it flows in whirlpools into the outer stream through Feishayan. The Bottle-Neck channel and the Flying-Sand weir play a key role in regulating the water automatically and safeguard the Chengdu plain as well as the irrigated regions. That is why we have had 「the land of abundance」.

T: What an extraordinary feat! A great contribution to Sichuan.

Q: Absolutely. Let's visit Dragon-Taming temple. There I'll tell the legend of Erlang, Li Bing's son, subduing an evil dragon down at the river and controlling the water flow. We can also see a stone statue of Li Bing. It was unearthed from the river base and is now placed in the middle of the main hall. Please hurry up.

Words and Phrases

irrigate ['ɪrɪgeɪt]　　*vt.* 灌溉；沖洗
infrastructure ['ɪnfrəstrʌktʃə(r)]　　*n.* 基礎設施；公共建設
Warring States Period　戰國時期
the Land of Abundance　天府之國
feat [fiːt]　　*n.* 功績
wonder ['wʌndə(r)]　　*n.* 奇跡；奇觀
UNESCO (abbr. for United Nations Educational, Scientific and Cultural Organization)　聯合國教科文組織
heritage ['herɪtɪdʒ]　　*n.* 遺產
ingenious [ɪn'dʒiːnɪəs]　　*adj.* 有獨創性的；天才的
ingenuity [ˌɪndʒə'njuːətɪ]　　*n.* 獨創性；巧思
levee ['levɪ]　　*n.* 堤壩
channel ['tʃænl]　　*n.* 通道；海峽
hydraulic [haɪ'drɔːlɪk]　　*adj.* 液壓的；水力的
maintenance ['meɪntənəns]　　*n.* 維護，維修
conserve [kən'sɜːv]　　*vt.* 保護；保存
conservancy [kən'sɜːvənsɪ]　　*n.* 保護
on the spot　現場
in person　親自
tributary ['trɪbjət(ə)rɪ]　　*n.* 支流
whitewater ['waɪtˌwɔːtə]　　*n.* 急流
torrent ['tɒrənt]　　*n.* 水流；洪流
destroy [dɪ'strɔɪ]　　*vt.* 破壞；毀滅
construct [kən'strʌkt]　　*vt.* 建造；施工
construction [kən'strʌkʃn]　　*n.* 建設；建築物
geographic [ˌdʒiːə'græfɪk]　　*adj.* 地理的；地理學的
approximately [ə'prɒksɪmətlɪ]　　*adv.* 大約，近似地
decrease [dɪ'kriːs]　　*vi.* 減少，減小
marvelous ['mɑːvɪləs]　　*adj.* 了不起的；非凡的
initially [ɪ'nɪʃəlɪ]　　*adv.* 最初，首先
renovation [ˌrenə'veɪʃn]　　*n.* 革新；修理

expansion [ikˈspænʃn]　　n. 擴展，擴大，擴張，擴充
tripod [ˈtraipɒd]　　n. 三腳架
take the advantage of　　利用
topography [təˈpɒgrəfi]　　n. 地勢
divert [daiˈvɜːt]　　vt. 轉移；轉入
orator [ˈɒrətə(r)]　　n. 演說者；雄辯家
flatter [ˈflætə(r)]　　vt. 恭維；奉承
motto [ˈmɒtəʊ]　　n. 格言；箴言
cliff [klif]　　n. 懸崖；絕壁
stela [ˈstelə]　　n. 石碑
inscribe [inˈskraib]　　vt. 題寫；銘刻
certificate [səˈtifikət]　　n. 證書；執照，文憑
isolate [ˈaisəleit]　　vt. 使隔離
mound [maʊnd]　　n. 堆
penetrate [ˈpenətreit]　　vt. 滲透；刺入
gunpowder [ˈgʌnpaʊdə(r)]　　n. 火藥
whirlpool [ˈwɜːlpuːl]　　n. 漩渦，渦流
automatically [ˌɔːtəˈmætikli]　　adv. 自動地
legend [ˈledʒənd]　　n. 傳奇；傳說
subdue [səbˈdjuː]　　vt. 徵服
unearth [ʌnˈɜːθ]　　vt. 發掘；出土

Additional Words and Phrases

Li Bing　　李冰
Er Lang　　二郎
Fish-Mouth Levee　　魚嘴
Sand-Flying Weir　　飛沙堰
Bottle-Neck Channel　寶瓶口
Two Kings Temple　　二王廟
Qin Weir Pavilion　　秦堰樓
Dragon-Taming Temple　　伏龍觀
Anlan Cable Bridge　　安瀾索橋
Li Dui Park　　離堆公園

Mount Yulei　玉壘山

South Bridge　南橋

Water-releasing ceremony　放水節

Useful Expressions

1. Divide the water into 40% and 60%, subdue floods and droughts. 分四六，平潦旱。

2. Dredge the shoal deep, make the dike low. 深掏灘，低作堰。

3. Cut off the bends of the river where it curves and dredge the middle of the river-bed where it runs straight across. 遇彎截角，逢正抽心。

Section 3　Exercises

I. Answer the following questions.

1. What lesson can be drawn from the annual maintenance of Dujiangyan Irrigation Project?

2. What were Zhulong and Macha used for?

3. Can you make some comment on the six-or eight-character mottos about water conservancy in Two Kings Temple?

4. What's the function of Sand-Flying Weir?

II. Translate the following sentences into English.

1. 都江堰是中國建設於古代並使用至今的大型水利工程。

2. 都江堰的創建開創了中國古代水利史上的新紀元。

3. 都江堰附近景色秀麗、文物古跡眾多。

4. 都江堰附近主要景點有伏龍觀、二王廟、安瀾索橋、玉壘山、離堆公園、玉壘山公園、靈岩寺、普照寺等。

5. 都江堰於2000年被聯合國確定為世界文化遺產，2007年被正式批准為國家5A級旅遊景區。

III. Write a brief introduction of Li Bing, who made a great contribution to the Dujiangyan irrigation project.

IV. Make dialogues according to the given situations.

Situation A: Li Hua is leading a group of tourists to walk across the Anlan cable bridge, and he is telling them about the story of He Xiande, who first built the bridge with his wife.

Situation B: Li Hua, the tour guide, is showing a group of tourists from America around the Two Kings temple.

Section 4　Extensive Reading

The Water-releasing Ceremony

The water-releasing ceremony on the Tomb-sweeping Day is a folk custom in Dujiangyan City. On that day every year, grand ceremonies are held in commemoration of the completion of the irrigation system and its builder Li Bing, and at the same time to mark the beginning of a busy spring plowing season. The celebrations include official ceremonies as well as sacrificial rituals held by ordinary people.

In ancient times, a grand water-releasing ceremony would be held as a wish for a bumper harvest. This ceremony has been kept alive as a tradition in the western Sichuan plain. At the ceremony, local officials are on hand to present the water-releasing spectacle, accompanied by large-scale celebrations.

This ceremony originated from the sacrificial ritual in honor of the God of Water before the irrigation system was built. At that time, there were frequently floods, causing great suffering to people on both banks of the river. To seek protection from the God of Water, sacrificial rituals would be regularly held along the river. After the construction of the Dujiangyan Irrigation System, the Chengdu Plain was free from floods and people had ample food and clothing. To commemorate Li Bing and his son for their great work, people dedicated the sacrificial ceremonies to the father and son instead of to the water. Local residents would spontaneously go to the Erwang (literally, two kings) Temple in honor of Li Bing and his son, where temple fairs (otherwise known as 「Qingming Festival Fairs」) would be held.

Unit 2　Mt. Qingcheng

Section 1　Introduction

　　Mt. Qingcheng, 15 kilometers from Dujiangyan Irrigation Project, is one of the most famous Taoist mountains in China. It is also a very attractive and intriguing scenic spot that is covered by luxuriant and verdant trees. Since ancient times it has enjoyed the fame of「the most tranquil mountain under heaven」.

　　Mt. Qingcheng is divided into two parts – the front mountain and the back mountain. The front part is the main part of the scenic spot, covering an area of approximately 15 square kilometers (about 3,706 acres) with great natural beauty as well as an abundance of cultural relics and historic sites of ancient Taoist temples. Among them, Jianfu Temple, Tianshi Cave, Zushi Temple and Shangqing Temple, together with the newly-rebuilt Lao-jun Pavilion on the top of the highest peak, are some of the most famous visiting spots.

Discussion

1. How do you define the word「幽」, referring to Mt. Qingcheng?
2. Can you say something about「Taoism」?

Section 2　Dialogues

Dialogue 1　Talking About Taoism

Scene: Li Qiao, a tour guide, is leading a group of tourists to the famous Taoist Mountain—Mt. Qingcheng, 65 kilometers west of Chengdu. She is explaining Taoism to the tourists.

(L= Li Qiao　T= Tourist)

L: I am glad you are so interested in Chinese Taoism. So I'll talk to you a little bit about it.

T: Great.

L: Anyone knows the Chinese character「道」(Dao)?

T: Does it mean「road」— Dao Lu?

L: Good for you! Tao, originally, meant「road」and then implied「rule」and「principle」or「the law of nature」. Lao Zi used Tao in his 5,000-word book-Dao De Jing — to propound his ideological system; therefore his school of thinking is called Taoism. He advocated preserving and restoring the Tao in the body and the cosmos.

T: How's that?

L: In Lao Zi's philosophy, Dao is the natural way of the universe, the driving force in nature, the order and the power behind all life and all living things. So he advocates a simple, honest life and noninterference with the course of natural events. For example, taoists believe in Wu Wei, that is, non-action. Non-action means to follow the law of nature and let everything be what it naturally will be, instead of trying to override it.

T: It works! I believe that.

L: It really helps sometimes, doesn't it? In fact, dialectic thinking is abundant in Lao Zi's system. He contended that things often turn to their opposites as they grow. We have a saying「things will develop in the opposite direction when they become extreme」, like existing and non-existing, fortune and misfortune, strong and weak. Lao Zi even cited the examples of 「water」, 「grass」, 「wood」 to prove that the weak and the flexible can defeat the strong and live long.

T: Very interesting philosophy. The Chinese people must have been quite influenced by Taoism.

L: Yes. It has a profound influence on us, in ideology, art, literature, medicine, and all the aspects, from personal life to state management. Some hold that without understanding Taoism, there can be no understanding of Chinese culture.

T: Lao Zi was a respectable creator. But why is the mountain connected with Taoism? Did he live here?

L: Good question. Lao Zi didn't live in Chengdu. He was said to have left a 5,000-word book and gone on his ox from Hangu Pass to nobody knows where! Mt. Qingcheng has been regarded as one of the places where the Taoist religion originated largely due to a famous Taoist named Zhang Lin. He was said to come to the mountain and practise the religion during the Eastern Han period, and there is a temple called Tianshi Cave in Mt. Qingcheng to enshrine his statue and to commemorate him. Since then, many famous Taoists came here and dozens of their temples were built on the mountain. Later we will visit many ancient Taoist temples. I will tell you more about their legendary stories.

T: Great. We love stories.

Dialogue 2 Visiting Shangqing Temple

Scene: Li Qiao, a tour guide, is leading a group of tourists to the famous Taoist temple in Mt. Qingcheng — Shangqing Temple. She is explaining some of the relics to the tourists.

(L= Li Qiao   T= Tourist)

L: Now we'll take the cable cars up the mountain. Each car for two passengers. Take care when you get in and out. The working staff will help you. Don't worry. I will meet you at the top station. Just enjoy the cable journey.

T: Ok, see you soon.

(After several minutes, they get out of the cars and gather together.)

L: How did you like the cable cars? Did you enjoy the scenery?

T: Fantastic! Is this the highest peak?

L: Not yet. It takes about 20 minutes to walk there. Does anyone want to buy some water or something? There are some shops there, on the left.

T: Me. Wait a minute.

L: Well, everyone is here. Now, let's move on. Take a deep breath of the fresh air, and we will climb up the stone stairs. Come on, here in the middle of the road is a huge rock. It fell down here in the massive earthquake in 2008.

T: Oh, what a huge stone! Unbelievable. How many casualties at that time?

L: Nearly eighty thousands were killed, ten thousand missing, and over four hundred thousand people injured. Deadly damage. The front mountain was not so badly damaged, but the back mountain was not so lucky. Some villages were buried. Several dozens of people were killed.

T: Good heavens.

L: Let's walk on. Look at this stele. You know the Chinese word now, don't you?

T: Dao.

L: Right. The doctrine of Taoism. Come to the back and look at the stone inscription 「大道無為」. Do you still remember what Wu Wei is in Taoism? Non-action?

T: To follow the law of nature, not to override it. What will be will be.

L: Exactly. Thank you for your attention. Turn back and look up. We are reaching the famous Shangqing temple near the highest peak of the mountain.

T: Hurray!

L: After having seen the green scenery along the way and an overlooking of the mountain from the cable cars, now we will enter the fairyland of an ancient Taoist temple.

T: When was it built?

L: It was first built in Jin Dynasty, more than 1,500 years ago. Later, in Tang Dynasty and the Wu Dai Period, it was rebuilt and enlarged, but was ruined in Ming Dynasty in the 18th century due to war. Most of the buildings we see now were built in late 19th century after Emperor Tongzhi's reign in Qing Dynasty.

T: It was centuries' work.

L: In a sense, it is. There is an ancient well in it which is said to have been dug in Wu Dai Period more than 1,000 years ago. There are many ancient cultural relics displayed as well. Mr. Zhang Daqian, one of the most famous Chinese artists, lived here for about four years during the anti-Japanese war.

T: Wow.

L: Please look at the three Chinese characters above the arch door. They were written by Chiang Kai-shek, former chairman of the Kuomintang (KMT), the Chinese

Nationalist Party in 1930s and 40s. He later retreated to Taiwan. You must have heard about him. He had another name Jiang Zhongzheng. Do you see it, on the left side? The two couplets on the sides were written by his men Yu Youren and Feng Yuxiang, a famous KMT literary man and a famous military man.

  T: Interesting couplets.

  L: Yes. As so many famous men in history came here or visited here, they left abundant relics: drawings, poems, handwriting, buildings, Taoist stories, philosophy, and so on. Let's appreciate them!

  T: How lucky we are! Which door is the entrance?

  L: This way. Follow me.

Words and Phrases

  intriguing [inˈtriːgiŋ] *adj.* 有趣的；迷人的

  luxuriant [lʌgˈʒʊəriənt] *adj.* 繁茂的；茂密的

  verdant [ˈvɜːdnt] *adj.* 青翠的；翠綠的

  tranquil [ˈtræŋkwil] *adj.* 安靜的；寧靜的

  approximately [əˈprɒksɪmətlɪ] *adv.* 大約，近似地

  abundance [əˈbʌnd(ə)ns] *n.* 充裕，豐富

  relic [ˈrelik] *n.* 遺跡，遺物

  propound [prəˈpaʊnd] *vt.* 提出；提議

  ideology [ˌaidiˈɒlədʒi] *n.* 意識形態；思想

  ideological [ˌaidiəˈlɒdʒikl] *adj.* 思想的；意識形態的

  cosmos [ˈkɒzmɒs] *n.* 宇宙

  override [ˌəʊvəˈraid] *vt.* 推翻；踐踏

  contend [kənˈtend] *vt.* 主張

  enshrine [inˈʃrain] *vt.* 供奉

  statue [ˈstætʃuː] *n.* 雕像；塑像

  commemorate [kəˈmeməreit] *vt.* 紀念

  legendary [ˈledʒəndri] *adj.* 傳說的；傳奇的

  massive [ˈmæsiv] *adj.* 巨大的

  casualty [ˈkæʒuəlti] *n.* 傷亡人員

  bury [ˈberi] *vt.* 埋葬

  doctrine [ˈdɒktrin] *n.* 教義；信條

inscription [inˈskripʃn]　　n. 碑文；刻印
reign [rein]　　vi. 統治 n. 統治；統治時期
in a sense　　在某種意義上
couplet [ˈkʌplət]　　n. 對聯；對句

Additional Words and Phrases

Taoism　　道教
Taoist　　道家；道士
Taoist Trinity　　三清
Jianfu Temple　　建福宮
Tianshi Cave　　天師洞
Zushi Temple　　祖師殿
Shangqing Temple　　上清宮
Sun-viewing Pavilion　　觀日亭
Echo Pavilion　　呼應亭
Laojun Pavilion　　老君閣
Zhangren Peak　　丈人峰
Pengzu Peak　　彭祖峰

Section 3　Exercises

I. Answer the following questions.

1. How did Mt. Qingcheng get its name?
2. Who is the founder of Taoism on Mt. Qingcheng?
3. Who is Taishang Laojun?
4. How long does it usually take tourists to complete the mountain trip?

II. Translate the following sentences into English.

1. 青城山距成都 68 千米，距都江堰僅 10 多千米。
2. 青城山是中國著名的道教名山，道教發源地之一。
3. 青城前山景色優美，文物古跡眾多。
4. 青城山有「三十六峰」「八大洞、七十二小洞」「一百八景」之說。
5. 1940 年前後，國畫大師張大千舉家寓居青城山上清宮。

III. Write a brief introduction of the scenic spot of the Jianfu temple in Mt. Qingcheng.

IV. Make dialogues according to the given situations.

Situation A: Zhang Lin, the tour guide, is leading the group of tourists to Mt. Qingcheng. Now they arrive here. Zhang Lin is telling the group about the route and the schedule.

Situation B: Zhang Lin, the tour guide, is introducing the Mandarin-duck wells to the visitor in Shangqing Temple of Mt. Qincheng.

Section 4 Extensive Reading

Post-Quake Reconstruction

In May, 2008, Dujiangyan and Mount Qingcheng were hit by a major earthquake. The devastation was massive. But only four days after the earthquake, the people of Dujiangyan began planning reconstruction work and future development. The city government issued a recovery blueprint that included infrastructure, public services, industries, social security and the environment.

A little over two years later, the city not only completed rebuilding the Dujiangyan irrigation system and Qingcheng Mountain, but also developed many new attractions.

Quake-damaged houses, temples and alleys have been rebuilt in traditional styles. At a cost of 2.8 billion yuan, a newly renovated ancient city zone highlights historical relics and the local water-themed culture. Modern service facilities, including hotels, shopping centers and restaurants, have been added to the area. In March 2010, workers in the scenic area of Mount Qingcheng were busy installing and testing a new electronic tour guide system. Beginning in May of this year, every tourist here was given a digital card valid for use on the digital tour guide service that can also contact the city's digital control center and even send out an SOS.

Unit 3　Leshan Giant Buddha

● Section 1　Introduction

  Leshan Giant Buddha, located to the east of Leshan City, Sichuan Province, sits at the confluence of the Minjiang, Dadu and Qingyi rivers. It is carved out of the cliff face of Mt. Lingyun. As the largest carved stone Buddha in the world, this colossal staue is three times higher than the biggest Buddha in the Yungang Grottoes (雲岡石窟) of Datong, Shanxi province. It is even higher than the standing Bamyan Buddha in Afghanistan (阿富汗巴米楊大佛), which was formerly considered the highest in the world.

  At 71 metres high, the statue depicts a seated Maitreya Buddha, a disciple of Sakyamuni, the founder of Buddhism, with his hands resting on his knees. The figure occupies the entire hillside. His head is 14.7 meters high. His shoulders are 28 metres wide and its 8.5 meters instep can hold more than a hundred people. There is a local saying,「The Mountain unveils a Buddha, while the Buddha fades into the mountain.」

  Leshan Giant Buddha was ratified as a China Key Cultural Relic Unit under protection by the State Council in 1982, and it was listed as the World Cultural Heritages by UNESCO in 1996. The Leshan Giant Buddha Scenic Area has been listed as China's 5A Class Scenic Area, and one of the「Best Forty」tourist places of China.

Discussion

1. What's the special characteristics of Leshan Giant Buddha?

2. Why was Leshan Giant Buddha listed as a UNESCO world cultural and natural heritage in 1996?

Section 2　Dialogues

Dialogue 1　*A Panoramic View of Leshan Giant Buddha*

Scene: The tourists from America, led by the guide, are taking the ferry to appreciate the panoramic view of Leshan Giant Buddha.

(G = Guide　　T = Tourist)

G: Today, we will enjoy a more panoramic view of Leshan Buddha from a tourist boat on the river. Have you heard a local saying 「The Mountain unveils a Buddha, while the Buddha fades into the mountain.」?

T: Yes. Does it mean the Buddha was carved into the mountain face?

G: Partly right. Please look at the three linked mountains whose names are Mt. Wuyou, Mt. Lingyu and Mt. Guicheng. Could you have some discovery?

T: No. Do they have any speciality?

G: Yes. Looking careful, you can find the three mountains are shaped like a slumbering Buddha when seen from the river. The Buddha lies asleep on the east bank of Minjiang river, extending roughly 1,300 meters with his head to the south and its feet to the north. Mt. Wuyou, Mt. Lingyun and Mt. Guicheng constitute the head, the body and the feet of the huge invisible Buddha respectively. Observed from the opposite bank or the river, Leshan Giant Buddha is appropritely seated in the bosom of the sleeping Buddha, presenting a miracle of the 「Buddha existing within Buddha」. The sleeping Buddha and the seated Buddha constitute the huge invisible spectacular of a slumbering Buddha.

T: Wow! It's amazing that the mountains are really like a slumbering Buddha.

G: From the ferry we can also view two carved stone warriors in battle robes, over 10 meters high, holding the halberd on the cliffs beside the Giant Buddha, which is not visible by foot. Besides, there are numerous smaller carvings of various buddhas on the Giant Buddha cliff road. When getting close to the Buddha, we can take the nine-turn plank road on the right to appreciate the dedicate sculpture of the head of the Buddha.

T: Are there any legends about the Buddha?

G: The Buddha, located to the east of Leshan City, is at the confluence of Minjiang River, Qingyi River, and Dadu River, where many boats had capsized because of the deep and swift torrents of the river at the foot of Lingyun Mountain. This led a Buddhist monk called Haitong from the Lingyun Temple to build a Buddha to seek his blessing. He hoped that the Buddha would subdue the turbulent currents that plagued the shipping vessels traveling down the river and protect the boatmen. This carving project begun in 713 A. D. and was completed in 803 A. D..

The Buddha is 71 meters high, with its head reaching the top of the cliffs, his hands resting on his knees and feet on the lotus. The Buddha has a serene expression, watching the river flowing below his feet.

T: Does the project work well?

G: Yes. Apparently so much stone was removed from the cliff face by the massive construction and deposited into the river below that the currents were indeed altered by the statue, making the waters safe for passing ships.

T: I heard that there was a big temple built to protect the Buddha. Is it true?

G: Yes. After the construction of the Giant Buddha, a huge thirteen-story wooden structure (The 「protecting umbrella」— Giant Buddha Pavilion 大佛阁), plated in gold, was built to shelter it from rain and sunshine. But unfortunately the pavilion was destroyed during the war at the end of the Ming Dynasty. From then on, the Buddha was oxidized. Now the government has promised restoration work to avoid severe erosion and degradation.

T: I find there are also a variety of temples and shrines scattered about the spot. It is meanwhile like a pilgrimage trip to visit the world heritages.

G: Yes. The Buddha not only has a cultural meaning but also a religious meaning. Various smaller buddhas carvings on the cliff road make the mountain a museum of buddhist carving. As a colossal statue, the Buddha is so awe-inspiring that every pious Buddhist feels compelled to fall to his knees and to pray for blessings and safety in life. This is why an increasing number of people come to visit the Buddha.

T: We hope we can also obtain the blessing of the Buddha.

G: Surely. The buddhist dogma that 「xin zhong you fo, fo zai wo xin」(心中有佛,佛在我心。) applies to everyone. Whenever you pray to Buddha, the buddha is in your heart.

Dialogue 2 *Leshan Giant Buddha*

Scene: A guide is introducing Leshan Giant Buddha to some tourists from America.
(G= Guide   T = Tourists)

G: Welcom to the Leshan Giant Buddha Scenic Area. Now, we are looking at the well-known Leshan Giant Buddha, also called the Lingyun Giant Buddha. It is a Maitreya sitting Buddha statue that has been carved from living rock. It is the greatest stone statue of Maitreya Buddha in the world.

T: Wow! How gorgeous and magical it is! The whole mountain is a Buddha. How high is it?

G: Looking solemn and stately, the Buddha is 71 meters high with 28 meters wide shoulders, a 10 meters wide and 14.7 meters long head, 7 meters long drooping ears, 3.3 meters wide eye, 5.6 meters long nose and 3.3 meters long mouth. Each chignon on the head is as big as a round table. Its middle finger is 8.3 meters long, and the nail of his big toe is 1.5 meters long. Eeach of its bare feet is 11 meters long and 8.5 meters wide, large enough for more than 100 people to sit on. Even his smallest toenail is large enough to easily accommodate a seated person.

T: When was it built?

G: The statue was to be built in the first year of the Emperor Tang Xuanzong (713 A.D.), led by a Buddhist monk called Haitong, who hoped that the Buddha would subdue the swift currents and protect the boatmen. It was finally completed by his disciples in the 19th year of Emperor Tang Dezong (803 A.D.), lasting 90 years. The Buddha has been sitting here for 1,200 years.

T: Does the Buddha have any special characteristics?

G: The charm of the Buddha lies not only in its size but also in its architectural artistry. There are 1,021 buns in the Buddha's coiled hair, each of which is as big as a huge round table. These have been skillfully embedded in the head. The skill is so wonderful that the 1,021 buns seem integral to the whole.

T: The Buddha has been here for over 1,000 years. Is it not eroded?

G: The Buddha has a sophisticated drainage system, which is made up of some hidden gutters and trenches scattered on the head and arms, behind the ears and in the clothes. All these hidden ditches and caves are linked with the left and the right to prevent the Buddha from being eroded by rainwater and spring. On the fourth, the ninth, and the eighteenth layers of the Buddha's hair bobs, there are three horizontal ditches. The unique system of drainage and ventilation has played a vital role in limiting the erosion of the giant statue for over a thousand years.

T: What a remarkable wisdom and vast creativity of the ancient people! Can we have a close visit?

G: To the right of the statue, a plank road with nine turns (also called nine-turn plank road) was built, paving with 173 steps that range from a maximum width of 1.45 meters to a minimum width of 0.6 meter. Walking from top to bottom (and back up again) along a staircase carved in the wall, we can overlook the Buddha. A popular activity near the head is for people to have their photo taken 「touching」 the nose or sticking their finger in the ear of the Buddha, supposedly for good luck. Now, you can have some free time to enjoy the Buddha. Two hours from now, we will meet at the gate of Lingyun Temple on the top of the Buddha. Then we will visit another famous cultural relic — The Mahao Cliff Tombs. Please pay attention to your safety.

Words and Phrases

China National Key Cultural Relic Unit　全國重點文化遺跡單位

China National 5A-class Scenic Area　國家5A級風景區

The List of World Culture Heritages　世界文化遺產名錄

turbulent ['tɜːbjələnt]　　*adj.* 騷亂的，混亂的；激流的，湍流的

plague [pleig]　　*n.* 瘟疫；*vt.* 使受災禍

vessel ['vesl]　　*n.* 容器；船

disciple ［diˈsaipl］　　n. 信徒，追隨者
buns ［bʌnz］　　n. 髮髻
cluster ［ˈklʌstə(r)］　　n. 叢；簇
accommodate ［əˈkɒmədeit］　　vt. 容納；向……提供住處
ratify ［ˈrætifai］　　vt. 批准；認可
relic ［ˈrelik］　　n. 遺物，遺跡
heritage ［ˈheritidʒ］　　n. 遺產；繼承物
panoramic ［ˌpænəˈræmik］　　adj. 全景的
carve ［kɑːv］　　vt. 切，切開
Mt. Wuyou　　烏尤山
Mt. Lingyu　　凌雲山
Mt. Guicheng　　龜城山
constitute ［ˈkɒnstitjuːt］　　vt. 構成
invisible ［inˈvizəbl］　　adj. 看不見的
slumber ［ˈslʌmbə(r)］　　vt. 微睡，睡眠
ferry ［ˈferi］　　n. 渡船
warrior ［ˈwɒriə(r)］　　n. 武士
battle robe　　n. 戰袍
halberd ［ˈhælbɜːd］　　n. 戟
the nine-turn plank road　　n. 九曲棧道
appreciate ［əˈpriːʃieit］　　vt. 欣賞
dedicate ［ˈdedikeit］　　vt. 奉獻
sculpture ［ˈskʌlptʃə(r)］　　n. 雕刻
confluence ［ˈkɒnfluəns］　　n.（河流的）匯合處
capsize ［kæpˈsaiz］　　vt. / vi. 翻車；傾覆
torrent ［ˈtɒrənt］　　n. 奔流
serene ［səˈriːn］　　adj. 沉靜的
deposit ［diˈpɒzit］　　vt. 放置
alter ［ˈɔːltə(r)］　　v. 改變
restoration ［ˌrestəˈreiʃn］　　n. 恢復
erosion ［ɪˈrəʊʒn］　　n. 腐蝕
degradation ［ˌdegrəˈdeiʃn］　　n. 退化
cowl ［kaʊl］　　n. 鬥篷；罩

lotus ['ləʊtəs] n. 蓮花
awe-inspiring adj. 令人敬畏的
pious ['paiəs] adj. 虔誠的
blessing ['blesiŋ] n. 祝福
Maitreya Buddha 彌勒佛
gorgeous ['gɔ:dʒəs] adj. 華麗的
coiled hair n. 盤髮
erode [i'rəʊd] vt. 侵蝕, 腐蝕
sophisticated [sə'fistikeitid] adj. 複雜的
drainage system 排水系統
gutter ['gʌtə(r)] n. 排水溝
trench 溝渠, 塹壕
horizontal ditch 橫溝
ventilation [ˌventi'leiʃn] n. 通風, 流通空氣
maximum ['mæksiməm] adj. 最大量
minimum ['miniməm] n. 最小量
The Mahao Cliff Tombs 麻浩崖墓

Section 3　Exercises

I. Answer the following questions.

1. What's the legend of Leshan Giant Buddha?
2. Why was Leshan Giant Buddha built as a Maitreya Buddha?
3. What's the meaning of the local saying「The Mountain unveils a Buddha, while the Buddha fades into the mountain.」?
4. What's the function of Leshan Giant Buddha's drainage system?

II. Translate the following sentences into English.

1. 樂山大佛是世界上最大的一尊石刻彌勒坐像。
3. 沿著大佛右邊的九曲棧道，人們可以欣賞樂山大佛頭部的精美雕刻藝術。
3. 早在隋朝和唐朝，大佛坐落的凌雲山就是著名的風景區和佛教聖地。
3. 樂山大佛的一對大耳朵，每只長達 7 米，是用木頭雕成並用泥裝飾安裝在面部的。
6. 樂山大佛和這一地區中許多的自然文化遺址一樣由於風雨剝蝕、空氣污染

和蜂湧而至的遊客而遭到了破壞。

III. Make dialogues according to the given situation.

Situation A: Suppose you are a guide. Tomorrow you will guide tourists from England to visit Leshan Giant Buddha. Please write a tour speech.

Situation B: As a tour guide, you will make a detailed description of Lingyun Temple on the top of Leshan Giant Buddha to the tourists.

Section 4　Extensive Reading

The Yungang Grottoes

The Yungang Grottoes (雲岡石窟), Longmen Grottoes (龍門石窟), and Mogao Grottoes (莫高窟) are the three major cave clusters in China. The Yungang Grottoes lie on the north cliff of Wuzhou Mountain (武周山), Datong (大同), Shanxi Province. They are an outstanding example of the Chinese stone carvings from the 5th and 6th centuries. As China's first major stone carved grottoes, it has a history of over 1,500 years. Altogether the site extends 1 kilometer (0.62 miles) from east to west and is composed of 252 grottoes with more than 51,000 Buddha stone statues.

The grottoes are divided into east, middle and west parts. Pagodas dominate the eastern parts; the western caves are small and mid-sized with niches; the caves in the middle are made up of front and back chambers with Buddha statues in the center. All the walls and ceilings are covered by embossing. Started in 450, the grottoes is a relic of the Northern Wei Dynasty (386-534). Originally, the carving of the grottoes was a link between the imperial sponsors and the Buddhist community. During the Northern Wei Dynasty (北魏), they made Pingcheng (平城), now called Datong, the capital city, and adapted Buddhism as the state religion. Through the ancient North Silk Road (北絲綢之路), Buddhism arrived in Pingcheng (Datong). Absorbing Indian Gandhara Buddhist art, the sculptures here developed traditional Chinese art melded with social features of the time. The five caves of Tanyao (曇曜五窟) with their strict unity of layout and design, constitute a classical masterpiece of the first peak of Chinese Buddhist art.

As an excellent example of rock-cut architecture, in 2001, the Yungang Grottoes became a UNESCO World Heritage Site. According to UNESCO, they are a masterpiece of early Chinese Buddhist cave art. The site is classified as a 5 A scenic area by the China National Tourism Administration.

Unit 4   Mt. Emei

Section 1   Introduction

　　Mt. Emei, located in Emeishan County, about 160 kilometers far from Chengdu, the capital city of Sichuan province, is one of the four sacred Buddhist mountains in China. Mt. Emei covers an area of 154 square kilometers, and can be divided into four scenic areas: Baoguo Temple, Wannian temple, Qinyin Pavilion and Jiulao Cave, Golden Summit. Mt. Emei is characterized by its grandeur, delicateness, uniqueness, steepness and sereneness, of which delicateness is the most famous, known as 「beauty under Heaven」 and a 「paradise of animals」 and a 「kingdom of plants」 because of the abundance of fauna and flora resources (with approximately 200 distinct plant species and 2,300 animal species). Its main peak, the Golden Summit, is 3,077 meters above the sea level. The Clouds Sea, the wonderful Sunrise, the Buddhist Halo and the Magic Lanterns constitude the 「four unique wonders」 of Emei.

　　As a world natural and cultural heritage, Mt. Emei is also notable for its Buddhist culture. Puxian (普贤, Samantabhadra, Bodhisattva of Universal Benevolence) was said to hold Buddhist rites on Emei (Bright Mountain). Around the Ten-Thousand-Buddha Peak, there are more than a hundred stone-shrine and forty caves from Eastern Han Dynasty to Ming Dynasty, there are more than hundred temples built on Mt. Emei. The mountain has thus remained the holy place for Buddhist believers since ancient times.

Mt. Emei was among the first batch of China National Key Tourist Resorts in 1982. In 1991, it was rated as one of China's 40 Top Tourist Resorts, and was inscribed on 「the List of the World Natural and Cultural Heritages」 by UNESCO on December 6, 1996. It was rated as a China National 5A-class Scenic Area in 2007.

Discussion

1. Why is Mt. Emei called a 「kingdom of plants」?
2. What's the historical connection between Buddhism and Taoism on Mt. Emei?

● Section 2 Dialogues

Dialogue 1 Wannian Temple

Scene: A guide is leading a group of tourists to visit Wannian Temple.

(G= Guide   T= Tourist)

T: I was very curious about the name of Mt. Emei. Why is the Mountain called Emei?

G: Mt. Emei consists of Mt. Da E, Mt. Er E, Mt. San E and Mt. Si E. Viewed from afar, its catchy Mt. Da E and Mt. Er E stand side by side in quite a symmetry, long and thin like the delicate eyebrows of a beautiful maid. Hence the mountain is called Emei, which literally means 「the charming eyebrow of a beautiful maid」 in Chinese.

T: I see. The name is vivid and imaginative.

G: Now, we are arriving at Wannian Temple. Do you know why it is called Wannian Temple?

T: No. Could you please explain it to us?

G: Wannian Temple, 1,020 meters above sea level, was built in the Jin Dynasty. It was originally called Puxian Temple (Temple of Samantabhadra, 普贤寺). Later in the Ming Dynasty, Emperor Shenzong renamed it Wannian Temple (Temple of 10,000 Years) to celebrate his mother's seventieth birthday.

T: I find there are many temples on Mt. Emei. Is this temple different from other temples?

G: It really has its specialty. Stepping through the gate of the temple, walking up the steps, you come to a flatland, on which stands the well-known Beamless Brick Hall. As the name suggests, the whole hall is made of bricks without a beam, imitating the architectural style of Rena Temple in India. The hall is 18.22 meters high with a round roof and a square floor of 16.02 meters on each side.

T: It's amazing and unbelievable. What's the name of the gilded statue sitting on a six-tooth white elephant?

G: It is called Puxian Bodhisattva. Vividly and skillfully cast, the statue is 7.35 meters high, and weighs 62,000 kilograms. As the largest temple on Mt. Emei, Wannian Temple reflects the profound Buddhist culture. Mt. Emei is traditionally regarded as the bodhidharma, or the place where Samantabhadra Bodhisattva (普贤, Puxian, Bodhisattva of Universal Benevolence) attained enlightenment.

T: How about the scenery here?

G: The scenery here is pleasant and attractive, especially in autumn when the maple leaves turn red all over the mountain. The red leaves are reflected in Baishui Pool, in which colorful ripples are trembling as the mountain wind blows. This beautiful view is called Autumn Wind on Baishui Pool (白水秋风), another one of the ten marvels of Mt Emei.

T: It's a pity it's summer. I can't enjoy the beautiful scenery in autumn. Next autumn, I'll definitely come here to enjoy it.

Dialogue 2 The Golden Summit

Scene: A guide is leading a group of tourists to enter the Golden Summit Scenic Area. He is introducing some information about Xixiang Pool Temple and the Golden Summit to the tourists.

(G= Guide   T = Tourist)

G: Now, we have entered the Golden Summit Scenic Area. We can appreciate a great number of scenic spots and historical sites, such as Huazang Temple (華藏寺), Xixiang Pool Temple (洗象池), Leidong Terrace (雷洞坪), Jieyin Hall (接引殿), Taiziping (the Prince Temple, 太子坪) and Woyun Nunnery (卧雲庵). Huazang Temple is the center of this scenic area.

T: What does Xixiang Pool Temple mean?

G: It is said that this is the place where Puxian used to bathe his white elephant before traveling up to the Golden Summit. When night falls, a bright moon hangs in the clear sky, casting silvery moonlight into the pool, you can enjoy the well-known scene of the Moonlit Night at Xixiang Pool.

(Two hours later, the tourists arrive at the Golden Summit.)

T: Could you please tell us why the place is called the Golden Summit? Is the hall made of gold?

G: The Golden Summit gets its name from the Gold Hall (金殿), made of gilded bronze, whose golden metallic roof dazzles and glitters in the sunshine like「countless golden rays over the whole summit」. Besides, you can appreciate the highest gold Samantabhadra statue in the world, which is 48 meters high and weighs 660 tons. The statue is decorated with granite relief on the base, which makes it delicate.

T: Thank you for your introduction. We are told we can enjoy the four marvelous spectacles of the Golden Summit. Is it true?

G: Yes. It may be fortunate enough for a tourist to watch the four marvelous spectacles-the clouds Sea, the Sunrise, the Buddhist Halo and the Magic Lanterns. People will be happy to regard Mt. Emei as their fortunate place. The Cliff of Self-Sacrifice is the best place to appreciate the four brilliant wonders. But you should look out to keep safe.

T: Thank you. By the way, what does the Buddhist halo stand for?

G: The sighting of the Buddha halo has a special significance for Buddhists, indicating a special blessing, spiritual insight, or the good karma of the observer. It is seen as a sign of good fortune, and has gained the name「The Auspicious Light of Golden Summit」. Furthermore it is believed that Samantabhadra Bodhisattva uses the Foguang「to manifest himself to those that are predestined to see him」in his「reward body」or baoshen.

T: It's magnificent. We will enjoy the wonder.

Word and Phrases

grandeur, delicateness, uniqueness, steepness and sereneness　雄、秀、奇、險、幽
paradise of animals　動物樂園
kingdom of plants　植物王國
Mt. Da E　大峨山
Mt. Er E　二峨山
Mt. San E　三峨山
Mt. Si E　四峨山
symmetry ['simətri]　*n.* 對稱
delicate eyebrows　蛾眉
Beamless Brick Hall　無梁磚殿
imitate ['imiteit]　*vt.* 模仿
Rena Temple　熱那寺
cast [kɑːst]　*vt.* 澆鑄
reflect [ri'flekt]　*vt.* 反射
maple ['meipl]　*n.* 楓樹
tremble ['trembl]　*vi.* 戰栗，發抖，震動
marvel ['mɑːvl]　*n.* 奇跡
Autumn Wind on Baishui Pool　白水秋風
the Golden Summit　金頂
Xixiang Pool Temple　洗象池
the Moonlit Night at Xixiang Pool　象池月夜
bronze [brɒnz]　*n.* 青銅
dazzle ['dæzl]　*vt.* 使目眩；耀眼
glitter ['glitə]　*vi.* 閃爍
marvelous ['mɑːviləs]　*adj.* 不凡的
spectacle ['spektəkl]　*n.* 奇觀
the Auspicious Light of Golden Summit　金頂祥光

Section 3　Exercises

I. Answer the following questions.

1. Where does the name Mt. Emei come from?

2. Why does Mt. Emei possess the five characteristics of「grandeur, delicateness, uniqueness, steepness and sereneness」?

3. What are the ten marvels of Mt. Emei?

4. Why does Puxian (Samantabhadra) Bodhisattva ride a white elephant with six tusks?

II. Translate the following sentences into English.

1. 峨眉山是世界著名的旅遊勝地。它不僅是世界文化與自然雙重遺產還因其佛教文化而揚名。

2. 峨眉山豐富的佛教文化遺產有記載的歷史是2,000多年，它與五臺山、普陀山、九華山共稱為中國佛教四大名山。

3. 峨眉佛光被看作是幸運的象徵，它因而有「金頂祥光」之稱。

4. 金頂海拔3,077米，是峨眉山第三大高峰。

5. 野生猴子是峨眉山上最令人興奮的動物了。它們一點都不怕人。

III. Make dialogues according to the given situations.

Situation A: Suppose you are a tour guide. You will introduce Baoguo Temple Scenic Area to a group of tourists from England.

Situation B: Suppose you are a tour guide. Please use the on-the-way introduction to introduce the Double-Bridge Spray at Qingyin Pavilion (雙橋清音).

Section 4　Extensive Reading

Sansu Memorial Temple（三蘇祠）

Sansu Memorial Temple is located at the west of Meishan City（眉山市）in Sichuan Province. It is the former residence of Su Xun（蘇洵）, Su Shi（蘇軾）and Su Zhe（蘇轍）. The memorial temple covers an area of 56800 square meters, encircled with a red wall and hovered by clean water.

Originally, it was a courtyard of about 5 Mu. The yard was rebuilt as an ancestral temple in the Yuan Dynasty (元朝) and expanded in the Hongwu years (洪武年間) of Ming Dynasty (明朝). In the late Ming Dynasty, the shrine hall was destroyed by fire. Afterwards, in the following dynasties the temple has been expanded and rebuilt.

In the temple there are the statues of members of the Su's family, the pavilions, terraces and towers of primitive simplicity and elegance. The main architectures in the temple are the Central Palace (正殿), Qixian Hall (啓賢堂), Laifeng Pavilion (來鳳軒), Pifeng Terrace (披鳳榭) and the South Hall (南堂).

In the Central Palace, there are the statues of Su Shi, Su Xun and Su Zhe. In the east part of the temple, there is a garden made up of a pond and Greenland Pavilion (綠洲亭), Ruilian Pavalion (瑞蓮亭), Baoyue Pavilion (抱月亭) and Yunyu Pavilion (雲雨樓). The ancient well, from which the Su family obtained their drinking water, has a history of more than 1,000 years. The water in the well is sweet and will never dry. It is said that one will be cleverer if he drinks the water of the well.

Sansu Memorial Temple is famous for Su Shi, Su Zhe and Su Xun, who are skilled in literature in the Song Dynasty (宋朝). What's more, the three Su conducted themselves honorably, showed sympathy to the poor people and did many good things for common people.

In Sansu Memorial Temple, there are more than 5188 cultural relics about the Su family. Among them are 3,256 ancient books containing the Su's articles and essays, and 1,044 paintings, all of which have great research value.

Unit 5　Jiuzhaigou Valley

● Section 1　Introduction

　　Jiuzhaigou Valley, located in Jiuzhaigou County of A'ba Tibetan and Qiang Autonomous Prefecture in Sichuan Province, northwest Sichuan, 435 kilometers from Chengdu, is the world-famous scenic area in China under the protection of the state. At the elevation of 2,000-4,760 meters and with an average annual temperature of 7.8℃ (with the average temperature of -3.7℃ in January and 16.8℃ in July), Jiuzhaigou Valley is well-known for its diversity in natural species and for its scenery with the pleasant climate and beautiful colors all year round. Jiuzhaigou Valley is 47 kilometers long from the south to the north, 29 kilometers wide from east to west, covering an area of 720 square kilometers. It is famous for the nine Tibetan villages that reside within its borders.

　　It is known as a 「Fairy Tale World」 and 「Dream Land」, for it is predominantly covered with primitive and dense forests that are scattered around 108 lakes sitting within the large valley. Jiuzhaigou consists of three main gullies — Shuzheng Gully (樹正溝), Rize Gully (日則溝) and Zechawa Gully (則查窪溝). The formation of the three main gullies is 「Y」-shaped, total length of more than 60 kilometers. There distributed 108 lakes, 17 splashing waterfalls, 47 springs, 5 shoals, 11 turbulent streams and 9 Tibetan villages.

　　Colorful and lucid Haizi (lakes plateau), splashing waterfalls, multicolored trees, flowers, leaves and snow-covered peaks present you a totally different but never-the-less amazing landscape at any time of the year. The main scenery includes: Potted Landscape Lake (盆景灘), Reed Lake (蘆葦海), Shuzheng Lakes, Shuzheng Waterfall, Changhai (Long) Lake, Five-color Pond, Mirror Lake, Five Flower Lake, Pearl Shoals, Panda Lake, Arrow Bamboo Lake, Rhinoceros Lake (犀牛海) and 320-meter-wide Nuorilang Falls. All these scenic sites create the unique landscape of Jiuzhaigou to China and the world.

In 1978, Jiuzhaigou Valley was ratified as the China National Nature Reserve for Giant Panda and for the forest ecosystem. In 1982, it was designated as one of the first group of China National Key Tourist Resorts by the State Council. In 1990, it was ratified as one of China Top40 Tourist Resorts. On October 14, 1992, it was inscribed on「the List of World Natural Heritages」by UNESCO. On October 29, 1997, it was admitted into「the List of the Man and Biosphere Nature Reserves」by the United Nations. In 2007, it was rated as a China National 5A-class Scenic Area.

Five-Flower Lake　　　　**Pearl Shoal Waterfall**　　　　**Nuorilang Falls**

Landscape of Jiuzhaigou 　　　　**Mirror Lake**

Discussion

1. Why is this scenic area named Jiuzhaigou?
2. How many main scenic spots are there in Jiuzhaigou? What are they?

Section 2　Dialogues

Dialogue 1　Shuzheng Lakes

Scene: A group of tourists from Australia arrives at the entrance of Jiuzhaigou Valley. The guide tells the itinerary and introduces Shuzheng Lakes to them.

(G = Guide　T = Tourists)

G: Good morning, ladies and gentlemen, I feel it a great honor to be your tour guide today. First, on behalf of my company, I warmly welcome all my distinguished australian guests to Jiuzhaigou.

T: Could you please tell us something about it?

G: Located in Jiuzhaigou County of A'ba Tibetan and Qiang Autonomous Prefecture in Sichuan Province, Jiuzhaigou is known as「Fairy Tale World」for its diversity in natural species and scenery. It is very famous for its high snow-coved peaks, the magnificent waterfalls, the dense colorful forests, the clear blue water and colorful lakes. you will find yourselves in the world's most exciting and unspoiled nature. As you know, Jiuzhaigou has been crowned with several titles: The World Natural Heritage, The World Biosphere Reserve, the Green Globe 21 and The State 5A-class Scenic Area.

T: Wonderful! We can't wait to see the beautiful scenery.

G: Today, our schedule for the trip to Jiuzhaigou is as follows: first, we will have 4 hours from 7:50 to 11:50 to experience the beautiful scenery-The Shuzheng Lakes. Then we'll assemble at the hall of Nuorilang Hotel at 12:00 to enjoy our lunch. After lunch, we will take a bus to Zezhawa Gully to continue to appreciate Five-color Pond, Seasonal Lakes and Changhai Lake. Please follow me and don't lag behind. If you have some problems, please call me. My phone number is 18258784236. (Half an hour later)

G: Ladies and gentlemen, now we enter the Shuzheng scenic site and arrive at the first lakes in Jiuzhaigou, called Shuzheng Lakes.

T: Why are they named Shuzheng Lakes?

G: The Shuzheng Lakes lies at the entrance to the magnificent Jiuzhaigou, leading into the rest of the gullies. Consisting of over 40 alpine lakes, Shuzheng Lakes extend as far as about 5 kilometers. With an elevation difference of over 100 meters, they form an ocean of lakes in a terrace-like distribution, separated from each other by calcium dykes. The main attractions are Mirror Lake, Reed Lake, Wolong Lake, Tiger Lake, Shuzheng Waterfall, Rhino Lake and Nuorilang Falls.

T: How do the lakes form?

G: Originating in glacial activity, earthquakes and calcification, they were dammed by rockfalls and other natural phenomena, then solidified by processes of carbonate deposition. The local Tibetan people call the dozens of blue, green and turquoise-colored lakes 「Haizi」 in Chinese, meaning 「son of the sea」. Some of the clear lakes are hidden in the valleys and some inlay the virgin forests. With a variety of shapes and sizes, these lakes look like gleaming mirrors projecting colorful light rings in the sunshine. The terraced lakes and waterfalls at different levels, combined with the weeping willows, pines, cypresses and metasequoia growing on the clay-colored calcium dykes and the white spray created by droping water straight down to the bottom of the valley, picture a splendid scenery, making tourists wonder whether they have stepped into a fairyland.

T: The scenery is indeed shocking and unforgetable. Looking at the fantastic blue water, we are almost dumb-struck.

G: The clean, green and colorful water can rated as the soul of Jiuzhaigou. It is so clean that you can see to the bottom even about 30 meters in depth. We can say Jiuzhaigou is a world of water, which brings Jiuzhaigou its most enchanting views. After the introduction, you can enjoy the scenery by yourselves and take photos.

T: Thank you very much. You have given us a detailed understanding of the Shuzheng Lakes.

G: You are always welcome. Hope you have a good time! I believe, whether you are a frequent visit or someone who simply enjoys beautiful places, the visit to Jiuzhaigou will be a perfect way to remember the unique sites and beauty of Jiuzhaigou in days to come.

Dialogue 2   Nuorilang Falls

Scene: A group of tourists arrives at Nuorilang Falls. The guide begins to introduce the waterfall to them.

(G = Guide　　T= Tourist)

G: Now we are arriving at the famous Nuorilang Falls — the symbol of Jiuzhaigou. You can appreciate the spectacular views.

T: Oh, that's really splendid. What's the meaning of 「Nuorilang」?

G: 「Nuorilang」 means 「magnificence」 in the Tibetan language. As its name suggests, its grandeur is breathtaking and deeply touches many tourists.

T: Could you please introduce Nuorilang Falls with more information?

G: Certainly. Nuorilang Falls, located at the juncture of three gullies-Shuzheng Gully, Rize Gully and Zechawa Gully, is one of China's largest calcium falls, with a vertical drop of 30 meters and a width of over 270 meters. Right above the waterfall are wide stretches of lakes, joined by travertine dykes which are overgrown with lush woods. Rushing over the cliff overgrown with willows, the massive water currents from Rize Gully drop some 30 meters down and form a chain of spectacular waterfalls of diverse shapes and sizes in a stair— like pattern.

T: How about the views of Nuorilang Falls in different seasons?

G: The views of Nuorilang Falls change with the seasons. The running waterfalls are the most majestic of all the seasons. During the rainy season, the terraced waterfall produces a tremendous roar reverberating unceasingly in the gully. When the sun is shining, the tourists can see the gorgeous rainbow above the waterfall. In the dry season of autumn, however, the waterfall presents another wonder. The tiny streams of the falls look like sheets of colorful silk fabric hanging over the cliff, contrasted by the surrounding multi-colored bushes which add radiant beauty to each other. In winter, it becomes a world of ice and snow. The abating currents are frozen, and become dazzling glacial cascades. Bunches of crystal icicles hang over the steep cliff. This is a wonderful and unique view that can rarely be seen anywhere else.

T: Thank you very much. I think I will come here again with my friends.

Words and Phrases

Jiuzhaigou Valley　*n.* 九寨沟

A'ba Tibetan and Qiang Autonomous Prefecture　*n.* 阿壩藏族羌族自治州

diversity ［daiˈvɜːsəti］　*n.* 多样性

Fairy Tale World　童话世界

primitive ［ˈprimətiv］　*adj.* 原始的

predominantly [pri'dɒminəntli]　　adv. 顯著地

splash [splæʃ]　　vt. 使（液體）濺起

shoal [ʃəʊl]　　n. 淺灘，沙洲

peak [piːk]　　n. 山峰；最高點

landscape ['lændskeip]　　n. 風景

China National Nature Reserve　　國家自然保護區

China National Key Tourist Resorts　　全國重點風景名勝區

China Top 40 Tourist Resorts　　中國旅遊勝地四十佳

List of the Man and Biosphere Nature Reserves　　人與生物保護圈名錄

distinguished [di'stiŋgwiʃt]　　adj. 卓越的；著名的

assemble [ə'sembl]　　vt. / vi. 集合，收集

gleaming ['gliːmiŋ]　　adj. 閃閃發光的

alpine ['ælpain]　　adj. 高山的

elevation [ˌeli'veiʃn]　　n. 海拔，仰角

terrace-like　　adj. 層疊式的

distribution [ˌdistri'bjuːʃn]　　n. 分配，分發

calcium ['kælsiəm]　　n. 鈣

dyke (=dike) [daik]　　n. 溝，渠，堤壩

inlay ['inlei]　　vt. 鑲嵌

weep [wiːp]　　vi. 滴落

weeping willows　　n. 垂柳

cypress ['saiprəs]　　n. 柏樹

metasequoia [ˌmetəsi'kwɔiə]　　n. 水杉

charming ['tʃɑːmiŋ]　　adj. 迷人的

interlace [ˌintə'leis]　　vt. 使交錯，使交織

fantastic [fæn'tæstik]　　adj. 異想天開的；奇異的

enchanting [in'tʃɑːntiŋ]　　adj. 迷人的

spectacular [spek'tækjələ(r)]　　adj. 壯觀的

juncture ['dʒʌŋktʃə(r)]　　n. 接合點，交匯處

grandeur ['grændʒə(r)]　　n. 莊嚴，偉大

breathtaking ['breθteikiŋ]　　adj. 驚人的，驚險的

travertine ['trævətiːn]　　n. 石灰華，鈣華

lush [lʌʃ]　　adj. 蔥翠的

willow ['wiləʊ]　　*n.* 柳樹
convergence [kən'vɜːdʒəns]　　*n.* 集中，收斂
reverberate [ri'vɜːbəreit]　　*vt.* 反響
fabric ['fæbrik]　　*n.* 織品，織物
abate [ə'beit]　　*vi.* 減少，減輕
glacial cascade　　*n.* 冰瀑
crystal icicles　　*n.* 冰凌

Section 3　Exercises

I. Answer the following questions.

1. Why is Jiuzhaigou known as a「fairyland in China」?
2. Why is the water in Jiuzhaigou commonly considered the soul of Jiuzhaigou?
3. Could you please talk about the legend of Jiuzhaigou?
4. What is the meaning of「Nuorilang」? Give an account of the Nuorilang Falls.

II. Translate the following sentences into English.

1. 景隨季換，多姿多彩，九寨溝終年向人們展示著不同的色彩和風韻。
2. 「黃山歸來不看山，九寨歸來不看水」，被譽為「地球之眼」的九寨溝之水是九寨溝美景的靈魂。
3. 因其湖泊眾多、植被豐富，九寨溝擁有自身完整的生態系統，為野生動物提供了最佳的棲息地。
4. 在冬天，冰雪已成為近年來九寨溝的一個旅遊亮點之一。
5. 每年十月黃金週期間，國內外的遊客紛紛來到九寨溝欣賞自然美景，使得這段時間成為旅遊旺季。

III. Make dialogues according to the given situations.

Situation A：Suppose you are a tour guide. You will introduce a group of tourists the Rize Gully Scenic Area（日則溝景區）where there are many exciting and astonishing scenic spots, including the Mirror Lake, the Pearl Shoal, the Five-Flower Lake, the Panda Lake, the Arrow Bamboo Lake and the Sword Cliff. You can choose one to introduce.

Situation B：Suppose you are a tour guide. You will introduce Wolong National Nature Reserve to the tourists. Please write a tour speech.

Section 4 Extensive Reading

Wolong National Nature Reserve

Wolong National Nature Reserve (卧龍自然保護區) is a protected area located in Wenchuan County (汶川縣), Sichuan Province. It extends 52 kilometers long from east to west and 62 kilometers wide from south to north, covering an area of about 700,000 hectares. Established in 1963, the Reserve joined the International Man and Biosphere Reserve Network of UNESCO in 1980. Its main targets for protection are forest ecosystem and precious animals like giant pandas.

Located in the alpine valley where the Tibetan Plateau descends into Sichuan Basin, Wolong National Nature Reserve has become China's largest and certainly the most important sanctuary for giant pandas and other rare and precious animals and plants during the climatic fluctuations of the ice age. The primitive forest and the original ecosystem here are well preserved, and therefore the Reserve is appraised as a rare genebank in the world as well as a natural park. According to relevant statistics, there are more than 4,000 plant species and over 50 species of animals and 300 species of birds.

Wolong National Nature Reserve is the most famous one among the 13 giant panda reserve centers established by the Chinese government with the help of the World Wildlife Fund (WWF). It is also identified as the homeland of the giant panda. The Wolong Panda Museum (卧龍大熊貓博物館) is the only museum in China that exhibits only a single species.

Part Five
Chinese Society and Culture

Unit 1　An Overview of China

Section 1　Introduction

China (The People's Republic of China) is regarded as one of the four great ancient civilizations in the world. It has a huge plenty of natural and cultural resources, which lies in the east of the Asian continent, on the western shore of the Pacific Ocean. China is a large country with a vast territory, including a land area of about 9.6 million square kilometers and a maritime territory is about 4.7 million square kilometers. It is the third largest country in the world, next only to Russia and Canada. China also has the largest population in the world, with approximately 1.3 billion people living in the mainland.

China has 14 neighboring countries in the land, it borders North Korea to the northeast; Mongolia to the north; Russia to the northeast and northwest; Tajikistan, Kyrgyzstan and Kazakhstan to the northwest; Pakistan and Afghanistan to the west; India, Bhutan and Nepal to the southwest; Laos, Burma and Vietnam to the south.

China's topography is likened to a four-step staircase if taking a bird's-eye view of it: the top one is Qinghai-Tibet Plateau in the Southwest China, with an average elevation of more than 4,000 meters and known as 「the roof of the world」. The second staircase consists of the Inner Mongolia Plateau, the Loess Plateau, the Yunnan-Guizhou Plateau, the Tarim basin, the Junggar Basin and the Sichuan Basin, with an average elevation between 1,000 and 2,000 meters. The third step features mostly plains, on an altitude of 500-1,000 meters, from north to south are the Northeast Plain, the North China Plain and the Middle-lower Yangtze Plain; the fourth step is the continental shelf, an extension of the land into the ocean, with a water depth of less than 200 meters.

China is rich in water-power resources, which has more than 1,500 rivers and 24,800 natural lakes. The Yangtze River and the Yellow River, flowing through 11 and 9 provinces, autonomous regions and municipalities respectively, are the main interior river system of China.

China is a socialist country. The nation is divided in a three-tier systems: provinces, counties and townships. At present there are 23 provinces, 5 autonomous regions, 4 municipalities and 2 Special Administrative Regions (SAR) in China. The Chinese celebrate the National Day on October 1st in honor of the founding of the People's Republic of China on October 1st, 1949. The five-starred red flag is the national flag of the PRC. Written by Nie Er in 1935, the March of Volunteers was officially adopted as the national anthem of the PRC on December 4th, 1982. Beijng was renamed by Beiping to be the capital of the PRC since September 27th, 1949. The Constitution of the PRC is the fundamental law of the state; the National People's Congress (NPC) is the highest organ of state power. The Communist Party is the sole party in power in China. Apart from it, there are eight democratic parties in China. The executive body of the highest organ of state power and the highest organ of state administration of the PRC respectively are the State Council and the Central People's Government.

The Chinese people are called as「the descendants of Yan and Huang」, which is distributed to 56 ethnic groups. Equality, Unity, Mutual assistance and Common prosperity are the basic principles of Chinese government in handling the relations between ethnic groups.

It has been 30 years since China started reform and began a policy of opening-up to the outside world. This has resulted in great changes taking place in various fields. In these years, China has made great progress in science and technology. As economy is developing fast, people's living conditions have greatly improved. In addition, the 29th Olympic Games were successfully hosted in Beijing and Chinese athletes won the most gold medals in 2008. It is the leadership of the Communist Party and the great efforts of the Chinese people that made all these successes possible. Nowadays, people are working hard towards an advanced and harmonious society.

Discussion

    1. What is the geographic position of China?

    2. How many countries border on China? What are they?

    3. What are the four-step staircases of China's topography?

    4. What is the political regime of China?

    5. What is the China's ethnic policy?

Section 2   Dialogues

Dialogue 1 How Many Wonders Does China Boast?

    Scene: The tour guide and the tourist are talking about China's wonders.

    (G = Tour Guide   T = Tourist)

    G: So, have you ever been to China before?

    T: No. This is the first time I have been to China.

    G: Have you travelled to other Asian countries?

    T: To be honest, I have never been to an Asian country before though I have visited many countries in Europe.

    G: How do you like China so far? What do you think of China?

    T: Well, China is a great country with its long history, beautiful natural landscape and profound culture. Everything is totally different from what I have heard before. You know, I think I should visit China earlier.

    G: Thank you, it seems that you are so satisfied with your journey to China.

    T: Yes, I am, for sure.

    G: Ok, Now would you like to know more information about China?

    T: Certainly. I'd like to.

    G: Do you know how many wonders does China boast?

    T: Um, I think it's out of count.

    G: Yes, you can say that in a way. There are incalculable wonders in every field. Let me make out the most gorgeous natural scenery in China to you.

    T: Ok, just do it.

    G: You know, Mount Everest is the highest moutain on earth. The Qinghai-Tibetan

Plateau is the highest plateau above sea level. The Brahmaputra Grand Canyon is the biggest canyon in the world. The Loess Plateau is the most tremendous loess landform of the world.

T: Wow, it sounds amazing! I hope I can visit all these wonders in the future.

G: Certainly, you will. Also there is a lot of unique cultural scenery in China, such as the terra cotta warriors and horses in Xi'an, which is given the honor of 「the eighth wonder of the world」; the Buddha Palace in Tibet and the Dunhuang Caves, to name just a few. It'll take you more than one year to visit all these places.

T: It's really fascinating! I can't wait to see these wonders.

G: I'm sure you will make your dream come true. Now let's continue our visit.

Dialogue 2   Chengdu — A Charming and Liveable City

Scene: The tourist is very interested in Chengdu city, now the tour guide is introducing it.

(G = Tour Guide   T = Tourist)

T: Well, so far as I know, people like to call Beijing a political city because it's the capital and there are lots of bureaucrats. Even taxi drivers talk politics. Shanghai, on the other hand, is viewed as a city of fashion. Ever since the 1930s, when Shanghai was under western rule, it has always been in the front line of fashion. Guangdong is the center of the economy where business has the priority as the saying goes, 「whether a cat is black or white, it is a good cat as long as it catches mice.」I heard that people say that Chengdu is a happy-go-lucky city. Could you please tell me something about Chengdu?

G: I'll be happy to. You know, Chengdu is the capital and the biggest city of Sichuan Province. The temperature is mild and the land is very productive, as they say: so fertile that even a stick will grow. The favorable environment has given rise to a very easy and relaxed life style. According to a survey, people's expectation of a monthly salary is 3,000 Yuan. They believe that amount of money is enough to lead a happy life in Chengdu.

T: Wow! That sounds very interesting! I also heard that Chengdu is especially known for its tea houses?

G: Yes, there are tea houses everywhere. It is the unique civil culture of Chengdu. Unlike some other big cities, where tea houses are specialized to serve different types of customers, tea houses in Chengdu offer a whole range of products. Everyone, yet a businessman, a migrant worker or a student, can find something they want. People can spend a day in the tea house, either to talk business or simply to relax.

T: Are there any other interesting games there?

G: Yes, have you ever heard of Mahjong?

T: Um, I've heard of it, but I don't know what it is actually.

G: Mahjong is a popular game among tea house goers in Chengdu. There is a joke on the Internet that says as soon as the plane enters the Chengdu airspace, passengers can hear the sound of mahjong shuffling. Chengdu is also known for its snacks. There are plenty of entertainment outlets. You don't always find a kind of restlessness in Chengdu as in other cities. But this doesn't mean Chengdu people have closed minds. On the contrary, they are very open-minded.

T: It's so funny, and it's good for a person to be happy and forget about fame and wealth. This reminds me of a Chinese saying, 「A lucky person doesn't have to chase luck.」

G: That's true!

Words and Phrases

shore ［ʃɔː(r)］　　n. 海濱；支柱

Pacific Ocean　n. 太平洋

maritime territory　n. 領海

border ［ˈbɔː(r)də(r)］　　n. 邊境；國界；邊界

topography ［təˈpɒɡrəfi］　　n. 地勢；地形學；地志

staircase ［ˈsteə(r)keis］　　n. 樓梯

plateau ［ˈplætoʊ］　　n. 高原

elevation ［eləˈveiʃ(ə)n］　　n. 高地；海拔

Tarim basin　塔里木盆地

Junggar basin　準格爾盆地

continental shelf　大陸架

interior ［inˈtiəriə(r)］　　adj. 內部的；國內的；本質的

respectively ［riˈspektivli］　　adv. 分別地；各自地

autonomous regions　自治區

municipality ［mjuːˌnisiˈpæləti］　　n. 自治市或區；直轄市

Special Administrative Region　特別行政區

National People's Congress   全國人民代表大會

Section 3　Exercises

I. Translate the following sentences into English.

1. 中國地形從西到東呈「四級階梯狀」分佈。

2. 中國的政黨組織結構模式是中國共產黨領導的多黨合作和政治協商制度。

3. 京杭大運河是中國著名的人工運河，南起浙江杭州，北至北京，全長 1,801 千米。

4. 通過十多年的扶貧開發，中國少數民族地區人民的生產和生活條件得到了明顯改善。

5. 中國改革開放 30 年來發生了巨大變化，人民的生活水平得到很大改善，政府的執政能力也在不斷增強。

II. Translate the following paragraphs into Chinese.

1. Provinces, counties, townships and villages are at different levels in the Chinese administration frame. At present China administers 34 province-level divisions, including twenty-three provinces, five autonomous regions, four municipalities, and two special administrative regions.

2. The Revolution of 1911 led by Dr. Sun Yat-sen was one of the greatest events in modern Chinese history, as it overthrew the 200-year-old Qing Dynasty, ending over 2,000 years of feudal monarchy, and established the Republic of China.

III. Make dialogues according to the given situations.

Situation A：You are a tour guide from CYTS, Beijing branch. Your name is Peter, you have met your tour group at the airport, now you are going to give them a brief introduction to China on the way to the hotel.

Situation B：You are a tour guide from CTS, Chengdu branch. Your name is Maggie, you are serving a tour group from Sweden, some group members know nothing about the policy of reform and opening-up of China, and you are going to explain it.

Section 4　Extensive Reading

The Han Nationality

China is a multinational country, with a population composed of a large number of ethnic and linguistic groups. So thoroughly did the Han dynasty (202 B. C. —220 A. D.) establish what was thereafter considered Chinese culture that「Han」became the Chinese word denoting someone who is Chinese. The Han is the largest ethnic group, and it outnumbers the minority groups or minority nationalities in every province or autonomous region except Tibet and Xinjiang. The Han, therefore, form the great homogeneous mass of the Chinese people, sharing the same culture, the same traditions, and the same written language. For this reason, the general basis for classifying the country's population is largely linguistic rather than ethnic.

Unit 2 Main Religions in China

Section 1 Introduction

China is a country with a great diversity of religions, with over 100 million followers of the various faiths. The main religions are Buddhism, Islam, Christianity and China's indigenous Taoism. The Hui, Uygur, Kazak, Kirgiz, Tatar, Ozbek, Tajik, Dongxiang, Salar and Bonan people adhere to Islam; the Tibetan, Mongolian, Lhoba, Moinba, Tu and Yugur people, to Tibetan Buddhism; and the Dai, Blang and Deang people to Theravada Buddhism. Quite a few Miao, Yao and Yi people are Christians. Religious Han Chinese tend to practice Buddhism, Christianity or Taoism.

Buddhism was originated and founded by Sakyamuni in India in the 6th BC. Buddhism was first introduced to China approximately in the 1st century A. D., then becoming increasingly popular and the most influential religion in China after the 4th century. The basic teachings of Buddhism are based on the theory of Samsara, meaning that living beings orbit around the six spheres of heaven, hell and earth, just like an ever-turning wheel. The nature of suffering, the origin of suffering, the cessation of suffering and the path are the basic doctrines of Buddhism, also known as Four Noble Truths (「Dukkha」). There are three main branches in Chinese Buddhism: the majority of Han people are the followers of Mahayana, whilst many minorities in Yunnan province such as Dai, Bulang, Deang and Wa peoples believe in Hinayana. Tibetan Buddhism, as a branch of Chinese Buddhism, is popular primarily in Tibet and Inner Mongolia. China now has more than 33,000 Buddhist temples. The four famous Buddhism Mountains in China are E'mei Mountain in Sichuan, Putuo Mountain in Zhejiang, Wutaishan Mountain in Shanxi and Jiuhuashan Mountain in Anhui.

Islam was founded by the Arabic prophet Mohammed and probably first reached China in the mid-7th century. 「Islam」 is the transliteration of Arabic, which simply means 「submission and obedience」. Islam is the religion of the world collectively. 「Muslim」, derived from 「Islamic」, refers to people who adhere to Allah, the only God of Islamic faith. The Yuan Dynasty (1271—1368) witnessed the zenith of prosperity of Islam. China has more than 35,000 muslim mosques at present.

Christianity is rooted in Judaism and was founded by Jesus in the Palestinian territory as an independent religion in 135 AD. Christianity is mainly composed by three principle divisions: the Roman Catholic Church, the various Protestant Churches, and the Eastern Orthodox Church. Catholic influence reached China at four times after the 7th century: Tang dynasty, Yuan dynasty, Ming dynasty and spread widely after the Opium War in 1840. Protestantism was introduced into China in the early 19th century. Christian classic is the Bible. The Bible, the accounts of God's revelation, is the Christian General principles of faith and life skills standards, and is the eternal truth. Major Christian festivals are Christmas, Easter, Ascension Day, and Halloween. Now there are more than 6,000 Catholic churches and over 56,000 Protestant churches and some other types of christian places of worship in China.

Taoism, or Daoism, is the indigenous religion of China, founded by Zhang Daoling in the Eastern Han Dynasty (during the 2nd century) and became very popular during the Southern and Northern Dynasties. It is based on the philosophy of Lao Zi and Zhuang Zi. The Taoist religion evolved out of witchcraft, necromancy and self-cultivation techniques. It emphasizes strongly the union of man and nature, suggesting that man controls his environment not by fighting it, but by cooperating with it. Taoism values the idea of Wu Wei, which means 「action by non-action」, is a core principle of Taoism and also plays an important role in Chinese philosophy. The school's doctrine is that the 「Dao」 is the course, the principle, the substance, and the standard of all things, to which all of them must conform. It also means simply the 「way」, the 「way of nature」. Tao Te Ching is regarded as its bible. Lao Zi is revered by the Taoists as the originator of Taoism and is often called 「Taishang Laojun」. China now has more than 9,000 Taoist temples. The most sacred four

Taoist mountains are Dragon-Tiger Mountain in Jiangxi, Qingcheng Mountain in Sichuan, Wudang Mountain in Hubei and Qiyun Mountain in Anhui.

Discussion

1. How many religions are popular in China at present? What are they?
2. Where and when was Buddhism founded?
3. What does 「Islam」 mean?
4. How many main principal divisions does Christianity comprise?
5. What does Taoism emphasize?

Section 2　Dialogues

Dialogue 1　Talking About China's Buddhism

Scene: The tourist wants to know more knowledge of Buddhism in China. Now the tour guide is talking about it with her/him.

(G = Tour Guide　T = Tourist)

T: Wow, the Chinese Buddhist culture is so extensive and profound!

G: Yes, it is. The Buddhism in China has been around for more than 2000 years.

T: But Buddhism originated from India, didn't it?

G: Yes, it did. But Buddhism is being carried forward in China. Now there are more than 200 millions Buddhists in China.

T: Such a huge number! Is Buddhism in China the same as in India now?

G: Actually there is a considerable difference between them. After thousands of years of development, there are three main branches of Buddhism in China.

T: Oh, what are they?

G: They are Mahayana, Hinayana and Tibetan Buddhism.

T: What is the difference among them?

G: Well, most of the Han people are the followers of Mahayana, because they believe that everyone can become a Buddha by devout practice. Many minorities in Yunnan province, such as Dai, Bulang, Deang and Wa people are the believers in Hinayana, they insist that there is only one Buddha, people can only be a bodhisattva by practice.

T: Wow, it sounds very interesting! How about the Tibetan Buddhism?

G: Tibetan Buddhism is a blend of Mahayana Buddhism and Tibetan indigenous Bonism. After a long history spread, it became very popular primarily in Tibet and Inner Mongolia.

T: Wow, now I can pick out the differences between them. Thank you so much.

G: My pleasure.

Dialogue 2　The Taoist Temple and the Five-Peck Rice Sect

Sense: The tour guide is introducing the origination of Taoism and a Taoist temple to the tourist.

(G = Tour Guide　T = Tourist)

T: What is that place? I've never seen anything like it!

G: Oh, it's a Taoist Temple. They are everywhere in China.

T: The temple is so colorful. It doesn't look like a Buddhist temple, does it? It seems that they are very difficult to separate.

G: No, but there is a nuance between them actually. Buddhist temples are much more modest in decoration.

T: I see. I remember that you have told us the Taoism is the indigenous religion of China, is that right?

G: Yes, it is. Taoism is founded by Zhang Daoling in the Eastern Han Dynasty. At the time of its of founding, it was not a religion, but an organization against the corrupt Han government. It was called the「Five-Peck Rice Sect」.

T: What a funny name! Why it is called「Five-Peck Rice Sect」?

G: Well, it is said that anyone who wanted to join the uprising needed to offer five pecks of rice, hence the name.

T: Hah! That is really interesting! So that Taoism is the most popular religion throughout China?

G: It depends on how you look at it. But in China, Buddhists are the largest group in terms of the number of believers, then the Christians, finally the Muslims and Taoists.

T: Oh, that's an eye-opener, thank you so much!

G: You're welcome. Let's continue our visit. This way, please.

Words and Phases

Buddhism [ˈbʊdizəm]　*n.* 佛教

Islam [ˈizlɑːm]　*n.* 伊斯蘭教

Christianity [ˌkristiˈænəti]　*n.* 基督教；基督教精神，基督教教義

Taoism [ˈtaʊizəm]　*n.* 道家的學說；道教

indigenous [inˈdidʒənəs]　*adj.* 本土的；土著的；國產的；固有的

adhere to　堅持；粘附；擁護，追隨

sakyamuni [ˈsɑːkjəmuni]　*n.* 釋迦牟尼

samsara [səmˈsɑːrə]　*n.* 輪迴

orbit [ˈɔːbit]　*n.* 軌道；眼眶；勢力範圍；生活常規

doctrine [ˈdɒktrin]　*n.* 主義；學說；教義；信條

Four Noble Truths　佛教四諦

mahayana [ˌmɑːhəˈjɑːnə]　*n.* 大乘佛教

hinayana [ˌhiːnəˈjɑːnə]　*n.* 小乘佛教

Tibetan Buddhism n. 藏傳佛教

Judaism [ˈdʒuːdeizəm]　*n.* 猶太教；猶太主義；（總稱）猶太人

Opium War　鴉片戰爭

Catholic [ˈkæθlik]　*n.* 天主教徒；羅馬天主教

Eastern Orthodox Christianity　東正教

Protestant [ˈprɒtistənt]　*n.* 新教；新教徒

prophet [ˈprɒfit]　*n.* 先知；預言者；提倡者

transliteration [ˌtrænzˌlitəˈreiʃn]　*n.* 音譯；直譯

zenith [ˈzeniθ]　*n.* 頂峰；頂點；最高點

mosque [mɒsk]　*n.* 清真寺

evolved out of　從…發展來的

witchcraft [ˈwitʃkrɑːft]　*n.* 巫術；魔法

necromancy [ˈnekrəʊmænsi]　*n.* 巫術，妖術

advocate [ˈædvəkeit]　*vt.* 提倡，主張，擁護

Section 3　Exercises

I. Translate the following sentences into English.

1. 在所有這些宗教中，特別在佛教中有另一個重要理念，那就是，人生在世就是來受苦的。

2. 道家崇尚自然無為，強調美與真的統一。

3. 根據基督教的說法，耶穌基督曾死而復生。

4. 觀音菩薩在中國擁有很多的信眾，是中國最為有名的菩薩。

5. 作為伊斯蘭教歷中的最神聖之月，傳統上齋月的開始取決於見到新月。

II. Translate the following paragraphs into Chinese.

1. The Great Buddha Hall is the main hall of a monastery. It usually has a number of huge stone pillars that support the roof, and each pillar is carved with famous Buddhist couplets. There is a board hangs on the top of the entrance hangs, which says Daxiong Baodian. Daxiong means 「Great Buddha」 or 「Great Hero」. The hall contains a central altar, on which a statue of Sakyamuni sits cross-legged on a lotus throne. His two closest disciples, Kasyap and Ananda flank him.

2. Chan Buddhism is a sect of Mahayana Buddhism. It asserts that enlightenment can be attained through meditation, self-contemplation and intuition rather than through faith and devotion. It aims to transmit the essence of Buddhism, and it advocates that the ability to achieve enlightenment is inherent within everyone. It holds that the universal 「Buddha-nature」 is immanent within ourselves and must be realized 「directly」 in mind-to-mind communication between master and disciple.

III. Make dialogues according to the given situations.

Section A: You are the tour guide from CYTS, Henan branch. Your name is Paul, you are serving a tour group from UK which is visiting Shaolin temple, the group members are very interested in Buddhism, and they ask you a question what is the difference between Mahayana and Hinayana.

Section B: You are a tour guide from CTS, Hubei branch. Your name is Susan, you are visiting Wudang Mountain with a tour group from Germany. The group members are very curious about the Taoist idea－「Wu Wei」, you are going to explain it.

Section 4　Extensive Reading

A Brief Summary of Confucianism

　　Confucianism became a major system of thought in Ancient China, developed from the teachings of Confucius and his disciples, and concerned with the principles of good conduct, practical wisdom, and proper social relationships. Throughout the feudal societies, it almost became dominant thinking. Confucianism has some extent influence on the Chinese attitude toward life, set the patterns of living and standards of social value. Its legacy and beliefs spread from China to Korea, Japan, Vietnam and other Asian nations.

Unit 3　Traditional Chinese Festivals

Section 1　Introduction

  Being one of the four great ancient civilizations, China has various traditional festivals characterized by diverse styles and themes, which are scheduled according to the Chinese lunar calendar and twenty-four solar terms. The traditional Chinese festivals are an essential part of harvests or prayer offerings, many of the customs connected with the traditional festivals have linked with religious devotions, superstitions and myths. The form which most of the festivals take today was established around the time of the Han Dynasty (206 B. C. — 202 A. D.) and for many years, various eminent poets have written countless masterpieces describing the festivals and are still recited regularly today. Almost every festival has its own unique origins and customs which reflect the traditional practices and morality of the whole Chinese nation and its people. The grandest and most popular festivals are the Spring Festival, the Lantern Festival, the Tomb-sweeping Day, the Dragon Boat Festival, and the Mid-autumn Festival.

  The Spring Festival, widely known as Chinese New Year in the West, is the most important traditional festival in China and a public holiday. It is also celebrated in South Korea, Vietnam, and some other Asian countries. The festival falls on the first day of the first lunar month (the corresponding date in the solar calendar varies from as early as January 21st to as late as February 19th), and is celebrated extensively until the 15th day (on

Chinese New Year—The Spring Festival

which comes from another Chinese traditional festival called the Lantern Festival). The historical reason for beginning the year during cold weather is that it is a time between the 「autumn harvest」 and 「winter storage」 and 「spring plowing」 and 「summer weeding」。

The Spring Festival is celebrated elaborately across the country with various cultural activities. Fireworks shows, dragon dancing and lion dancing are the most common Chinese New Year activities. Days before the festival, Chinese families clean their houses. The practice of house cleaning before the New Year is believed to sweep away bad luck and bring good fortune in the coming year. Children are given money inside red envelopes for good luck and prosperity. In the evening, families gather for a dinner of traditional cuisine, mostly round fruits that symbolize prosperity and sticky foods that symbolize unity.

The Lantern Festival

The Lantern Festival, also called Shangyuan festival, is celebrated on the 15th day of the first lunar month. It is the first full moon night in the Chinese lunar year, symbolizing the end of Chinese New Year festivities. The Lantern Festival dates back to legends of the Eastern Han Dynasty over 2,000 years ago. During the Lantern Festival, people gather together to celebrate the beginning of spring by watching lanterns, setting off fireworks and eating Yuanxiao (sweet stuffed dumplings made of glutinous rice flour with sesame, bean paste, jujube paste or walnut meat served in soup). Guessing riddles written on lanterns is a Lantern Festival tradition from the Song Dynasty.

As time goes by, the Lantern Festival has enjoyed more and more celebrating activities. Some places even add traditional folk-custom performance such as playing dragon lantern, lion dancing, stilting, striking land boat, doing the Yangko, and striking the Peach Drum.

The Tomb-sweeping Day

The Tomb-sweeping Day, or Pure Brightness Day, is a day for mourning the dead. Also it is one of the 24 seasonal division points in the lunar calendar. After the festival, the temperature rises and rainfall increases in readiness for spring plowing and sowing.

The Tomb-sweeping Day, Originally-called 「cold food day」, is the most important day for people to offer sacrifice to ancestors and mourn the dead. It started in the Zhou Dynasty, and has a history of over 2,500 years. Qingming is one of the 24 solar terms in China, indicating the coming of late spring, falling on April 4th-6th each year, thus the best plowing and growing time, while 「cold food day」 is a day when folks sweep the ancestors' tombs and eat cold food. Qingming was adjacent to cold food day, so later on they gradually became one festival, and thus 「cold food」 became another name for Qingming, and dusting the tomb and eating cold food turned into a custom of Qingming. Qingming has evolved into a culture-rich and meaning-deep remembrance day.

In ancient times, people celebrated Qingming with dancing, singing, picnics, and kite flying. Colored boiled eggs would be broken to symbolize the opening of life. In the capital, the Emperor would plant trees on the palace grounds to celebrate the renewing nature of spring. In the villages, young men and women would court each other.

With the passing of time, this celebration of life became a day to honor past ancestors. Following folk religion, the Chinese believed that the spirits of deceased ancestors looked after the family. Sacrifices of food and spirit money could keep them happy, and the family would prosper through good harvests and have more children. Today, Chinese visit their family graves to tend any underbrush that has grown. Weeds are pulled and dirt swept away, and the family will set out offerings of food and spirit money. Unlike the sacrifices at a family's home altar, the offerings at the tomb usually consist of dry, bland food. One theory is that since any number of ghosts around a grave area, this less appealing food will be consumed by the ancestors, and not be plundered by strangers.

The Dragon Boat Festival

The Dragon Boat Festival, also named 「Chongwu festival」, 「Calamus festival」 or 「Daughter's festival」, takes place on the 5th day of the fifth lunar month. It is a folk festival widely passed down with a history of over two thousand years, and is one of the most important festivals as well. There are various celebrating activities on the day of Dragon Boat festival, among which eating rice dumplings (zongzi, steamed glutinous rice wrapped in bamboo leaves) and dragon boat race are important customs.

There are many legends about the origin of the Dragon Boat Festival. Some people say it is to commemorate the great poet Qu Yuan, who lived in the Spring and Artumn Period; while some people think it is to memorialize Wu Zixu, a famous official in the Warring States Period, still there are some others regarding May 5th in the lunar calendar as the date when the Wuyue people held a memorial totem ceremony in ancient times. However, the legend of Qu Yuan is the most widely spread. People praise highly the lofty sentiment and outstanding talent toward this patriotic poet and take more pity on the finale that he drowned himself in a river. In the minds of most Chinese people, the convention of eating rice dumplings and the Dragon Boat Race in the festival are all related to the commemoration of Qu Yuan. There are also other conventions, such as drinking realgar wine, wearing sachets and flying kites.

The Mid-autumn Festival

The Mid-autumn Festival is another important Chinese traditional festival. It falls on the 15th day of the 8th lunar month, when the moon is fullest and brightest, and on this day relatives and friends send each other moon cakes, wish each other good luck and then have a big dinner together enjoying the full moon. The Mid-autumn Festival, as well as the Spring Festival, symbolizes reunion, so it is also called「Reunion festival」. Those unable to get home to join the get-together miss their family even more on this festival.

The origin of the Mid-autumn Festival derived from the tradition of worshipping the Goddess of the Moon back to more than 2,000 years ago. This festival is also a time to celebrate a good autumn harvest. It dates back thousands of years, and the modern-day festive customs were gradually formed over the years. Generally speaking, eating moon cakes, enjoying the moon and lighting up lanterns are common traditions in this festival.

There are many Chinese legends about the moon. The story of Goddess Chang'e, Wu Gang and the Jade Rabbit living on the moon is still popular today. The festival was a time to enjoy the successful reaping of rice and wheat with food offerings made in honor of the moon. Today, it is still an occasion for outdoor reunions among friends and relatives to eat moon-cakes and watch the moon, a symbol of harmony and unity.

Discussion

1. Why do Chinese people celebrate the Spring Festival?

2. What kinds of activities do Chinese people usually do on the day of the Lantern Festival?

3. Does the Tomb-sweeping Day have the same meaning as Qingming? Why?

4. What are the main legends of the origin of the Dragon-Boat Festival?

5. When is the Middle-autumn Festival and why is it as important as the Spring Festival in China?

Section 2 Dialogues

Dialogue 1 The Legend of Mid-autumn Festival — The Archer and the Suns

Scene: The tourist is interested in the legends of Mid-autumn Festival, the tour guide now is explaining it.

(G = Tour Guide   T = Tourist)

T: I heard of that tomorrow is the Chinese Mid-autumn Festival, what is the meaning behind this festival?

G: Well, the Mid-autumn Festival is one of the most important festivals in the Chinese lunar calendar, and is a legal national holiday in China, also in other Asian countries. In ancient times, the Mid-autumn Festival was the folklore to celebrate the end of the summer harvest season through sacrificing to the Moon Goddess. But nowadays, this festival represents the reunion of family members.

T: Oh, I think because it is more likely that the full moon symbolizes the gathering of family and friends, is that right?

G: Exactly!

T: Who is the goddess you just mentioned?

G: Well, her name is Chang'e. There is a legend about her and her husband Houyi.

T: Wow, what is that? I'd like to know.

G: It is said that a long time ago, there were ten suns in the sky.

T: What? Ten suns? That's so incredible. Nothing can be alive on the earth in that case.

G: Yes. But I told you it was only a legend. One day, all the ten suns appeared at the same time in the sky, and the temperature of the earth went up quickly. At this time, there was a legendary archer who shot down nine suns and saved the world.

T: Who was that?

G: It was Houyi.

T: He did a good job.

G: Yes. As his reward, the Heavenly Queen Mother gave him a magic pill to make him live forever. But it was a pity that he didn't follow her advice, he became a selfish man in front of the fame and fortune. So his wife Chang'e could not bear to live with her husband. So she stole his pill, ate it and fled to the moon. This is the myth of the beautiful woman in the moon.

T: Oh, I see. This story is fascinating!

G: This is the only legend that I know. Actually there are many other stories like this. But I'm not sure.

T: Thank you so much.

G: You're welcome!

Dialogue 2   Guessing Riddles — The Traditional Activity of the Lantern Festival

Scene: The tour guide is introducing the traditional activities of the Lantern Festival to the tourist.

(G = Tour Guide   T = Tourist)

T: Wow, the street is so busy! The beautiful lanterns are everywhere. It seems we are in a magic world. Now, I can see why it's called the Lantern Festival. It deserves its name.

G: Yes. Today is the last day of celebrating the Spring Festival, Chinese people always enjoy the lighted lanterns and the gala performances.

T: That's amazing! Look, why are so many people gathered over there?

G: Oh, it is because of guessing riddles! Did you notice the characters on the lanterns?

T: Sure. What is guessing riddles?

G: It's a traditional activity on the Lantern Festival. If is anyone can solve the riddles on the lanterns, he may get a prize.

T: Interesting! But you know, I don't know any Chinese characters, so I'm afraid we'd better do something else. Hey, look! There is a huge lantern there. Let's get close to it.

G: It's really eye-catching. It's the biggest dragon lantern I've ever seen in my life.

T: Really? Then I'm really lucky. Oh, it's spewing fireworks from its huge mouth.

G: Very impressive. It's made of glass, which makes it even brighter.

T: There are many Chinese characters on its body, too. What do they say? Riddles?

G: Let me have a look. Oh, no. They are Chinese poems which describe this happy scene.

T: The design is wonderful! I wonder how the designer comes up with all these great ideas. I want to take a picture with it and twitter it to my friends.

G: Sure, let me take pictures for you!

T: Thank you so much!

Words and Phrases

diverse [di'vɜːs]　　*adj.* 不同的；多種多樣的；變化多的
lunar ['luːnə(r)]　　*adj.* 月亮的，月球的；陰歷的
solar ['səʊlə(r)]　　*adj.* 太陽的；日光的；利用太陽光的
devotion [di'vəʊʃn]　　*n.* 獻身，奉獻；忠誠；熱愛
superstition [ˌsuːpə'stiʃn]　　*n.* 迷信
eminent ['eminənt]　　*adj.* 傑出的；有名的；明顯的
fall on　　（節日等）適逢（某日），正當（某日）
prosperity [prɒ'sperəti]　　*n.* 繁榮，成功
jujube ['dʒuːdʒuːb]　　*n.* 棗子，棗樹；棗味糖
Yangko　　秧歌
mourn [mɔːn]　　*vt.* 哀悼；憂傷；服喪
deceased [di'siːst]　　*n.* 死者；[法] 被繼承人
prosper ['prɒspə(r)]　　*vt.* (使) 成功；(使) 昌盛；(使) 繁榮
altar ['ɔːltə(r)]　　*n.* 祭壇；聖壇；聖餐臺
plunder ['plʌndə(r)]　　*n.* 搶奪；戰利品；掠奪品
glutinous rice　　糯米
commemorate [kə'meməreit]　　*vt.* 慶祝，紀念；成為……的紀念

sentiment ['sentimənt]　　n. 感情，情緒；情操；觀點；多愁善感
patriotic [ˌpætri'ɔtik]　　adj. 愛國的
final ['fainl]　　n. 結局；終曲；最後一場；最後樂章
realgar [ri'ælgə]　　n. 雄黃（二硫化二砷）；雞冠石
worship ['wɜːʃip]　　n. 崇拜；禮拜；尊敬
reap [riːp]　　vt. 收穫；收割

Section 3　Exercises

I. Matching the English festivals with the correct Chinese. Use a dictionary when necessary.

1. 小年　　　　　　　　A. International Working Women's Day
2. 重陽節　　　　　　　B. New Year's Day
3. 七夕節　　　　　　　C. Army Day
4. 臘八節　　　　　　　D. Lunar Year
5. 元旦　　　　　　　　E. Laba Festival
6. 國際勞動婦女節　　　F. International Labor Day
7. 國際勞動節　　　　　G. International Children's Day
8. 中國青年節　　　　　H. National Day
9. 國際兒童節　　　　　I. Double Seventh Festival
10. 建軍節　　　　　　　J. Chinese Youth Day
11. 國慶節　　　　　　　K. Double Ninth Festival

II. Translate the following sentences into English.

1. 關於元宵節的起源之說多種多樣，但是最確切的一種說法是它跟宗教信仰有關。
2. 春節又被稱為過年，意思就是驅趕一種叫「年」的怪獸。
3. 清明節是掃墓拜祭先人的日子，在中國大陸地區是法定節假日。
4. 中秋節的習俗很多，形式也各不相同，但都寄託著人們對生活無限的熱愛和對美好生活的向往。
5. 端午節、春節和中秋節並列為中國三大節日。

III. Translate the following paragraphs into Chinese.

1. The Dragon Boat Festival, which originated more than 2,500 years ago and is widely known to commemorate patriot poet Qu Yuan (278 B.C. — 340 B.C.) in the Warring States period, is celebrated annually in many parts of China. People eat Zongzi, a pyramid-shaped dumpling made of glutinous rice and wrapped in reed leaves, and watch dragon boat competitions.

2. The 23rd day of the 12th lunar month is Preliminary Year. Sacrifices are offered to the Kitchen God with families sharing delicious food followed by preparations for the coming Spring Festival.

IV. Make dialogues according to the given situations.

Section A: You are a tour guide from U-tour, Chengdu Branch. Your name is Li Yang. You are serving an American tourist group in Chengdu. Tomorrow is the 7th day of the 7th lunar month of Chinese calendar, the group members want to know the beautiful legend of「Chinese Valentine's day」, and you are going to tell them the story.

Section B: You are the tour guide from China Space, Beijing Branch. Now you are serving a tourist group from Australia in Beijing, the tourists are very interested— in the Chinese Double Ninth Festival, and you are going to explain it.

● Section 4 Extensive Reading

The History of the Spring Festival

The Spring Festival has a history of more than 4,000 years. It is said that the custom of Spring Festival originated from belief in deities. When the solar terms changed, dictating farming activities, especially at the end of a year, people would sacrifice to the deities and pray for good harvests. Nian was not a word for describing time originally. It was used to describe the cycle of crop cultivation until the Xia Dynasty (2070 B.C. —1600 B.C.).

The beginning of a year changed during different dynasties until the Han Dynasty (206 B.C.— 220 A.D.). For example, people in the Xia Dynasty celebrated New Year's Day in the first lunar month of a year, while people in the Qin Dynasty (221 B.C.— 206 B.C.) celebrated New Year's Day in the tenth lunar month.

The exact celebration period of the Spring Festival was fixed in 104 B.C. and was given the name Suishou (the beginning of the year), when China was ruled by Emperor Wudi (156 B. C. — 87 B. C.), and the lunar calendar was promulgated. This calendar made the beginning of a year and the 24 solar terms coincident. So, in ancient China, the first day of the lunar year was called Yuan Dan (「The first dawn」, 元旦).

On January 1st, 1912, the Republic of China introduced the Gregorian calendar, and named January 1st as Yuan Dan. The traditional New Year's Day was given another name — Chun Jie (The「Spring Festival」, 春節).

Unit 4　Chinese Cuisine

Section 1　Introduction

China's vast territory and extensive contact with other nations and cultures have given birth to the distinctive Chinese culinary art. The history of Chinese cuisine stretches back for thousands of years and has changed from period to period in each region. Different from the cuisine in western world, Chinese people cook food in various ways such as frying, boiling, steaming and stir frying. Also Chinese people put a high premium on the taste, color and smell of food. Chinese cuisine enjoys the same international reputation as the 「kingdom of cuisine」 to that of France and Italy for its scent, taste and design.

Due to the diversity of availability of resources, climate, geography, history, cooking techniques and lifestyles are quite different from region to region in China, the flavor differs from one region to another, and sometimes two areas which are geographical neighbors may have completely different styles of cuisine. There is a popular saying that the flavor of Chinese food is 「sweetness in the south, saltiness in the north, freshness in the east and hotness in the west」. As such, a number of different styles contribute to Chinese cuisine. Perhaps the typical known and most influential are the 「Four Cuisines」 or the 「Eight Cuisines」. These are all quite representative as follows: Guangdong cuisine, Shandong cuisine, Sichuan cuisine, Jiangsu cuisine (specifically Huaiyang cuisine) and Anhui cuisine, Fujian cuisine, Zhejiang cuisine and Hunan cuisine.

Shandong cuisine, which is also called Lu cuisine, is very famous in northern China. It consists of Jinan cuisine and Jiaodong cuisine, and is characterized by its emphasis on aroma, freshness, crispness and tenderness. Soups are given much emphasis in Shandong cuisine. Jinan cuisine is adept at deep-frying, grilling, frying and stir-frying, while Jiaodong cuisine is famous for cooking seafood with fresh and light taste.

Sichuan cuisine is popular in Sichuan province and Chongqing municipality, which is mainly characterized by its spicy and pungent flavor. It has to do with the wet weather of that region and people need hot food to dispel the wet. Pepper and prickly ash produce typical exciting tastes. Fermented soybean, garlic and ginger are common-used in the cooking process. Sichuan cuisine also features a wide range of materials, various seasonings and different cooking techniques, 「Every dish has its own flavor」 is the essential feature of Sichuan cuisine, and Sichuan hotpots is perhaps the most famous hotpots in the world.

Jiangsu cuisine, also called Huaiyang cuisine, is popular in the lower reaches of the Yangtze River. It is moderately salty and sweet and is quite delicious, which is in keeping with the mild weather in that region. Cooking techniques consist of stewing, braising, roasting, and simmering. Jiangsu cuisine is famous for its delicate carving techniques, of which the melon carving technique is especially well known.

Guangdong cuisine, known as Cantonese cuisine, features exquisite, plentiful and varied raw materials, novel and strangely cooked foods, light, delicious, tender and refreshing taste, sour, sweet, bitter, hot and salty flavoring. Guangdong cuisine, which doesn't use much spice, emphasizes on bringing out the natural flavor of the raw materials, is easily one of the most diverse and richest cuisines in China.

Zhejiang cuisine originated from the local dishes of Hangzhou, Ningbo and Shaoxing. Food in Zhejiang is fragrant, tender and fresh, and most of them are highly sophisticated made. Fujian cuisine often takes marine products as its raw material. It tastes light and delicious and the color is beautiful. The most distinct features are the 「pickled taste」。 Hunan cuisine is mostly seasoned with chili, and features sour, dry hot, delicious and fragrant tastes. Anhui cuisine is made of the choicest delicacies of mountain and wilderness, and always keeps the original flavor of food.

Besides, roast duck and dip-boiled mutton slices of Beijing, doupi (a kind of fried pancake made of glutinous rice, minced meat, cubes of bamboo shoots, etc. wrapped in sheets of rice and bean flour mixed with eggs) of Hubei Province, and 「white meat with pickled Chinese cabbage」of the Northeast are all famous dishes in terms of their bright color and good taste.

Discussion

1. What are the「four cuisines」and「eight cuisines」in China?
2. Why do Chinese cuisines differ from region to region?
3. What is the essential feature of Sichuan cuisine?
4. Generally speaking, what are the basic features of Chinese cuisines in different areas?
5. What is the most famous cooking technique of Jiangsu cuisine?

Section 2　Dialogues

Dialogue 1　Ordering Sichuan Food at a Restaurant

Scene: The tour guide and the tourist are having a meal at a restaurant. They are preparing to order some Sichuan dishes.

(G = Tour Guide　　T = Tourist)

(At the restaurant)

T: I'd like to try some real Chinese cuisine. Do you have any recommendations?

G: Well, it depends. You see, there are eight famous distinctive cuisines in China. For instance, Sichuan cuisine, and Hunan cuisine.

T: I've heard of they are both spicy and hot, is that right?

G: That's right. If you like hot dishes, you can try some. Then there's Cantonese cuisine and Jiangsu cuisine. Most southerners like them because of the light taste.

T: What a tough choice! Well, I prefer the Sichuan food. Sometimes you have to challenge yourself, right?

G: Ok, let's order some Sichuan dishes. Here is the menu.

(The tourist is looking through the menu.)

T: Oh, what is this? It looks so delicious.

G: It's shredded pork with garlic sauce, a representative Sichuan dish.

T: Well, is it fairly spicy?

G: In fact, no. Different Sichuan dishes taste different, they are not only spicy and hot. This dish is made of pork meat, celery and agaric with sour sauce, which smells and tastes like fish. It is not very greasy, very nutritious.

T: Great! I will order one. Any other dishes could you recommend?

G: Sure. Spicy diced chicken with peanuts and stewed beancurd with minced pork in pepper sauce, they are the famous Sichuan dishes as well.

T: Sounds good! I'll take them.

G: Also you should have some vegetables. How about salted dried string beans. I'm sure you'll love it.

T: Um, it looks very interesting. Thank you for your recommendation, I'd love to try it.

G: You're welcome.

Dialogue 2 Tasting Beijing Roast Duck

Scene: The tour guide is teaching the tourist how to eat Beijing roast duck at a restaurant.

(G = Tour Guide   T = Tourist)

T: The magnificent Forbidden City is awesome. But I'm a little bit starving right now, shall we go to eat?

G: Sure, I've already arranged the lunch at Quanjude Roast Duck restaurant.

(30 minutes later, the tour group is at the restaurant).

T: Wow, the duck looks delicious. Is this what we ordered?

G: Yes, Beijing roast duck is well known by most foreigners, not only for its taste, but for the performance. Look, the chef is slicing the duck into thin pieces. There will be around one hundred and twenty pieces of both skin and meat for each.

T: That is incredible! The chef is so skillful with his knife.

G: Absolutely. It is said that they serve 3,000 ducks every day.

T: Unbelievable! By the way, what are these things in the plates?

G: Oh, they are pancakes, hollowed sesame buns, scallions, cucumbers and the sweet sauce made of fermented flour. I will show you how to make one.

T: Thank you. I couldn't wait any longer to have a taste.

G: Actually you can follow me. Look, just wrap all these food materials up in the pancake.

T: Oh, it's terrific. I love the flavor. Can you tell me how it is prepared?

G: Certainly. First, a Beijing duck is specially selected. After it is cleaned and dressed, it will be roasted in an open oven. Only wood of fruit trees is used to fuel the fire to give the duck a unique fragrance. When the skin turns golden brown, it is ready to be served.

T: It sounds really complicated. No wonder it tastes so great.

G: Yes, please have some more.

Words and Phrases

extensive [ik'stensiv]　*n.* 廣泛的，大量的
distinctive [di'stiŋktiv]　*adj.* 有特色的，與眾不同的
stir frying　用大火炒
aroma [ə'rəʊmə]　*n.* 芳香
crispness [krispnəs]　*n.* 酥脆
tenderness ['tendənis]　*n.* 細嫩
grill [gril]　*n.* 燒，烤
pungent ['pʌndʒənt]　*adj.* 辛辣的
prickly ash　四川花椒
fermented soybean　豆豉
delicate ['delikət]　*adj.* 微妙的；清淡可口的
stew [stju:]　*vt.* 炖；燜
braise [breiz]　*vt.* 燜；燴
simmer ['simə(r)]　*vt.* 煨；用文火熬
melon carving technique　瓜雕技術
exquisite [ik'skwizit]　*adj.* 精致的；細膩的
fragrant ['freigrənt]　*adj.* 芳香的
sophisticated [sə'fistikeɪtid]　*adj.* 精致的
marine [mə'ri:n]　*adj.* 海生的，海產的
pickled taste　鹵味
dip-boiled mutton slices　涮羊肉
white meat with pickled Chinese cabbage　酸菜白肉

Section 3　Exercises

I. Match the Column A with Column B correctly.

Column A	Column B
1. 鮑汁海鮮燴飯	1. Noodles with sesame paste and pea
2. 冰糖銀耳炖雪梨	2. Stewed sweet pear with white fungus
3. 擔擔面	3. Twice-cooked pork slices
4. 百合炒南瓜	4. Eggplants with garlic sauce
5. 白灼時蔬	5. Noodles with bean paste
6. 虎皮尖椒	6. Steamed bun stuffed with red bean paste
7. 蚝油生菜	7. Sauteed lettuce in oyster sauce
8. 回鍋肉	8. Hot and peppery chicken
9. 魚香茄子	9. Sauteed pumpkin with lily
10. 白粥	10. Stewed meatball with brown sauce
11. 炸醬面	11. Dumpling soup
12. 豆沙包	12. Sauteed green chili pepper
13. 麻辣仔雞	13. Boiled seafood and rice
14. 冬菜扣肉	14. Boiled seasonal vegetables
15. 紅燒獅子頭	15. Plain rice porridge
16. 榨菜肉絲面	16. West lake fish in vinegar
17. 椰汁炖雪蛤	17. Spicy salty pork spareribs
18. 椒鹽排骨	18. Coconut harsmar stew
19. 西湖醋魚	19. Pork, pickled mustard green noodles
20. 上湯水餃	20. Braised sliced pork with preserved vegetables in casserole

II. Translate the following sentences into English.

1. 治大國若烹小鮮。
2. 宣威火腿，產於雲南省宣威市，在國內外都享有盛名。
3. 淮揚菜在烹制過程中選材精細，非常重視刀工和火候，並且強調保留材料的原汁原味。
4. 川菜世界聞名，自成一家。中國人認為它包括5,000多道菜，其中300多

道都很有名氣。

　　5. 徽菜的突出特色不僅在於食材細緻，還在於烹調過程精細。

III. Translate the following paragraphs into Chinese.

　　1. Hunan cuisine, is also known as「Xiang cuisine」, consists of local cuisines of the Xiangjiang region, Dongting lake and Xiangxi coteau. It is characterized by thick and pungent flavor. Chili, pepper and shallot are usually necessaries in this division.

　　2.「Colorful」,「varied」,「delicious」and「complex」are often used to describe Chinese food. Great attention is paid to aesthetic appreciation of the food because the food should be good not only in flavor and smell but also in color and appearance.

IV. Make dialogues according to the given situations

　　Situation A：You are a tour guide from CYTS, Zhejiang Branch. Your name is Judy. You are serving a tour group from Canada at the famous restaurant of Hangzhou—Shizilou, you are going to give them a brief introduction to Zhejiang cuisine.

　　Situation B：You are the tour guide from STA, Shandong Branch. Your name is Leo. You are guiding a tour group to visit Qingdao city, and you are going to introduce some representative dishes and common-used cooking techniques of Shandong cuisine to them.

Section 4　Extensive Reading

Jiaozi—Chinese Dumpling

　　Jiaozi (Chinese Dumpling) is a traditional Chinese food, which is essential during holidays in northern China and some areas of Southern China. It is one of the most widely popular foods in China and has become a part of Chinese culture.

　　Since the shape of a Chinese dumpling is similar to ancient Chinese gold or silver ingots, they represent wealth. Traditionally, the members of a family get together to make dumplings during the Spring festival's eve. They may hide a coin in one of the dumplings. The person who finds the coin will likely have good fortune in the New Year.

　　The Chinese dumpling is a delicious food. It can be made by various fillings based on one's taste. Making dumplings is really teamwork. Usually all family members will join the work. Some people have stated to make dumplings when they were kids in the family, so many Chinese know how to make dumplings.

Unit 5   Chinese Art

Section 1   Introduction

    The art of ancient Egypt, India and Babylon has become mists of the past. But that of China, on the other hand, has developed continuously for thousands of years. Chinese art is richly diverse and highly comprehensive, encompassing various forms and styles. Calligraphy, painting, opera, martial art, porcelain and others are the essences of Chinese art.

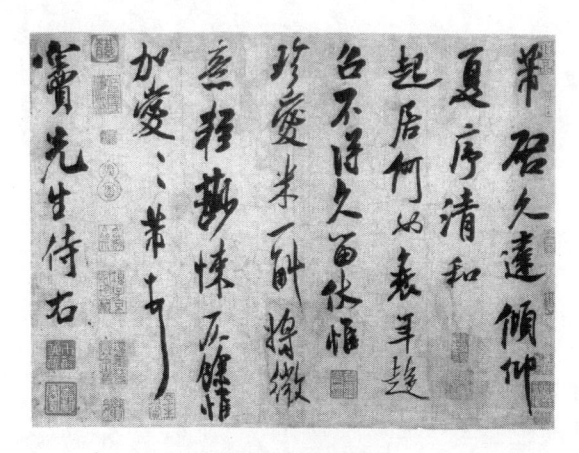

Chinese Calligraphy

In China calligraphy occupies a distinguished position in the field of traditional art. It is regarded as the most abstract and sublime form of art in Chinese culture. Calligraphy, or Shufa, is one of the four basic skills and disciplines of the Chinese literati, together with painting, stringed musical instruments and board games. It is not only a means of communication, but also a means of expressing a person's inner world in an aesthetic sense. According to an old Chinese saying,「The way characters are written is a portrait of the person who writes them.」In China, a person who can produce beautiful calligraphy is considered to be highly cultured.

Through the centuries Chinese characters have changed constantly and are mainly divided into five categories today: seal script (zhuan shu), official script (li shu), regular script (kai shu), running script (xing shu) and cursive script (cao shu).

To practice calligraphy one needs a brush, paper, ink stick and ink stone, commonly referred to as the「Four Treasures of the Study」. They are also good souvenirs for tourists from overseas.

Chinese Painting

Different from Western painting, traditional Chinese painting is characterized by unique forms of expression. It involves the same techniques as Chinese calligraphy and is done with a brush dipped in black or colored ink; oils are not used. Figure, landscape, and flower-and-bird paintings are important traditional Chinese painting genres.

There are two main techniques used in Chinese painting. One is Gong-bi, meaning「meticulous」. It uses highly detailed brushstrokes that delimit details very precisely. It is often highly colored and usually depicts figural or narrative subjects. It was traditionally practiced by artists working for the royal court or in independent workshops. Another is ink and wash painting, this style is also referred to as 「xie yi」or freehand style. Just as the famous painter Qi Baishi said that a painting should be between likeness and unlikeness.

Opera

Chinese opera is a traditional form of stage entertainment, with a history of more than 800 years. It evolved from folk songs, dances, talking, masques, and especially distinctive dialectical music. For Chinese, especially older folks, to listen to this kind of opera is a real pleasure.

What appeals to foreigners most might be the different styles of facial make-up, which is one of the highlights of opera and requires distinctive techniques of painting. Exaggerated designs are painted on each performer's face to symbolize a character's personality, role, and fate. Generally, red symbolizes loyalty and courage; black represents a bold and fearless character; blue shows a calculating nature; and white portrays a deceitful and conniving individual. Silver and gold are for the exclusive use of spirits and gods. Another technique that fascinates people is the marvelous acrobatics. Players can make fire spray out of their mouths when they act as a spirit, or can gallop while squatting to act as a dwarf. This reflects a saying among actors: 「One minute's performance on the stage takes ten years' practice behind the scenes.」

Over the past 800 years, Chinese opera has evolved into many different regional varieties based on local traits and accents. Now there are over 300 regional opera styles. Beijing Opera, Kun Opera, Qinqiang Opera, Yu Opera, Yue Opera, Sichuan Opera and Huangmei Opera are all very popular.

Martial Art

The origins of martial art (also known as Wushu or Kong Fu) can be found over 6,000 years ago, when men learned to hunt and fight. It is probably one of the earliest and longest lasting sports which utilizes both brawn and brain. During its development, many divisions were formed. Among there, Shaolin, Wudang and Emei styles are very famous.

Although being fighting styles, Kung Fu advocates virtue and peace, not aggression or violence. This has been the common value upheld by martial artists from generation to generation. Chinese literary works always praise the knight-errant's spirit of fighting against tyranny and helping good people.

Kung Fu movies have been a powerful medium to show Chinese martial art to the world. In the 1970s, Bruce Lee, a world famous Kung Fu master and film star, successfully introduced Chinese martial arts films to the world. Nowadays, Jackie Chan, Jet Li and some other actors have played many great masters' characters with their skills. These movies have created a cultural genre known as 「Kung Fu Theater」.

Porcelain

China is the home of porcelain and the invention of porcelain was China's great contribution to world civilization. The word 「china」 when capitalized, is recognized as the name of the country.

Porcelain originally derived from pottery. Firing porcelain requires the following three conditions: first, the materials must be porcelain stone, porcelain clay or kaolin; second, the temperature of the kiln stove must be up to 1,200 ℃; third, the surface of the vessels must be coated with glaze fired at a high temperature. Among all porcelain products, the most representative is blue-white porcelain.

Porcelain was one of the earliest artworks introduced to the western world through the Silk Road. Due to its durability and luster, it rapidly became a necessity of daily life, especially in the middle and upper classes. Now it is still a brilliant art that attracts many people's interest.

Discussion

1. What is the 「Four Treasures of the Study」?
2. Do you think computers would lead to the disappearance of Chinese calligraphy in the future? Why or why not?
3. Do you like watching Chinese opera? Why or why not?
4. What are the benefits of practicing martial arts?
5. Do you know the difference between porcelain and pottery?

● Section 2　Dialogues

Dialogue 1　Talking about Kung Fu Movies

Scene: Mr. Tom and Mrs. Susan are both fans of Kung Fu movies. Now they are talking about them.

(T= Mr. Tom　S=Mrs. Susan)

T: Could you recommend some popular Chinese Kung Fu movies to me?

S: No problem. I think 「Crouching Tiger, Hidden Dragon」 is quite good. It was directed by Ang Lee and it has become popular internationally.

T: I have seen that movie before. It won four Academy Awards, including Best Foreign Language Film.

S: Yes, it caused a sensation back then. By the way, what do you think of Chen Long's movies?

T: Who is this Chen Long?

S: Chen Long is a very famous movie star in Hong Kong. His English name is Jackie Chan.

T: Ha, I know Jackie Chan. He has made over 100 movies. And he is praised as the new Bruce Lee. But I didn't know his Chinese name.

S: OK. Then tell me what else do you know.

T: Some movie stars measure their worth by how many millions of dollars they have made. Do you know how Jackie Chan measures his worth?

S: He measures his worth by how many of his bones he has fractured while executing his films. The stunts in his movies are incredible.

T: That's true.

Dialogue 2 At a Souvenir Shop

Scene: Mr. Brown wants to buy some souvenirs before leaving China. Now he is in a souvenir shop. Miss Alice, the assistant, is serving him.

(A = Miss Alice   B = Mr. Brown)

A: Good Morning, sir. How can I help you?

B: I am just wondering what I should buy here for my souvenirs. Do you have any recommendations?

A: Sure, we have a variety of articles, such as glazed pottery, embroidery, wood carvings, braiding, and so forth.

B: I want something typically Chinese.

A: How about this tea set? It was made in Jingdezhen.

B: Jingdezhen? Oh I know. Isn't it called the 「Porcelain Capital」? This set is extremely beautiful. It is the very thing I've been dreaming of. I'll take it.

A: Yes, sir. Is there anything else you want?

B: I also want some scrolls or traditional paintings.

A: Good idea. Scrolls with Chinese cursive calligraphy will look great on your wall. And they might even bring you luck! Let me show you some scrolls written by young artists. The quality is quite good and the prices are reasonable.

B: I like this one. It's vigorous and forceful.

A：You really have a good taste.

B：How much in all?

A：430 dollars in total. If you want, we can post them for you. Next to ours is a post office.

B：That's a good idea. Here is ＄450.

A：Here is your change. Thank you.

B：That's all right. Bye.

Words and Phrases

encompass ［inˈkʌmpəs］　　vt. 包含；包圍

essence ［ˈes(ə)ns］　　n. 本質，實質；精華；香精

sublime ［səˈblaim］　　adj. 莊嚴的；令人崇敬的

discipline ［ˈdisəplin］　　n. 學科

literati ［litəˈrɑːtiː］　　n. 文人

souvenir ［ˌsuːvəˈniər(r)］　　n. 紀念品；禮物

be characterized by　　具有……的特徵

genre ［ˈʒɒnrə］　　n. 類型；流派

meticulous ［miˈtikjʊləs］　　adj. 一絲不苟的；小心翼翼的

brushstroke　　n. 一筆；筆的一畫；繪畫技巧

delimit ［diːˈlimit］　　vt. 劃界；定界限

masque ［ˈmɑːsk］　　n. 滑稽戲

dialectical ［ˌdaiəˈlektikl］　　adj. 方言的

appeal to　　對…有吸引力

deceitful ［diˈsiːtf(ə)l］　　adj. 欺騙的；虛偽的

conniving ［kəˈnaiviŋ］　　adj. 縱容的；默許的

acrobatics ［ækrəˈbætɪks］　　n. 雜技

gallop ［ˈgæləp］　　vi. 飛馳

dwarf ［dwɔː(r)f］　　n. 侏儒，矮子

brawn ［brɔːn］　　n. 發達的肌肉；臂力

advocate ［ˈædvəkeɪt］　　vt. 提倡，主張

in praise of　　歌頌

knight-errant ［ˈnaitˈerənt］　　n. 俠客

tyranny ［ˈtir(ə)ni］　　n. 暴政；專橫

porcelain ['pɔːs(ə)lin]　n. 瓷；瓷器
derived from　來自於
kiln [kiln]　n. 窯；爐
glaze [gleiz]　vt. 上釉於　n. 釉
durability [ˌdjʊərə'biləti]　n. 耐久性
luster ['lʌstɚ]　n. 光澤；光彩
Crouching Tiger, Hidden Dragon　臥虎藏龍
Ang Lee　李安
Academy Awards　奧斯卡金像獎
sensation [sen'seiʃ(ə)n]　n. 感覺；轟動
fracture ['fræktʃə]　n. 斷裂；骨折
stunt [stʌnt]　n. 絕技，特技
glazed pottery　釉陶
embroidery [im'brɒid(ə)ri; em-]　n. 刺繡；刺繡品
wood carving　木雕，木刻
braiding ['breidiŋ]　n. 編結物
scroll [skrəʊl]　n. 卷軸，畫卷
vigorous ['vig(ə)rəs]　adj. 有力的；精力充沛的

Section 3　Exercises

I. Translate the following Chinese expressions into English.

1. 文房四寶
2. 青花瓷
3. 變臉
4. 京劇
5. 草書
6. 硯臺
7. 水墨畫
8. 絲綢之路
9. 武術
10. 釉陶

II. Translate the following sentences into English.

1. 中國書法不但是美的藝術，而且練習書法也是享受健康生活和長壽的有效方法。

2. 京劇的人物角色是由性別、年齡和個性來區分的。四種主要的人物類型是生、旦、淨、醜。

3. 中國功夫是中國文化不可或缺的一部分，而且具有全球的吸引力。

4. 國畫按照主題分為三種流派：人物畫、山水畫和花鳥畫。

5. 瓷器起源於中國，它是由絲綢之路傳到西方世界的藝術品之一。

III. Translate the following paragraphs into Chinese.

1. Chinese calligraphy is an Oriental art. Like chopsticks, calligraphy was once entirely Chinese, but as Chinese culture spread to Korea, Japan, and Singapore, calligraphy has became a unique feature of the Oriental art.

2. In traditional Chinese society, opera was used to spread knowledge and ethical teachings. Most operas were based on historical events or classical novels. They promoted traditional values and moral principles such as punishing evil and eulogizing virtue, loyalty and kindness.

IV. Make dialogues according to the given situations.

Section A: You are in a souvenir shop for your parents' gifts. You would like to ask for some information from a shop assistant.

Section B: You're having a conversation about Chinese opera with a foreign friend.

Section 4　Extensive Reading

Sichuan Opera

Sichuan Opera (Chuan Ju) originated at the end of the Ming (1368—1644) and the beginning of the Qing Dynasty (1644—1911). With immigrants flooding into Sichuan, different dramas were brought in to blend with the local dialect, customs, folk music and dances. Gradually, brisk humorous Sichuan Opera, reflecting Sichuan culture, came into being.

Face changing is the highlight of Sichuan Opera. It is said that ancient people painted their faces to drive away wild animals. Sichuan Opera absorbs this ancient skill and perfects it into an art.

Face changing is a magical art. Actors are able to change more than 10 masks in less than 20 seconds. By raising the hand, swinging a sleeve or tossing the head, an actor uses different masks to show different emotions, expressing invisible and intangible feelings through visible and tangible masks. From green to blue, red, yellow, brown, black, dark and gold, these masks show fear, tension, relaxation, slyness, desperation, outrage, and so on.

Sichuan Opera master Peng Denghuai could change 14 masks in 25 seconds, and reverted to four masks after revealing his true face. This was his latest Guinness World record, breaking his previous one.

Unit 6　Traditional Chinese Medicine

Section 1　Introduction

Traditional Chinese medicine

China was one of the first countries to have a medical culture. In comparison with Western medicine, the Chinese method takes a far different approach. With a history of 5,000 years, China has formed a deep and immense knowledge of medical science, theory, diagnostic methods, prescriptions and cures. Chinese philosophers regarded man as an integral part of his surroundings. He was composed not only of the five elements - metal, water, wood, fire and earth — but subject to the interplay of the elemental forces of the universe. He was 「a small world within a large world」, a microcosm within a macrocosm.

One of the most important valuable ideas and views of traditional Chinese medicine is that, rather than treat only the symptoms, as Western medicine often does, it takes into account every aspect of a patient's condition to form a unified idea of it under the theories of Yin and Yang and the five elements before deciding on its treatment. Diagnoses are made within a complete observational system, in which the nature of a patient's disease is determined by the 「four methods of diagnosis」— observing the overall way the patient looks, listening to the voice and observing any odor, asking questions, and feeling the patient's pulse. Treatment then proceeds to balance the 「eight principal syndromes」— Yin and Yang, exterior and interior, cold and heat, underactivity and overactivity.

In China, foreign visitors are often amazed at the variety of Chinese medical techniques. Take acupuncture and moxibustion for example. Acupuncture, known as zhenci in Chinese, is an ancient technique involving the insertion of needles into the body. The needles themselves can be stainless steel, silver or gold, and of course have to be sterilized, and used only by a qualified practitioner. Acupuncture is capable of treating a wide range of illnesses, including muscular complaints which are not easy to control using Western methods. The theory of acupuncture involves the belief in the existence of channels in the body called jingluo, often translated as 「meridians」. These meridians are the routes through which energy, qi, travels through the body. If there is a blockage in the jingluo, the inability of the qi to move freely causes symptoms of disease. The needles are inserted at certain points, Xuewei, where the needles can stimulate the flow of qi. Acupuncture can even be used as an anaesthetic, numbing certain parts of the body without using drugs and with the patient fully conscious. Moxibustion aijiu is another important technique in Chinese medicine. The Chinese mugwort, when dry, is known as moxa, and this material gives out a steady heat when burned. It is the heat which is used, often in conjunction with acupuncture, to treat certain illnesses. The combination is called zhenjiu.

Even more widespread than the use of acupuncture and moxibustion is the use of herbal medicine. By and large, herbal treatments are preferred as alternatives to Western-type medications. Herbal formulations are cheaper, and more effective to some ailments. What is more, they usually have little or no side effects compared with Western medicine. Still, there are many other wonderful folkways of treatment and secret recipes which are often handed down in families.

In both traditional Chinese cuisine and herbal medicine, there has never been a strict distinction between the roles of 「food」 and 「medicine」 in the kitchen or the clinic.

One of the most basic premises of traditional Chinese medical therapy states, ⌈When illness occurs, first try to cure it with food; only when food fails should one resort to herbal medicines.⌋ This means two things: first, that properly prepared food which has been correctly balanced for specific conditions is always the best cure; second, that food is always the best means for delivering medicinal herbs, especially tonics, into the human system. Tonics such as ginseng and wolfberry, for example, are more therapeutically effective and readily absorbed into the body when they are taken with fortifying foods such as chicken and pigeon than when administered alone. Only when a person's condition precludes, such foods are the herbs prescribed alone as decoctions, powders, or pills.

Many of the common tonic herbs, such as Chinese wolfberry, cinnamon, gingko nuts, lotus seeds, white fungus, dried lily bulb and red dates are available in Chinese food markets, or stocked in supermarkets. Others can be purchased in any Chinese herb shop.

Discussion

1. What are the unique features of traditional Chinese medicine?
2. Some people argue that Chinese medicine is not a science. Do you agree with them? Why or why not?
3. What are the five elements of Chinese culture?
4. Do you know how acupuncture works?
5. Can you name some common tonics?

● Section 2 Dialogues

Dialogue 1 How to Keep Colds away

Scene: Miss Kelly has a cold and David tells her a good way to avoid catching a cold.

(D = Mr. David   K = Miss Kelly)

D: Hi, Kelly, you look a bit under the weather. What happened to you?

K: I feel terrible. Yesterday I had a runny nose. Now my nose is stuffy and I have a sore throat.

D: You must have a cold.

K: I think so. Maybe it's because I went for a walk in the rain yesterday. All I can do now is take some medicine.

D: Actually there is no miracle drug to cure a common cold. But I know how to avoid catching a cold.

K: Really? Tell me.

D: Maybe you should try some traditional Chinese medicine. It might not make a difference with this cold, but it can make your whole body stronger so you won't catch colds so often.

K: What are the benefits of taking traditional Chinese medicine?

D: One benefit is that it's all natural. Chinese medicine is made from plants, not chemicals, which means there are few side effects. Another advantage is that Chinese medicine considers the human body as a whole and cure diseases on the basis of the symptoms and the root causes. Chinese medicine works slowly, but it keeps your body healthy in the long run.

K: It makes sense. Each medical method has its own advantages.

D: Another thing, compared with Western medicine's high fees, Chinese medicine has a more reasonable price that ordinary people can afford. So more and more people prefer seeing a Chinese doctor or taking Chinese medicine.

D: That sounds like just what I need. So where can I get Chinese medicine? Can I buy it in any pharmacy?

D: First, you have to see a traditional doctor. I know a good doctor just around the corner.

K: That's wonderful. It would be a very interesting experience for me.

Dialogue 2　Talking About Chinese Medicine

Scene: Miss Grace is curious about why more and more Westerners are trying Chinese medicine. She is talking with Jack about Chinese medicine.

(G = Miss Grace　　J = Mr. Jack)

G: Are you familiar with Chinese medicine? I've heard that many Westerners are really interested in it.

J: Yes, Chinese medicine is very popular in Britain now. It falls under the banner of 「alternative medicine」. It's totally different from Western medicine.

G: Is it effective?

J: Of course. Many people, including me, had a positive experience with Chinese medicine.

G: Oh, really. Can you tell me a little bit about it?

J: You know, I was a heavy smoker before, and one friend of mine recommended an acupuncturist to me. She said he could help me stop smoking. I was skeptical about it at first. But I still tried it. And in sixteen weeks, I stopped smoking completely.

G: Did it have any side effects?

J: Actually, unlike Western medicine, Chinese medicine has fewer side effects. I had no cravings, no bad temper, I didn't gain weight. These are some common problems experienced by people who are trying to stop smoking.

G: That's amazing!

J: Now, more and more Westerners are willing to try Chinese medicine. It is more commonly available in Britain now than it was 10 years ago.

G: Thank you very much. I have learned a lot from you today.

Words and Phrases

Traditional Chinese Medicine　傳統中國醫藥
subject to　使服從；受……管制
microcosm ['maikrə(ʊ)kɒz(ə)m]　n. 微觀世界
macrocosm ['mækrə(ʊ)kɒz(ə)m]　n. 宏觀世界
take into account　考慮，重視
acupuncture and moxibustion　針灸；針灸療法
sterilize ['stɛrəlaiz]　vt. 消毒；殺菌
practitioner [præk'tiʃ(ə)nə]　n. 執業醫生
meridian [mə'ridiən]　n. 子午線，經絡
anaesthetic [ˌænəs'θetik]　n. 麻藥
numb [nʌm]　vt. 使麻木
mugwort ['mʌgwɜːt]　n. 艾蒿
moxa ['mɒksə]　n. 艾
conjunction [kən'dʒʌŋ(k)ʃ(ə)n]　n. 結合
herbal medicine　草藥
side effect　副作用
resort to　依靠，求助於

tonic ['tɒnik]   n. 補藥
ginseng ['dʒinseŋ]   n. 人參
wolfberry ['wʊlfbəri]   n. 枸杞
therapeutically [ˌθerə'pjuːtiklɪ]   adv. 在治療上
decoction [dɪ'kɒkʃ(ə)n]   n. 煎煮
gingko ['giŋkəʊ]   n. 銀杏
lotus seed   蓮子
white fungus   銀耳
lily bulb   百合
red date   紅棗
runny nose   流鼻涕
root cause   根源
make sense   言之有理
under the weather   身體不適
alternative medicine   替代療法

Section 3　Exercises

I. Translate the following expressions into Chinese.

1. the Yin and Yang theory
2. the theory of the five elements
3. the four methods of diagnosis
4. the eight principal syndromes
5. acupuncture anesthesia
6. secret recipe
7. alternative medicine
8. herbal medicine
9. Chinese wolfberry
10. white fungus

II. Translate the following sentences into English.

1. 傳統中醫使用大量的動植物製品來治療疾病。
2. 許多中國人從孩提時代就瞭解到食物的不同重要價值。

3. 針刺療法從中國向其他國家的傳播大約是自六世紀由日本開始的。

4. 針刺療法可以醫治許多的疾病，包括一些用西醫難以治療的疾病。

5. 通常來說每一次針灸治療要 20 到 30 分鐘。

III. Translate the following paragraphs into Chinese.

1.「If Yin and Yang are not in harmony it is as though there were no autumn opposite the spring, no winter opposite the summer.」(Yellow Emperor's Classic of Internal Medicine).

2. Traditional Chinese medicine is an indispensable part of Chinese culture. It has made great contributions to the prosperity of China. Nowadays, both traditional Chinese medicine and Western medicine are being used to cure people all around the world. Traditional Chinese medicines, with its unique diagnostic methods, long history and remarkable effects, have been used to treat a variety of diseases.

3. Herbal cuisine is the cuisine with food cooking ingredients and herbs. Herbal cuisine is a special dietary cuisine which combines the effect of medicines and the taste of foods. It enables the consumer to enjoy the delicious food with body nourishing and disease treatment.

IV. Make dialogues according to the given situations.

Section A：Your friend, Susan, has caught a cold and you are giving her some advice on how to avoid catching a cold.

Section B：You are a tour guide from CITS, Chengdu branch. A tourist from USA is very interested in herbal medicine. You try to provide him with some basic knowledge about this subject.

Section 4　Extensive Reading

Massage

Besides acupuncture and herbal medicine which are very popular in China and the rest of the world, massage is a therapy that has been around for centuries.

Traditional Chinese massage is done with clothes on and hence there is no need for essential oils. Different massage parlors—each with its own theory, training, style, and practice— have been established in various regions of China. In southern China where the weather is warm, the techniques of massage are gentle and slow. On the contrary, in northern China where the weather is cold, the techniques used are firm and vigorous. Some use rolling movements, while others focus on bone setting and digital point pressure. Some aim at health preservation, while others are designed to treat specific ailments. Generally speaking, all massage methods promote blood circulation, remove blood stasis, restore and treat injured soft tissues, and correct deformities and abnormal positions of bones and muscles.

Tui Na is one kind of basic massage technique in China. Tui Na, literally meaning pushing and pulling, refers to a system of massage, manual stimulation and manipulation of muscles, tendons, ligaments, and joints. The relationships between Qi Gong, acupuncture, and Tui Na are quite close, as they are all based on the same theoretical basis of Chinese traditional medicine.

Appendix
Useful Vocabulary for Hotel English

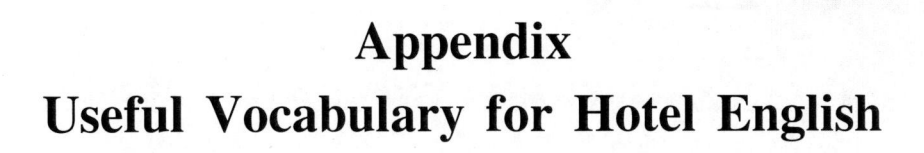

酒店前廳常用詞彙：

Front Office Manager　前廳部經理
Assistant Manager　大堂經理
Duty Manager　值班經理
Night Manager　夜班經理
Chief Concierge　禮賓部
Reception　接待處
Cashier　收銀處
Accounting　帳務處
Information　問詢處
Lost & Found　失物招領
The Cloak Room　寄存處
Early arrival　提前抵達
No-show　沒有按預定抵店
ETA (Estimated Time of Arrival)　預計到達時間
ETD (Estimated Time of Departure)　預計離開時間
Late check out　延遲退房

Extension　續住

Permanent room　長包房

Skipper　（逃帳）指客人沒有付帳就離開酒店

Check in　入住

Check out　退房

VIP guest　貴賓

Walk-in guest / current guests　散客

Regular guest　常客

Group guests　團體客人

Corporate clients　公司客戶

Price list　價目表

Average room rate　房間平均價格

Corporate rate　合同價

Full price　全價

Discounted price　折扣價

Rack rate　標準價

Special price　優惠價

Complimentary rate　免費

Shuttle bus　班車

Advance deposit　預付訂金/押金

Check / cheque　支票

Traveller's cheque　旅行支票

Voucher　證件

Passport　護照

Identification card (I. D.)　身分證

Rate of exchange　兌換率

Conversion rate　換算率

Bank draft　匯票

Procedure fee　手續費

Fill in the form　填表

Charge　收費

Bill　帳單

Interest　利息

King-size　特大號床
Queen-size　大號床
Twin beds　雙床房
Single bed　單床房
Double room　雙人間
Single room　單人間
Suite　套房
Extra bed　加床
Studio suite　公寓套房
Adjoining room　相鄰房
Connecting room　連通房
Turn down　夜床服務
Morning call　叫早服務
Luggage rack　行李架
Luggage office　行李房
Luggage label　行李標籤
Porter　行李員
Bellman　門童

客房部常用詞彙：

Housekeeping Manager　客房部經理
Executive Housekeeper / Head Housekeeper　客房部主管
Head Waiter / Captain　領班
Floor Captain　樓層領班
Room / Floor Attendant　客房／樓層服務員
Chambermaid　客房女服務員

客房設備、用品：

Electronic lock　電子門鎖
Room card　房卡
Cabinet　櫥櫃
Venetian blind　百葉窗簾
Curtain　窗簾

Carpet　地毯
Smoke reaction　菸感應器
Tea table　茶幾
Ashtray　菸缸
Thermos　熱水瓶
Electric kettle　電熱水壺
Folding screen　屏風
Wallplate　壁上掛盤
Chinese painting　國畫
Painting　裝飾畫
Spring　彈簧
Cushion　靠墊，墊子
Armchair　扶手椅
Sitting room　起居室
Carpentry　（總稱）木器
Bed table　床頭櫃
Bed board　床背
Bedclothes　床上用品
Quilt　被子
Mattress　席夢思床墊
Cover sheet　床單
Pillow　枕芯；枕頭
Pillowcase　枕套
Quilt inside　被芯
Quilt cover　被套
Bed cushion　床墊
Switch　開關
Socket　插座，插口
Telephone set　電話機
TV set　電視機
TV table　電視櫃
TV remote　電視遙控器
Air-condition remote　空調遙控器

Mirror light　鏡前燈
Reading lamp　臺燈
Wall lamp（fixed）　壁燈（固定）
Wall lamp（moveable）　壁燈（雙搖）
Stand lamp　落地燈
Lamp shade　燈罩
Workdesk　寫字臺
Stationery holder　文具夾
Leather folder　皮具夾
Drawer　抽屜
Table chair　書桌櫃
Wall mirror　掛壁鏡
Service directory　服務指南
Luggage frame　行李架
Hanger　掛勾/衣架
Bathroom　衛生間
Toilet mirror　衛生間鏡子
Bath towel　浴巾
Bath robe　浴衣
Face towel　面巾
Bath mat　浴室地席
Soap tray　肥皂碟
Bathroom cup　漱口杯
Bathtub　浴缸
Shower door　淋浴房
Shower　淋浴龍頭
Shower curtain　浴簾
Shower cap　浴帽
Tissue　面巾紙
Toilet paper　卷紙
Towls shelf　浴巾架
Bracket　托架
Laundry bag　洗衣袋

Plug　插頭
Hairdryer　電吹風
Taps　水龍頭
Basin　臺下盆
Water closet　抽水馬桶
Waste basket　字紙簍
Dustbin　垃圾桶
Voltage　電壓

飲料：

Beverages　飲料
Mineral water　礦泉水
Distilled water　蒸餾水
Soda water　蘇打水
Ice water　冰水
Soya bean milk　豆漿
Orangeade / orange squash　桔子水
Lemon juice　檸檬汁
Lemonade　檸檬汽水
Soft drinks　不含酒精的飲料
Coco-cola（coke）　可口可樂
Pepsi cola　百事可樂
Sprite　雪碧
Pineapple juice　菠蘿汁
Tomato juice　番茄汁
Orange juice　橘子汁
Coconut plum　椰子汁
Watermelon juice　西瓜汁
Grapefruit juice　葡萄柚汁
Vegetable juice　蔬菜汁
Ginger ale　姜汁；姜味汽水
Cocoa　可可（粉）
Sarsaparilla　沙士

Tea leaves　茶葉
Black tea　紅茶
Tea bag　茶包
Lemon tea　檸檬茶
Jasmine tea　茉莉茶
White goup tea　冬瓜茶
Oolong tea　烏龍茶
Tie-guan-yin tea　鐵觀音
Longjin tea　龍井
Pu'er tea　普洱茶
Ice candy　冰棒
Milk-shakes　奶昔
Milk　牛奶
Yoghurt　酸奶
Coffee　咖啡
Iced coffee　冰咖啡
White coffee　牛奶咖啡
Black coffee　純咖啡
Espresso　意式特濃咖啡
Irish coffee　愛爾蘭咖啡
Chlorella yakult　養樂多
Essence of chicken　雞精
Ice-cream cone　甜筒
Sundae　聖代
Ice-cream　雪糕；冰淇淋
Vanilla ice-cream　香草冰淇淋
Straw　吸管

水果：

Cherry　櫻桃
Lemon　檸檬
Clove　丁香
Pineapple　菠蘿

Lichee　荔枝
Longan　龍眼
Grape　葡萄
Banana　香蕉
Loquat　枇杷
Strawberry　草莓
Olive　橄欖
Mint　薄荷
Grapefruit　葡萄柚
Betel nut　檳榔
Coconut　椰子
Chestnut　栗子
Haw　山楂
Orange　橘子
Persimmon　柿子
Pear　梨子
Juice peach　水蜜桃
Plum　李子
Apple　蘋果
Mango　芒果
Fig　無花果
Durian　榴蓮
Watermelon　西瓜
Honey-dew melon　哈密瓜
Papaya　木瓜
Cucumber　黃瓜

酒：

Bar　酒吧
Counter　吧臺
Bar chair　酒吧椅
Barman　酒吧男招待
Barmaid　酒吧女招待

Bottle opener 開瓶刀
Champagne bucket 香檳桶
Appetizer 餐前葡萄酒
Great wall white wine 長城白葡萄酒
Red wine 紅葡萄酒
Claret 波爾多紅葡萄酒
Cider 蘋果酒
Champagne 香檳酒
Cocktail 雞尾酒
Vermounth 苦艾酒
Sake 日本清酒
Liqueur 白酒
Vodka 伏特加
Whisky 威士忌
Brandy 白蘭地
Cognac 法國白蘭地
Gin flzz 杜松子酒
Martini 馬丁尼酒
Gin 金酒
Gordon's 哥頓
Rum 朗姆酒
Bacardi 百家得
Smirnoff 皇冠
Calvados 蘋果酒
Glenfiddich 格蘭菲迪
VSOP Hennessy VSOP 軒尼詩
Cognac L'or De Martell 金王馬爹利
Martell Cognac Gobelet Royal 極品馬爹利
Martell Cordon Blue 藍帶馬爹利
Martin Louis XIII 路易十三
Remy Martin XO (Big) 人頭馬
Bailey's 百利甜酒
Drought beer 生啤

Stout　黑啤
Qinqindao beer　青島啤酒
Heineken　喜力啤酒
Budweiser　百威啤酒
Foster's　福士啤酒
Beck's　貝克啤酒
Carlsbery　嘉士伯啤酒
Guinness stout　健力士啤酒

主食及糕點：

Steamed bread　饅頭
Steamed stuffed bread　包子
Steamed twisted roll　花卷
Stuffed dumpling　餃子
Steamed dumpling　蒸餃
Lightly fried dumpling　鍋貼
Deep-fried twisted drough ticks　油條
Shao-mai　燒賣
Spring roll　春卷
Glutionus rice balls for Lantern Festival　元宵
Wonton　餛飩
Pickled cucumbers　醬瓜
Preserved egg　皮蛋
Salted duck egg　咸鴨蛋
Sesame seeds cake　燒餅
Scallion cake　蔥油餅
Meat pie　肉餡餅
Crisp cake　酥餅
Almond biscuit　杏仁餅干
Assorted biscuit　什錦餅干
Gingerbread　姜餅
Oatmeal　燕麥片
Bran-bread　麥麩麵包

Brown bread　黑麵包
French fires　炸薯條
French bread　法式麵包
Ham sandwich　火腿三明治
Hamburger　漢堡包
Hotdog　熱狗
Pizza　比薩
Macaroni　義大利通心粉
Spaghetti　義大利麵條
Fried noodles　炒面
Noodles with sesame paste and pea　擔擔面
Noodles with gravy　打鹵面
Plain noodles　陽春面
Fried rice with mixed meat and eggs　什錦蛋炒飯
Rice curry　咖喱飯
Mush　玉米粥
Porridge　麥片粥

中餐：

Boiled salted duck　鹽水鴨
Preserved meat　臘肉
Barbecued pork　叉燒
Fried pork flakes　肉松
Bird's nest　燕窩
Braised chicken with shallot　紅蔥頭蒸雞
Braised fish head in Pottery pot　砂鍋魚頭煲
Spicy salty pork spareribs　椒鹽排骨
Diced chicken with green pepper　辣子雞丁
Sichuan style chicken meat ball　川汁雞球
Fried pork tripe with chicken gizzard　醬爆雙脆
Poached beef with hot chili　水煮牛肉
Boiled fish head with bean curd　豆腐魚頭煲
Steam spare ribs/fish with black bean sauce　豉汁蒸排骨/魚

Stir-fried beef with ginger and shallot　姜葱爆牛肉
Stir-fried beef with black pepper　黑椒炒牛肉
Steam beef and mushroom　茶樹菇蒸牛柳
Stir-fried beef in bean sauce　醬爆牛柳
Braised pork with preserved vegetables　梅菜扣肉
Mud-baked chicken　叫化雞
Roast Beijing duck　北京烤鴨
Roast meat　鐵板烤肉
Steamed minced pork with salted fish　咸魚蒸肉餅
Braised pork in brown sauce　紅燒肉
Pork chops with sweet and sour sauce　糖醋排骨
Sauté pork dices with hot pepper　宮保肉丁
Stewed black-boned chicken with Chinese Herbs　鍋仔藥膳烏雞
Tomato and bean curd soup　番茄豆腐湯
Laver and egg soup　紫菜蛋花湯
Three delicious ingredient soup　三鮮湯
Stewed white gourd soup with eight ingredients　八寶冬瓜盅
Mushroom soup　清炖冬菇湯

西餐：

French cuisine　法國菜
Continental cuisine　歐式西餐
Today's special　今日特餐
Specialty　招牌菜
Chef's special　主廚特餐
Buffet　自助餐
Fast food　快餐
Aperitif　飯前酒
Dim sum　點心
Baked potato　烘馬鈴薯
Mashed potatoes　馬鈴薯泥
Salad　色拉
Ham omelet　火腿蛋卷

Pudding　布丁
Pastries　甜點
Pickled vegetables　泡菜
Kimchi　韓國泡菜
Ham and Sausage　火腿香腸
Crab meat　蟹肉
Deviled crab　炒蟹
Prawn　明蝦
Conch　海螺
Escargots　田螺
Sardines　沙丁魚
Caviar　魚子醬
Sashimi　生魚片
Corn beef　咸牛肉
Roasted beef　燒牛肉
Braised beef　炖牛肉
Beef steak　牛排
Mutton chops　羊排
Roasted pork chop　燒豬排
Steamed fish　蒸魚
Bacon　熏肉

Reference

[1] 孫小珂. 新編飯店英語［M］. 武漢：武漢大學出版社，2007.

[2] 陳嘉隆. 臺灣地區旅行社的經營與管理［M］. 北京：旅遊教育出版社，2001.

[3] 袁智敏，仇向明. 領隊英語［M］. 3版. 北京：旅遊教育出版社，2010.

[4] 李東升，楊麗萍. 接待英語應急一本通［M］. 濟南：山東科學技術出版社，2009.

[5] 易婷婷，王曉寧. 導遊實務［M］. 北京：北京大學出版社，2013.

[6] 魏新民，申延子. 酒店情景英語［M］. 北京：北京大學出版社，2011.

[7] 李靜波. 旅遊服務實用英語［M］. 成都：電子科技大學出版社，2009.

[8] 劉金舉，等. 中英日三語對照旅遊日語：中英日［M］. 廣州：廣東旅遊出版社，2000.

[9] 何陽，許蘭娟，田力. 全新涉外醫療英語［M］. 鄭州：河南人民出版社，2007.

[10] 蘇靜. 導遊英語［M］. 北京：化學工業出版社，2007.

[11] 胡朝慧. 酒店英語［M］. 北京：北京大學出版社，2011.

[12] 張麗君. 酒店英語［M］. 北京：清華大學出版社，2010.

[13] 郭兆康，吳雲. 飯店英語［M］. 北京：旅遊教育出版社，2010.

[14] BILBOW G T. 朗文現代酒店業英語［M］. 北京：外語教學與研究出版社，2005.

[15] 郭兆康. 飯店情景英語［M］. 上海：復旦大學出版社，2008.

［16］王肇華. 飯店情景英語［M］. 上海：格致出版社，2008.

［17］唐曉莉，NACY SCHAFFINER. 360°全景酒店英語［M］. 濟南：齊魯電子音像出版社，2010.

［18］浩瀚，李志剛. 飯店英語900句［M］. 北京：中國古籍出版社，2006.

［19］林群，安錦蘭. 旅遊服務英語［M］. 北京：清華大學出版社，2010.

［20］林瀚. 會展英語實務［M］. 北京：北京師範大學出版社. 2011.

［21］孫國風. 旅遊英語景點教程［M］成都：西南交通大學出版社，2008.

［22］夢幻四季九寨溝編委會. 夢幻四季九寨溝［M］. 成都：四川民族出版社，2006.

［23］朱華. 四川英語導遊景點講解［M］. 北京：旅遊教育出版社，2010.

［24］林竹梅. 旅遊英語［M］. 北京：對外經濟貿易大學出版社，2011.

［25］朱華. 四川英語導遊：景點與文化［M］. 成都：四川科學技術出版社，2011.

［26］Kathleen K (Eds). Understanding China：The culture of China［M］. Britannica Educational Pubulishing and Rosen Educational Services. 2011.

［27］關肇遠. 導遊英語口語［M］. 2版. 北京：高等教育出版社，2009.

［28］楊天慶. 和老外聊中國文化——沿途英語導遊話題［M］. 成都：天地出版社，2010.

［29］龍江. 英語漫談中國文化［M］. 大連：大連理工大學出版社，2010.

［30］李飛，袁露，阮蓓. 旅遊英語［M］. 天津：天津大學出版社，2010.

［31］周毅. 旅遊英語教程［M］. 成都：四川大學出版社，2004.

［32］A Guide to Tour［EB/OL］.［2014-02-19］http://www.sccom.gov.cn/wszs/page/english/htm/zjsc.htm.

［33］Les Clefs d'Or USA［EB/OL］.［2014-05-10］http://www.Icdusa.org/characteristics -of - a- Les Clefs -d'or concierge.

［34］The Yungang Grottoes［EB/OL］.［2014-2-12］http://www.foreignercn.com/index. php? option = com_content&view = article&id = 7833；the - yungang - grottoes&catid = 103；travel-in-shanxi&Itemid = 237.

［35］Wolong National Nature Reserve［EB/OL］.［2014-02-16］http://www.foreignercn.com/index.php? option = com_content&view = article&id = 6842；wolong-national-nature-reserve&catid = 99；travel-in-sichuan&Itemid = 202.

［36］Sansu Memorial Temple［EB/OL］.［2014-03-10］http://bbs.chinadaily.com.cn/forum.php? mod = viewthread&tid = 724772&page = 1&authorid = 785897.

[37] The Canton Fair [EB/OL]. [2014-02-24] http://www.cantontradefair.com/cantonfair/index.aspx.

[38] WonderWorks Orlando [EB/OL]. [2014-02-24] http://www.smartdestinations.com/orlando-attractions-an d-tours/wonderworks/_attr_Orl_Att_WonderWorks.html.

[39] The Dujiangyan Water-Releasing Ceremony [EB/OL]. [2014-01-18] http:// traditions.cultural-china.com.

[40] Confucianism-teachings of Confucius [EB/OL]. [2014-05-19] http://www.chinadaily.com.cn/china/2007-12/25/content_6346639.htm.

國家圖書館出版品預行編目(CIP)資料

旅遊服務英語 / 許酉萍，張科 主編. -- 第一版.
-- 臺北市：崧博出版：財經錢線文化發行，2018.10

面；　公分

ISBN 978-957-735-613-0(平裝)

1. 英語 2. 旅遊 3. 會話

805.188　　107017332

書　名：旅遊服務英語
作　者：許酉萍、張科 主編
發行人：黃振庭
出版者：崧博出版事業有限公司
發行者：財經錢線文化事業有限公司
E-mail：sonbookservice@gmail.com
粉絲頁　　　　　　網　址：
地　址：台北市中正區延平南路六十一號五樓一室
8F.-815, No.61, Sec. 1, Chongqing S. Rd., Zhongzheng Dist., Taipei City 100, Taiwan (R.O.C.)
電　話：(02)2370-3310　傳　真：(02) 2370-3210
總經銷：紅螞蟻圖書有限公司
地　址：台北市內湖區舊宗路二段 121 巷 19 號
電　話：02-2795-3656　　傳真：02-2795-4100　網址：
印　刷：京峯彩色印刷有限公司（京峰數位）

　　本書版權為西南財經大學出版社所有授權崧博出版事業有限公司獨家發行電子書及繁體書繁體版。若有其他相關權利及授權需求請與本公司聯繫。

定價：400元

發行日期：2018 年 10 月第一版

◎ 本書以POD印製發行